IMAGINE . . .
A brilliant writer losing h

IMAGINE . . .
A congregation of SF aficionados who owns the stars and the future.

IMAGINE . . .
What an ambitious author would be willing to trade for his own survival.

IMAGINE . . .
A writer and his editor sharing the astonishing secret of a simian with an extraordinary gift.

Stories by

ISAAC ASIMOV	ERIC NORDEN
AVRAM DAVIDSON	PATRICIA NURSE
PHILIP K. DICK	FREDERIK POHL
GEORGE ALEC EFFINGER	FRANK RAMIREZ
EDMOND HAMILTON	MIKE RESNICK
C.M. KORNBLUTH	ALLEN STEELE
JACK LEWIS	IAN WATSON
BARRY N. MALZBERG	JANE YOLEN

INSIDE THE FUNHOUSE

17 SF STORIES ABOUT SF

edited by
MIKE RESNICK

AVON BOOKS • NEW YORK

INSIDE THE FUNHOUSE is an original publication of Avon Books. This work has never before appeared in book form. This is a work of fiction. Any similarity to actual persons or events is purely coincidental.

Additional copyright notices appear on the acknowledgments pages, which serve as an extension of this copyright page.

AVON BOOKS
A division of
The Hearst Corporation
1350 Avenue of the Americas
New York, New York 10019

Copyright © 1992 by Mike Resnick
Published by arrangement with the editor
Cover illustration by Tim O'Brien
Library of Congress Catalog Card Number: 91-92457
ISBN: 0-380-76643-4

First AvoNova Printing: August 1992

AVONOVA TRADEMARK REG. U.S. PAT. OFF. AND IN OTHER COUNTRIES, MARCA REGISTRADA, HECHO EN U.S.A.

Printed in the U.S.A.

RA 10 9 8 7 6 5 4 3 2 1

To Carol, as always,

And to Barry Malzberg, who came awfully close
to perfecting recursive science fiction,
And Tony Lewis, who codified and cataloged it

Acknowledgments

"Science Fiction" by Jane Yolen. Copyright © 1987 by Jane Yolen. Reprinted by permission of the author.

"A Galaxy Called Rome" by Barry N. Malzberg. Copyright © 1975 by Mercury Press, Inc. First published in *The Magazine of Fantasy & Science Fiction* in July 1975. Reprinted by permission of the author.

"Who's Cribbing?" by Jack Lewis. Copyright © 1953 by Better Publications, Inc. Copyright renewed © 1981 by Jack Lewis. Reprinted by permission of Forrest J. Ackerman, 2495 Glendower Avenue, Hollywood, California 90027.

"The Merchant of Stratford" by Frank Ramirez. Copyright © 1979 by Davis Publications, Inc. First published in *Isaac Asimov's Science Fiction Magazine*. Reprinted by permission of the author.

"One Rejection Too Many" by Patricia Nurse. Copyright © 1978 by Davis Publications, Inc. Reprinted by permission of the author.

"The Pinch Hitters" by George Alec Effinger. Copyright © 1979 by Davis Publications, Inc. Reprinted by permission of the author.

"Mute Inglorious Tam" by Frederik Pohl and C.M. Kornbluth. Copyright © 1974 by Mercury Press, Inc. Reprinted by permission of the authors.

"The Curse of Mhondoro Nkabele" by Eric Norden. Copyright © 1982 by Eric Norden. Reprinted by permission of the author.

"The Pro" by Edmond Hamilton. Copyright © 1964 by Mercury Press, Inc. Reprinted by permission of the author and the author's agent, Scott Meredith Literary Agency, Inc., 845 Third Avenue, New York, New York 10022.

"The Reunion at the Mile-High" by Frederik Pohl. Copyright © 1989 by Frederik Pohl. Reprinted by permission of the author.

Contents

INTRODUCTION

RECURSIVE SCIENCE FICTION (i.e., science fiction *about* science fiction) has been around for almost as long as science fiction itself.

Tarzan and the Lion Man ends with Tarzan going to Hollywood and failing to land the lead role in a Tarzan movie because he's the wrong type.

In E. E. "Doc" Smith's *Children of the Lens*, the immortal Kimball Kinnison goes undercover as Sybly White, a science fiction writer.

Frederic Brown's classic *What Mad Universe*, an expansion of an earlier novelette of the same title, was probably the first full-length recursive science fiction novel, but it was followed by many more over the years. Some of the more notable titles include Brown's own *Martians, Go Home*, Barry Malzberg's *Galaxies* and *Herovit's World*, Tim Powers's *The Stress of Her Regard*, Larry Niven and Jerry Pournelle's *Inferno*, Philip Jose Farmer's *Venus on the Half Shell*, Philip K. Dick's *The Man in the High Castle*, Michael Bishop's *The Secret Ascension*, and Jonathan Carroll's *The Land of Laughs*.

In fact, to give you an idea of just how specialized recursive science fiction has become, Barry Malzberg's *Gather in the Hall of the Planets*, Robert Coulson and Gene DeWeese's *Now You See It/Him/Them* and *Charles Fort Never Mentioned Wombats*, Sharyn McCrumb's *Bimbos of the Death Sun*, Richard Purtill's *Murdercon*, and William Marshall's *Sci Fi* are all novels set at science fiction conventions.

Almost every major name in our field—including Robert A.

1

Heinlein, Ray Bradbury, Robert Silverberg, Philip K. Dick, Frederik Pohl, and Isaac Asimov—has written recursive science fiction stories or novels, as have some major names from outside the field, such as Kurt Vonnegut. Probably the man who has explored the limits of recursive science fiction the most thoroughly is Barry Malzberg, with four novels and more than half a dozen shorter pieces.

In fact, recursive science fiction has become such an important subgenre of the field that Anthony R. Lewis, a longtime fan, occasional pro, and former worldcon chairman, has actually published an index to it: *An Annotated Bibliography of Recursive Science Fiction.*

Well, sez I, any field with its own index deserves its own anthology, especially when there are so many delightful and thought-provoking stories from which to choose. I hope you have as much fun reading them as I had selecting them.

—MIKE RESNICK

SCIENCE FICTION

Jane Yolen owns an old rambling farmhouse with so many rooms and levels that I managed to get lost for almost half an hour inside it. Her other, more respectable claims to fame are the more than one hundred novels she has sold, her own publishing imprint, and her term as president of the Science Fiction Writers of America.

I can't think of a better invocation to this anthology than the following brief poem by the illustrious Ms. Yolen.

Meadow was never our metaphor.
Sky and the circling stars,
The meter of Venus and slow Mars,
The spangles of lofty Heaven's core

All spoke their poems into our ears.
We listened and rode the good ship
Wonder. All through the trip
The clanking of the shifting gears

Were haiku, sonnets, sestinas, rhyme.
We lived the poetry of space and of time.

—Jane Yolen

A GALAXY CALLED ROME

Barry N. Malzberg

Galaxies, *by the brilliant and prolific Barry Malzberg, was one of the two or three most powerful novels to come out of the science fiction field in the 1970s, an ascerbic critique of the genre couched in fictional form. But before* Galaxies *was a novel, it was an absolutely stunning novelette, which I am proud to present to you as the leadoff story for this anthology.*

I

THIS IS NOT a novelette but a series of notes. The novelette cannot be truly written because it partakes of its time, which is distant and could be perceived only through the idiom and devices of that era.

Thus the piece, by virtue of these reasons and others too personal even for this variety of True Confession, is little more than a set of constructions toward something less substantial . . . and, like the author, it cannot be completed.

II

The novelette would lean heavily upon two articles by the late John Campbell, for thirty-three years the editor of *Astounding/Analog,* which were written shortly before his untimely death on July 11, 1971, and appeared as editorials in his magazine later that year, the second being perhaps the last piece which will ever bear his byline. They imagine a black galaxy which would result from the implosion of a neutron star, an implosion so mighty that gravitational forces unleashed would contain not only light itself but space and time; and *A Galaxy Called Rome* is his title, not mine, since he envisions a spacecraft that might be trapped within such a black galaxy and be unable to get out . . . because escape velocity would have to exceed the speed of light. All paths of travel would lead to this galaxy, then, none away. A galaxy called Rome.

III

Conceive then of a faster-than-light spaceship which would tumble into the black galaxy and would be unable to leave. Tumbling would be easy, or at least inevitable, since one of the characteristics of the black galaxy would be its *invisibility,* and there the ship would be. The story would then pivot on the efforts of the crew to get out. The ship is named *Skipstone*. It was completed in 3892. Five hundred people died so that it might fly, but in this age life is held even more cheaply than it is today.

Left to my own devices, I might be less interested in the escape problem than that of adjustment. Light housekeeping in an anterior sector of the universe; submission to the elements, a fine, ironic literary despair. This is not science fiction however. Science fiction was created by Hugo Gernsback to show us the ways out of technological impasse. So be it.

IV

As interesting as the material was, I quailed even at this series of notes, let alone a polished, completed work. My personal life is my black hole, I felt like pointing out (who would listen?); my daughters provide more correct and sticky implosion than any neutron star, and the sound of the pulsars is as nothing to the music of the paddock area at Aqueduct racetrack in Ozone Park, Queens, on a clear summer Tuesday. "Enough of these breathtaking concepts, infinite distances, quasar leaps, binding messages amidst the arms of the spiral nebula," I could have pointed out. "I know that there are those who find an ultimate truth there, but I am not one of them. I would rather dedicate the years of life remaining (my melodramatic streak) to an understanding of the agonies of this middle-class town in northern New Jersey; until I can deal with those, how can I comprehend Ridgefield Park, to say nothing of the extension of fission to include progressively heavier gases?" Indeed, I almost abided to this until it occurred to me that Ridgefield Park would forever be as mysterious as the stars and that one could not deny infinity merely to pursue a particular that would be impenetrable until the day of one's death.

So I decided to try the novelette, at least as this series of notes, although with some trepidation, but trepidation did not unsettle me, nor did I grieve, for my life is merely a set of notes for a life, and Ridgefield Park merely a rough working model of Trenton, in which, nevertheless, several thousand people live who cannot discern their right hands from their left, and also much cattle.

V

It is 3895. The spacecraft *Skipstone*, on an exploratory flight through the major and minor galaxies surrounding the Milky Way, falls into the black galaxy of a neutron star and is lost forever.

The captain of this ship, the only living consciousness of it, is its commander, Lena Thomas. True, the hold of the ship carries five hundred and fifteen of the dead sealed in gelatinous fix who will absorb unshielded gamma rays. True, these rays will at some time in the future hasten their reconstitution. True, again, that another part of the hold contains the prosthesis of seven skilled engineers, male and female, who could be switched on at only slight inconvenience and would provide Lena not only with answers to any technical problems which would arise but with companionship to while away the long and grave hours of the *Skipstone*'s flight.

Lena, however, does not use the prosthesis, nor does she feel the necessity to. She is highly skilled and competent, at least in relation to the routine tasks of this testing flight, and she feels that to call for outside help would only be an admission of weakness, would be reported back to the Bureau and lessen her potential for promotion. (She is right; the Bureau has monitored every cubicle of this ship, both visually and biologically; she can see or do nothing which does not trace to a printout; they would not think well of her if she was dependent upon outside assistance.) Toward the embalmed she feels somewhat more. Her condition rattling in the hold of the ship as it moves on tachyonic drive seems to approximate theirs; although they are deprived of consciousness, that quality seems to be almost irrelevant to the condition of hyperspace, and if there were any way that she could bridge their mystery, she might well address them. As it is, she must settle for imaginary dialogues and for long, quiescent periods when she will watch the monitors, watch the rainbow of hyperspace, the collision of the spectrum, and say nothing whatsoever.

Saying nothing will not do, however, and the fact is that Lena talks incessantly at times, if only to herself. This is good because the story should have much dialogue; dramatic incident is best impelled through straightforward characterization, and Lena's compulsive need, now and then, to state her condition and its relation to the spaces she occupies will satisfy this need.

In her conversation, of course, she often addresses the embalmed. "Consider," she says to them, some of them dead eight hundred years, others dead weeks, all of them stacked in the hold in relation to their status in life and their ability to hoard assets to pay for the process that will return them their lives, "Consider what's going on here," pointing through the hold, the colors gleaming through the portholes onto her wrist, colors dancing in the air, her eyes quite full and maddened in this light, which does not indicate that she is mad but only that the condition of hyperspace itself is insane, the Michelson-Morley effect having a psychological as well as physical reality here. "Why it could be *me* dead and in the hold and all of you here in the dock watching the colors spin, it's all the same, all the same faster than light," and indeed the twisting and sliding effects of the tachyonic drive are such that at the moment of speech what Lena says is true.

The dead live; the living are dead, all slide and become jumbled together as she has noted; and were it not that their objective poles of consciousness were fixed by years of training and discipline, just as hers are transfixed by a different kind of training and discipline, she would press the levers to eject the dead one-by-one into the larger coffin of space, something which is indicated only as an emergency procedure under the gravest of terms and which would result in her removal from the Bureau immediately upon her return. The dead are precious cargo; they are, in essence, paying for the experiments and must be handled with the greatest delicacy. "I will handle you with the greatest delicacy," Lena says in hyperspace, "and I will never let you go, little packages in my little prison," and so on, singing and chanting as the ship moves on somewhat in excess of one million miles per second, always accelerating; and yet, except for the colors, the nausea, the disorienting swing, her own mounting insanity, the terms of this story, she might be in the IRT Lenox Avenue local at rush hour, moving slowly uptown as circles of illness move through the fainting car in the bowels of summer.

VI

She is twenty-eight years old. Almost two hundred years in the future, when man has established colonies on forty planets in the Milky Way, has fully populated the solar system, is working in the faster-than-light experiments as quickly as he can to move through other galaxies, the medical science of that day is not notably superior to that of our own, and the human lifespan has not been significantly extended, nor have the diseases of mankind which are now known as congenital been eradicated. Most of the embalmed were in their eighties or nineties; a few of them, the more recent deaths, were nearly a hundred, but the average lifespan still hangs somewhat short of eighty, and most of these have died from cancer, heart attacks, renal failure, cerebral blowout, and the like. There is some irony in the fact that man can have at least established a toehold in his galaxy, can have solved the mysteries of the FTL drive, and yet finds the fact of his own biology as stupefying as he has throughout history, but every sociologist understands that those who live in a culture are least qualified to criticize it (because they have fully assimilated the codes of the culture, even as to criticism), and Lena does not see this irony any more than the reader will have to in order to appreciate the deeper and more metaphysical irony of the story, which is this: that greater speed, greater space, greater progress, greater sensation has not resulted in any definable expansion of the limits of consciousness and personality and all that the FTL drive is to Lena is an increasing entrapment.

It is important to understand that she is merely a technician; that although she is highly skilled and has been trained through the Bureau for many years for her job as pilot, she really does not need to possess the technical knowledge of any graduate scientists of our own time . . . that her job, which is essentially a probe-and-ferrying, could be done by an adolescent; and that all of her training has afforded her no protection against the boredom and depression of her assignment.

When she is done with this latest probe, she will return to Uranus and be granted a six-month leave. She is looking forward to that. She appreciates the opportunity. She is only twenty-eight, and she is tired of being sent with the dead to tumble through the spectrum for weeks at a time, and what she would very much like to be, at least for a while, is a young woman. She would like to be at peace. She would like to be loved. She would like to have sex.

VII

Something must be made of the element of sex in this story, if only because it deals with a female protagonist (where asepsis will not work); and in the tradition of modern literary science fiction, where some credence is given to the whole range of human needs and behaviors, it would be clumsy and amateurish to ignore the issue. Certainly the easy scenes can be written and to great effect: Lena masturbating as she stares through the port at the colored levels of hyperspace; Lena dreaming thickly of intercourse as she unconsciously massages her nipples, the ship plunging deeper and deeper (as she does not yet know) toward the Black Galaxy; the Black Galaxy itself as some ultimate vaginal symbol of absorption whose Freudian overcast will not be ignored in the imagery of this story . . . indeed, one can envision Lena stumbling toward the Evictors at the depths of her panic in the Black Galaxy to bring out one of the embalmed, her grim and necrophiliac fantasies as the body is slowly moved upwards on its glistening slab, the way that her eyes will look as she comes to consciousness and realizes what she has become . . . oh, this would be a very powerful scene indeed, almost anything to do with sex in space is powerful (one must also conjure with the effects of hyperspace upon the orgasm; would it be the orgasm which all of us know and love so well or something entirely different, perhaps detumescence, perhaps exaltation?), and I would face the issue squarely, if only I could, and in line with the very real need of the story to have powerful and effective dialogue.

"For God's sake," Lena would say at the end, the music of her entrapment squeezing her, coming over her, blotting her toward extinction, "for God's sake, all we ever needed was a screw, that's all that sent us out into space, that's all that it ever meant to us, I've got to have it, got to have it, do you understand?" jamming her fingers in and out of her aqueous surfaces—

—But of course this would not work, at least in the story which I am trying to conceptualize. Space *is* aseptic; that is the secret of science fiction for forty-five years; it is not deceit or its adolescent audience or the publication codes which have deprived most of the literature of the range of human sexuality but the fact that in the clean and abysmal spaces between the stars sex, that demonstration of our perverse and irreplaceable humanity, would have no role at all. Not for nothing did the astronauts return to tell us their vision of otherworldliness, not for nothing did they stagger in their thick landing gear as they walked toward the colonels' salute, not for nothing did all of those marriages, all of those wonderful kids undergo such terrible strains. There is simply no room for it. It does not fit. Lena would understand this. "I never thought of sex,'' she would say, ''never thought of it once, not even at the end when everything was around me and I was dancing.''

VIII

Therefore it will be necessary to characterize Lena in some other way, and that opportunity will only come through the moment of crisis, the moment at which the *Skipstone* is drawn into the Black Galaxy of the neutron star. This moment will occur fairly early into the story, perhaps five or six hundred words deep (her previous life on the ship and impressions of hyperspace will come in expository chunks interwoven between sections of ongoing action), and her only indication of what has happened will be when there is a deep, lurching shiver in the gut of the ship where the embalmed lay and then she feels herself falling.

To explain this sensation it is important to explain normal hyperspace, the skip-drive which is merely to draw the curtains and to be in a cubicle. There is no sensation of motion in hyperspace, there could not be, the drive taking the *Skipstone* past any concepts of sound or light and into an area where there is no language to encompass nor glands to register. Were she to draw the curtains (curiously similar in their frills and pastels to what we might see hanging today in lower-middle-class homes of the kind I inhabit), she would be deprived of any sensation, but of course she cannot; she must open them to the portholes, and through them she can see the song of the colors to which I have previously alluded. Inside, there is a deep and grievous wretchedness, a feeling of terrible loss (which may explain why Lena thinks of exhuming the dead) that may be ascribed to the effects of hyperspace upon the corpus; but these sensations can be shielded, are not visible from the outside, and can be completely controlled by the phlegmatic types who comprise most of the pilots of these experimental flights. (Lena is rather phlegmatic herself. She reacts more to stress than some of her counterparts but well within the normal range prescribed by the Bureau, which admittedly does a superficial check.)

The effects of falling into the Black Galaxy are entirely

different, however, and it is here where Lena's emotional equipment becomes completely unstuck.

IX

At this point in the story great gobs of physics, astronomical and mathematical data would have to be incorporated, hopefully in a way which would furnish the hard-science basis of the story without repelling the reader.

Of course one should not worry so much about the repulsion of the reader; most who read science fiction do so in pursuit of exactly this kind of hard speculation (most often they are disappointed, but then most often they are after a time unable to tell the difference), and they would sit still much longer for a lecture than would, say, readers of the fictions of John Cheever, who could hardly bear sociological diatribes wedged into the everlasting vision of Gehenna which is Cheever's gift to his admirers. Thus it would be possible without awkwardness to make the following facts known, and these facts could indeed be set off from the body of the story and simply told like this:

It is posited that in other galaxies there are neutron stars, stars of four or five hundred times the size of our own or "normal" suns, which in their continuing nuclear process, burning and burning to maintain their light, will collapse in a mere ten to fifteen thousand years of difficult existence, their hydrogen fusing to helium then nitrogen and then to even heavier elements until with an implosion of terrific force, hungering for power which is no longer there, they collapse upon one another and bring disaster.

Disaster not only to themselves but possibly to the entire galaxy which they inhabit, for the gravitational force created by the implosion would be so vast as to literally seal in light. Not only light but sound and properties of all the stars in that great tube of force . . . so that the galaxy itself would be sucked into the funnel of gravitation created by the collapse and be absorbed into the flickering and desperate heart of the extinguished star.

It is possible to make several extrapolations from the fact of the neutron stars—and of the neutron stars themselves we

have no doubt; many nova and supernova are now known to
have been created by exactly this effect, not *ex-* but *im-*
plosion—and some of them are these:

(a) The gravitational forces created, like great spokes
wheeling out from the star, would drag in all parts of the
galaxy within their compass; and because of the force of
that gravitation, the galaxy would be invisible . . . these
forces would, as has been said, literally contain light.

(b) The neutron star, functioning like a cosmic vacuum
cleaner, might literally destroy the universe. Indeed, the
universe may be in the slow process at this moment of
being destroyed as hundreds of millions of its suns and
planets are being inexorably drawn toward these great vor-
texes. The process would be *slow,* of course, but it is seemingly inexorable. One neutron star, theoretically, could
absorb the universe. There are many more than one.

(c) The universe may have, obversely, been *created* by such
an implosion, throwing out enormous cosmic filaments
that, in a flickering instant of time which is as eons to us
but an instant to the cosmologists, are now being drawn
back in. The universe may be an accident.

(d) Cosmology aside, a ship trapped in such a vortex, such
a ''black,'' or invisible, galaxy, drawn toward the deadly
source of the neutron star, would be unable to leave it
through normal faster-than-light drive . . . because the
gravitation would absorb light, it would be impossible to
build up any level of acceleration (which would at some
point not exceed the speed of light) to permit escape. If it
was possible to emerge from the field, it could only be
done by an immediate switch to tachyonic drive without
accelerative buildup . . . a process which could drive the
occupant insane and which would, in any case, have no
clear destination. The black hole of the dead star is a literal
vacuum in space . . . one could fall through the hole, but
where, then, would one go?

(e) The actual process of being in the field of the dead star
might well drive one insane.

For all of these reasons Lena does not know that she has

fallen into the Galaxy Called Rome until the ship simply does so.

And she would instantly and irreparably become insane.

X

The technological data having been stated, the crisis of the story—the collapse into the Galaxy—having occurred early on, it would now be the obligation of the writer to describe the actual sensations involved in falling into the Black Galaxy. Since little or nothing is known of what these sensations would be—other than that it is clear that the gravitation would suspend almost all physical laws and might well suspend time itself, time only being a function of physics—it would be easy to lurch into a surrealistic mode here; Lena could see monsters slithering on the walls, two-dimensional monsters that is, little cut-outs of her past; she could re-enact her life *in full consciousness* from birth until death; she could literally be turned inside-out anatomically and perform in her imagination or in the flesh gross physical acts upon herself; she could live and die a thousand times in the lightless, timeless expanse of the pit . . . all of this could be done within the confines of the story, and it would doubtless lead to some very powerful material. One could do it picaresque fashion, one perversity or lunacy to a chapter—that is to say, the chapters spliced together with more data on the gravitational excesses and the fact that neutron stars (this is interesting) are probably the pulsars which we have identified, stars which can be detected through sound but not by sight from unimaginable distances. The author could do this kind of thing, and do it very well indeed; he has done it literally hundreds of times before, but this, perhaps, would be in disregard of Lena. She has needs more imperative than those of the author, or even those of the editors. She is in terrible pain. She is suffering.

Falling, she sees the dead; falling, she hears the dead; the dead address her from the hold, and they are screaming, "Release us, release us, we are alive, we are in pain, we are in torment"; in their gelatinous flux, their distended limbs sutured finger and toe to the membranes which hold them, their decay has been reversed as the warp into which they have fallen has reversed time; and they are begging Lena from a torment which they cannot phrase, so profound is it; their voices are in her head, pealing and banging like oddly shaped bells. "Release us!" they scream, "we are no longer dead, the trumpet has sounded!" and so on and so forth, but Lena literally does not know what to do. She is merely the ferryman on this dread passage; she is not a medical specialist; she knows nothing of prophylaxis or restoration, and any movement she made to release them from the gelatin which holds them would surely destroy their biology, no matter what the state of their minds.

But even if this were not so, even if she could by releasing them give them peace, she cannot because she is succumbing to her own responses. In the black hole, if the dead are risen, then the risen are certainly the dead; she dies in this space, Lena does; she dies a thousand times over a period of seventy thousand years (because there is no objective time here, chronology is controlled only by the psyche, and Lena has a thousand full lives and a thousand full deaths), and it is terrible, of course, but it is also interesting because for every cycle of death there is a life, seventy years in which she can meditate upon her condition in solitude; and by the two hundredth year or more (or less, each of the lives is individual, some of them long, others short), Lena has come to an understanding of exactly where she is and what has happened to her. That it has taken her fourteen thousand years to reach this understanding is in one way incredible, and yet it is a kind of miracle as well because in an infinite universe with infinite possibilities, all of them reconstituted for her, it is highly unlikely that even in fourteen thousand years she would stumble upon the answer, had it not been for the fact that she is unusually strong-willed and that some of the personalities through which she has lived are highly creative and controlled and have been able to do some serious thinking. Also there is a carry-over from life to life, even with the differing personalities, so that she is able to make use of preceding knowledge.

Most of the personalities are weak, of course, and not a few are insane, and almost all are cowardly, but there is a little residue; even in the worst of them there is enough residue to carry forth the knowledge, and so it is in the fourteen-thousandth year, when the truth of it has finally come upon her and she realizes what has happened to her and what is going on and what she must do to get out of there, and so it is [then] that she summons all of the strength and will which are left to her, and stumbling to the console (she is in her sixty-eighth year of this life and in the personality of an old, sniveling, whining man, an exferryman himself), she summons one of the prostheses, the master engineer, the controller. All of this time the dead have been shrieking and clanging in her ears, fourteen thousand years of agony billowing from the hold and surrounding her in sheets like iron; and as the master engineer, exactly as he was when she last saw him fourteen thousand years and two weeks ago, emerges from the console, the machinery whirring slickly, she gasps in relief, too weak even to respond with pleasure to the fact that in this condition of antitime, antilight, anticausality the machinery still works. But then it would. The machinery always works, even in this final and most terrible of all the hard-science stories. It is not the machinery which fails but its operators or, in extreme cases, the cosmos.

"What's the matter?" the master engineer says.

The stupidity of this question, its naivete and irrelevance in the midst of the hell she has occupied, stuns Lena, but she realizes even through the haze that the master engineer would, of course, come without memory of circumstances and would have to be apprised of background. This is inevitable. Whining and sniveling, she tells him in her old man's voice what has happened.

"Why that's terrible!" the master engineer says. "That's really terrible," and lumbering to a porthole, he looks out at the Black Galaxy, the Galaxy Called Rome, and one look at it causes him to lock into position and then disintegrate, not because the machinery has failed (the machinery never fails, not ultimately) but because it has merely recreated a human substance which could not possibly come to grips with what has been seen outside that porthole.

Lena is left alone again, then, with the shouts of the dead carrying forward.

Realizing instantly what has happened to her—fourteen thousand years of perception can lead to a quicker reaction time, if nothing else—she addresses the console again, uses the switches and produces three more prostheses, all of them engineers barely subsidiary to the one she has already addressed. (Their resemblance to the three comforters of Job will not be ignored here, and there will be an opportunity to squeeze in some quick religious allegory, which is always useful to give an ambitious story yet another level of meaning.) Although they are not quite as qualified or definitive in their opinions as the original engineer, they are bright enough by far to absorb her explanation, and, this time, her warnings not to go to the portholes, not to look upon the galaxy, are heeded. Instead, they stand there in rigid and curiously mortified postures, as if waiting for Lena to speak.

"So you see," she says finally, as if concluding a long and difficult conversation, which in fact she has, "as far as I can see, the only way to get out of this black galaxy is to go directly into tachyonic drive. Without any accelerative build-up at all."

The three comforters nod slowly, bleakly. They do not quite know what she is talking about, but then again, they have not had fourteen thousand years to ponder this point. "Unless you can see anything else," Lena says, "unless you can think of anything different. Otherwise, it's going to be infinity in here, and I can't take much more of this, really. Fourteen thousand years is enough."

"Perhaps," the first comforter suggests softly, "perhaps it is your fate and your destiny to spend infinity in this black hole. Perhaps in some way you are determining the fate of the universe. After all, it was you who said that it all might be a gigantic accident, eh? Perhaps your suffering gives it purpose."

"And then too," the second lisps, "you've got to consider the dead down there. This isn't very easy for them, you know, what with being jolted alive and all that, and an immediate vault into tachyonic would probably destroy them for good. The Bureau wouldn't like that, and you'd be liable for some pretty stiff damages. No, if I were you I'd stay with the dead," the second concludes, and a clamorous murmur seems to arise from the hold at this, although whether it is one of approval or of terrible pain is difficult to tell. The dead are not very expressive.

"Anyway," the third says, brushing a forelock out of his eyes, averting his glance from the omnipresent and dreadful portholes, "there's little enough to be done about this situation. You've fallen into a neutron star, a black funnel. It is utterly beyond the puny capacities and possibilities of man. I'd accept my fate if I were you." His model was a senior scientist working on quasar theory, but in reality he appears to be a metaphysician. "There are corners of experience into which man cannot stray without being severely penalized."

"That's very easy for you to say," Lena says bitterly, her whine breaking into clear glissando, "but you haven't suffered as I have. Also, there's at least a theoretical possibility that I'll get out of here if I do the build-up without acceleration."

"But where will you land?" the third says, waving a trembling forefinger. "And when? All rules of space and time have been destroyed here; only gravity persists. You can fall through the center of this sun, but you do not know where you will come out or at what period of time. It is inconceivable that you would emerge into normal space in the time you think of as contemporary."

"No," the second says, "I wouldn't do that. You and the dead are joined together now; it is truly your fate to remain with them. What is death? What is life? In the Galaxy Called Rome all roads lead to the same, you see; you have ample time to consider these questions, and I'm sure that you will come up with something truly viable, of much interest."

"Ah, well," the first says, looking at Lena, "if you must know, I think that it would be much nobler of you to remain here; for all we know, your condition gives substance and viability to the universe. Perhaps you *are* the universe. But you're not going to listen anyway, and so I won't argue the point. I really won't," he says rather petulantly and then makes a gesture to the other two; the three of them quite deliberately march to a porthole, push a curtain aside and look out upon it. Before Lena can stop them—not that she is sure she would, not that she is sure that this is not exactly what she has willed—they have been reduced to ash.

And she is left alone with the screams of the dead.

Note similarity to Malzberg trying to get out of SF & into mainstream

XI

It can be seen that the satiric aspects of the scene above can be milked for great implication, and unless a very skillful controlling hand is kept upon the material, the piece could easily degenerate into farce at this moment. It is possible, as almost any comedian knows, to reduce (or elevate) the starkest and most terrible issues to scatology or farce simply by particularizing them; and it will be hard not to use this scene for a kind of needed comic relief in what is, after all, an extremely depressing tale, the more depressing because it has used the largest possible canvas on which to imprint its messages that man is irretrievably dwarfed by the cosmos. (At least, that is the message which it would be easiest to wring out of the material; actually I have other things in mind, but how many will be able to detect them?)

What will save the scene and the story itself, around this point will be the lush physical descriptions of the Black Galaxy, the neutron star, the altering effects they have had upon perceived reality. Every rhetorical trick, every typographical device, every nuance of language and memory which the writer has to call upon will be utilized in this section describing the appearance of the black hole and its effects upon Lena's (admittedly distorted) consciousness. It will be a bleak vision, of course, but not necessarily a hopeless one; it will demonstrate that our concepts of "beauty" or "ugliness" or "evil" or "good" or "love" or "death" are little more than metaphors, semantically limited, framed in by the poor receiving equipment in our heads; and it will be suggested that, rather than showing us a different or alternative reality, the black hole may only be showing us the only reality we know, but *extended*, infinitely extended so that the story may give us, as good science fiction often does, at this point some glimpse of possibilities beyond ourselves, possibilities not to be contained in word rates or the problems of editorial qualification. And also at this point of the story it might be worthwhile to characterize Lena in a "warmer" or more "sympathetic" fashion so that the reader can see her as a distinct and admirable human being, quite plucky in the face of all her disasters and fourteen thousand years, two hundred lives. This can be done through conventional fictional technique: individuation through defining idiosyncrasy, tricks of speech, habits, mannerisms, and so on. In common everyday fiction we could give her an affecting stutter, a dimple on her left breast, a love of policemen, fear of red convertibles, and leave it at that; in this story, because of its considerably extended theme, it will be necessary to do better than that, to find originalities of idiosyncrasy which will, in their wonder and suggestion of panoramic possibility, approximate the black hole . . . but no matter. No matter. This can be done; the section interweaving Lena and her vision of the black hole will be the flashiest and most admired but in truth the easiest section of the story to write, and I am sure that I would have no trouble with it whatsoever if, as I said much earlier, this were a story instead of a series of notes for a story, the story itself being unutterably beyond our time and space and devices and to be glimpsed only in empty little flickers of light much as Lena can glimpse the black hole, much as she knows the gravity of the neutron star. These notes are as close to the vision of the story as Lena herself would ever get.

As this section ends, it is clear that Lena has made her decision to attempt to leave the Black Galaxy by automatic boost to tachyonic drive. She does not know where she will emerge or how, but she does know that she can bear this no longer.

She prepares to set the controls, but before this it is necessary to write the dialogue with the dead.

XII

One of them presumably will appoint himself as the spokesman of the many and will appear before Lena in this new space as if in a dream. "Listen here," this dead would say, one born in 3361, dead in 3401, waiting eight centuries for exhumation to a society that can rid his body of leukemia (he is bound to be disappointed), "you've got to face the facts of the situation here. We can't just leave in this way. Better the death we know than the death you will give us."

"The decision is made," Lena says, her fingers straight on the controls. "There will be no turning back."

"We are dead now," the leukemic says. "At least let this death continue. At least in the bowels of this galaxy where there is no time we have a kind of life or at least that non-existence of which we have always dreamed. I could tell you many of the things we have learned during these fourteen thousand years, but they would make little sense to you, of course. We have learned resignation. We have had great insights. Of course all of this would go beyond you."

"Nothing goes beyond me. Nothing at all. But it does not matter."

"Everything matters. Even here there is consequence, causality, a sense of humanness, one of responsibility. You can suspend physical laws, you can suspend life itself, but you cannot separate the moral imperatives of humanity. There are absolutes. It would be apostasy to try and leave."

"Man must leave," Lena says, "man must struggle, man must attempt to control his conditions. Even if he goes from worse to obliteration, that is still his destiny." Perhaps the dialogue is a little florid here. Nevertheless, this will be the thrust of it. It is to be noted that putting this conventional viewpoint in the character of a woman will give another of those necessary levels of irony with which the story must abound if it is to be anything other than a freak show, a cascade of sleazy wonders shown shamefully behind a tent . . . but irony will give it legitimacy. "I don't care about the dead," Lena says. "I only care about the living."

"Then care about the universe," the dead man says, "care about that, if nothing else. By trying to come out through the center of the black hole, you may rupture the seamless fabric of time and space itself. You may destroy everything. Past and present and future. The explosion may extend the funnel of gravitational force to infinite size, and all of the universe will be driven into the hole."

Lena shakes her head. She knows that the dead is merely another one of her tempters in a more cunning and cadaverous guise. "You are lying to me," she says. "This is merely another effect of the Galaxy Called Rome. I am responsible to myself, only to myself. The universe is not at issue."

"That's a rationalization," the leukemic says, seeing her hesitation, sensing his victory, "and you know it as well as I do. You can't be an utter solipsist. You aren't God, there is no God, not here, but if there was it wouldn't be you. You must measure the universe about yourself."

Lena looks at the dead and the dead looks at her; and in that confrontation, in the shade of his eyes as they pass through the dull lusters of the neutron star effect, she sees that they are close to a communion so terrible that it will become a weld, become a connection . . . that if she listens to the dead for more than another instant, she will collapse within those eyes as the *Skipstone* has collapsed into the black hole; and she cannot bear this, it cannot be . . . she must hold to the belief, that there is some separation between the living and the dead and that there is dignity in that separation, that life is not death but something else because, if she cannot accept that, she denies herself . . . and quickly then, quickly before she can consider further, she hits the controls that will convert the ship instantly past the power of light; and then in the explosion of many suns that might only be her heart she hides her head in her arms and screams.

And the dead screams with her, and it is not a scream of joy but not of terror either . . . it is the true natal cry suspended between the moments of limbo, life and expiration, and their shrieks entwine in the womb of the *Skipstone* as it pours through into the redeemed light.

XIII

The story is open-ended, of course.

Perhaps Lena emerges into her own time and space once more, all of this having been a sheath over the greater reality. Perhaps she emerges into an otherness. Then again, she may never get out of the black hole at all but remains and lives there, the *Skipstone* a planet in the tubular universe of the neutron star, the first or last of a series of planets collapsing toward their deadened sun. If the story is done correctly, if the ambiguities are prepared right, if the technological data is stated well, if the material is properly visualized . . . well, it does not matter then what happens to Lena, her *Skipstone* and her dead. Any ending will do. Any would suffice and be emotionally satisfying to the reader.

Still, there is an inevitable ending.

It seems clear to the writer, who will not, cannot write this story, but if he did he would drive it through to this one conclusion, the conclusion clear, implied really from the first and bound, bound utterly, into the text.

So let the author have it.

XIV

In the infinity of time and space, all is possible, and as they are vomited from that great black hole, spilled from this anus of a neutron star (I will not miss a single Freudian implication if I can), Lena and her dead take on this infinity, partake of the vast canvas of possibility. Now they are in the Antares Cluster flickering like a bulb; here they are at the heart of Sirius the Dog Star five hundred screams from the hold; here again in ancient Rome watching Jesus trudge up carrying the Cross of Calvary . . . and then again in another unimaginable galaxy dead across from the Milky Way a billion light-years in span with a hundred thousand habitable planets, each of them with their Calvary . . . and they are not, they are not yet satisfied.

They cannot, being human, partake of infinity; they can partake of only what they know. They cannot, being created from the consciousness of the writer, partake of what he does not know but what is only close to him. Trapped within the consciousness of the writer, the penitentiary of his being, as the writer is himself trapped in the *Skipstone* of his mortality, Lena and her dead emerge in the year 1975 to the town of Ridgefield Park, New Jersey, and there they inhabit the bodies of its fifteen thousand souls, and there they are, there they are yet, dwelling amidst the refineries, strolling on Main Street, sitting in the Rialto theatre, shopping in the supermarkets, pairing off and clutching one another in the imploded stars of their beds on this very night at this very moment, as that accident, the author, himself one of them, has conceived them.

It is unimaginable that they would come, Lena and the dead, from the heart of the Galaxy Called Rome to tenant Ridgefield Park, New Jersey . . . but more unimaginable still that from all the Ridgefield Parks of our time we will come and assemble and build the great engines which will take us to the stars and some of the stars will bring us death and some bring life and some will bring nothing at all but the engines will go on and on and so—after a fashion, in our fashion—will we.

Note similarities between the story situation & Malzberg's apparent fear that he will be absorbed by the fans, the field. Note his struggles (which always fail) to leave the field. Note his expressed concern with money — only by being wealthy can he continue to write SF with some self-respect.

WHO'S CRIBBING?

Jack Lewis

Time for a change of pace, courtesy of Jack Lewis, who wrote this hilarious tale of a science fiction author's living nightmare almost forty years ago. And while others have borrowed both the form and the theme over the years, no one has ever done it better.

February 4, 1953

Mr. Jack Lewis
90-26 219 St.
Queens Village, N. Y.

Dear Mr. Lewis:

We are returning your manuscript "The Ninth Dimension." At first glance, I had figured it a story well worthy of publication. Why wouldn't I? So did the editors of *Cosmic Tales* back in 1934 when the story was first published.

As you no doubt know, it was the great Todd Thromberry who wrote the story you tried to pass off on us as an original. Let me give you a word of caution concerning the penalties resulting from plagiarism.

It's not worth it. Believe me.

Sincerely,
Doyle P. Gates
Science Fiction Editor
Deep Space Magazine

February 9, 1953

Mr. Doyle P. Gates
Editor, Deep Space Magazine
New York, N. Y.

Dear Mr. Gates:

I do not know, nor am I aware of the existence of any Todd Thromberry. The story you
rejected was submitted in good faith, and I re-
sent the inference that I plagiarized it.

"The Ninth Dimension" was written by me not
more than a month ago, and if there is any similarity between it and the story written by this
Thromberry person, it is purely coincidental.

However, it has set me thinking. Some time
ago, I submitted another story to *Stardust
Scientifiction,* and received a penciled notation
on the rejection slip stating that the story was,
"too Thromberryish."

Who in the hell is Todd Thromberry? I don't
remember reading anything written by him in the
ten years I've been interested in science fiction.

Sincerely,
Jack Lewis

February 13, 1953

Mr. Jack Lewis
90-26 219 St.
Queens Village, N. Y.

Dear Mr. Lewis:

Re: Your letter of February 9.
While the editors of this magazine are not in
the habit of making open accusations and are
well aware of the fact in the writing business

there will always be some overlapping of plot ideas, it is very hard for us to believe that you are not familiar with the works of Todd Thromberry.

While Mr. Thromberry is no longer among us, his works, like so many other writers', only became widely recognized after his death in 1941. Perhaps it was his work in the field of electronics that supplied him with the bottomless pit of new ideas so apparent in all his works. Nevertheless, even at this stage of science fiction's development it is apparent that he had a style that many of our so-called contemporary writers might do well to copy. By "copy," I do not mean rewrite word for word one or more of his works, as you have done. For while you state this has been accidental, surely you must realize that the chance of this phenomenon actually happening is about a million times as great as the occurrence of four pat royal flushes on one deal.

Sorry, but we're not that naïve.

Sincerely yours,
Doyle P. Gates
Science Fiction Editor
Deep Space Magazine

February 18, 1953

Mr. Doyle P. Gates
Editor, Deep Space Magazine
New York, N. Y.

Sir:

Your accusations are typical of the rag you publish.

Please cancel my subscription immediately.

Sincerely,
Jack Lewis

February 18, 1953

Science Fiction Society
144 Front Street
Chicago, Ill.

Gentlemen:

    I am interested in reading some of the works
of the late Todd Thromberry.
    I would like to get some of the publications
that feature his stories.

                     Respectfully,
                      Jack Lewis

February 24, 1953

Mr. Jack Lewis
90-26 219 St.
Queens Village, N. Y.

Dear Mr. Lewis:

    So would we. All I can suggest is that you
contact the publishers if any are still in business, or haunt your second-hand bookstores.
    If you succeed in getting any of these maga-
zines, please let us know. We'll pay you a handsome premium on them.

                     Yours,
                      Ray Albert
                      President,
                      Science Fiction Society

February 27, 1953

Mr. Sampson J. Gross, Editor
Strange Worlds Magazine
St. Louis, Mo.

Dear Mr. Gross:

I am enclosing the manuscript of a story I have just completed. As you can see on the title page, I call it "Wreckers of Ten Million Galaxies." Because of the great amount of research that went into it, I must set the minimum price on this one at not less than two cents a word.

Hoping you will see fit to use it for publication in your magazine, I remain,

Respectfully,
Jack Lewis

March 5, 1953

Mr. Jack Lewis
90-26 219 St.
Queens Village, N. Y.

Dear Mr. Lewis:

I'm sorry, but at the present time we won't be able to use "Wreckers of Ten Million Galaxies." It's a great yarn though, and if at some future date we decide to use it we will make out the reprint check directly to the estate of Todd Thromberry.

That boy sure could write.

Cordially,
Sampson J. Gross
Editor,
Strange Worlds Magazine

March 10, 1953

Mr. Doyle P. Gates
Editor, Deep Space Magazine
New York, N. Y.

Dear Mr. Gates:

While I said I would never have any dealings with you or your magazine again, a situation has arisen which is most puzzling.

It seems all my stories are being returned to me by reason of the fact that except for the by-line, they are exact duplicates of the works of this Todd Thromberry person.

In your last letter you aptly described the odds on the accidental occurrence of this phenomenon in the case of one story. What would you consider the approximate odds on no less than half a dozen of my writings?

I agree with you—astronomical!

Yet in the interest of all mankind, how can I get the idea across to you that every word I have submitted was actually written *by me!* I have never copied any material from Todd Thromberry, nor have I ever seen any of his writings. In fact, as I told you in one of my letters, up until a short while ago I was totally unaware of his very existence.

An idea has occurred to me however. It's a truly weird theory and one that I probably wouldn't even suggest to anyone but a science fiction editor. But suppose—just suppose—that this Thromberry person, what with his experiments in electronics and everything, had in some way managed to crack through this time-space barrier mentioned so often in your magazine. And suppose—egotistical as it sounds—

he had singled out my work as being the type
of material he had always wanted to write.

Do you begin to follow me? Or is the idea of
a person from a different time cycle looking
over my shoulder while I write, too fantastic
for you to accept?

Please write and tell me what you think of
my theory?

Respectfully,
Jack Lewis

March 18, 1953

Mr. Jack Lewis
90-26 219 St.
Queens Village, N. Y.

Dear Mr. Lewis:

We think you should consult a psychiatrist.

Sincerely,
Doyle P. Gates
Science Fiction Editor
Deep Space Magazine

March 23, 1953

Mr. Sam Mines
Science Fiction Editor
Standard Magazines Inc.
New York, 16, N. Y.

Dear Mr. Mines:

While the enclosed is not really a manuscript
at all, I am submitting this series of letters,
carbon copies, and correspondence, in the hope

that you might give some credulity to this seemingly unbelievable happening.

The enclosed letters are all in the proper order and should be self-explanatory. Perhaps if you publish them, some of your readers might have some idea how this phenomenon could be explained.

I call the entire piece "Who's Cribbing?"

> Respectfully,
> Jack Lewis

March 27, 1953

Mr. Jack Lewis
90-26 219 St.
Queens Village, N. Y.

Dear Mr. Lewis:

Your idea of a series of letters to put across a science fiction idea is an intriguing one, but I'm afraid it doesn't quite come off.

It was in the August 1940 issue of *Macabre Adventures* that Mr. Thromberry first used this very idea. Ironically enough, the story title also was: "Who's Cribbing."

Feel free to contact us again when you have something more original.

> Yours,
> Samuel Mines
> Science Fiction Editor
> Standard Magazines Inc.

THE MERCHANT OF STRATFORD

Frank Ramirez

Did you ever wonder what Shakespeare was really like?
For example, what did he think of the works of Isaac
Asimov and Roger Zelazny? How would he have ghost-
written a Cordwainer Smith novel?
  But that's crazy, you say? Not really. It's just another
way to peek inside the funhouse, this time with Frank
Ramirez as your guide.

I TENSED WITH anticipation as the straps were tightened. The moment had finally come.

Gone from my mind were the agonies of years in planning, months in engineering, days in language training.

All thoughts were swept behind as I focused my attentions on the task at hand. Imagine! The wonder of it! Traveling back in time to speak with none other than the Immortal Bard himself! Unbelievable!

The greatest poet of all time, the man whose plays were still box-office hits after four hundred years, a man who could speak to and move humanity across the span of centuries— and to think he did it all by accident! For surely he had only written those masterpieces to fill a specific demand, writing parts to be performed by specific actors on a specific stage. What a genius!

In my storage compartment were volumes for his perusal— a concise history of the world through the year 2000, a selection of the greatest poets since the master, selected volumes of Shakespearean criticism, and the massive one-volume *Armstead Shakespeare*, the *definitive* Shakespeare, published in 1997.

What would the Bard think of the changes in technology, of the new direction art had taken, of the advance of our scholarship? I had hopes that the praise of four centuries would comfort him during his declining years, bringing a peace to his soul.

And I wondered, would he accept my offer and return with me to the twenty-first century?

I remembered the trepidation of my staff with regards to the so-called dangers of time-travel. Would my presence in the early seventeenth century change the course of history? It took many days to convince all concerned that their fears were groundless. I was going to visit the *past*. Therefore, if I had succeeded, I had already been there. I had always been there. With a little help from a philosopher of the university, I made my point.

I slept little the night before. I paced furiously, thoughts racing. The fruits of the ages were to be laid humbly at his feet. Would he find the specially bound volumes worthy? Lord grant he would accept and enjoy.

Would our lifestyle shock his sensibilities? Surely not, for he was the universal man.

These and many other questions passed through my mind that night.

After an eternity—morning.

I ate, then donned the costume provided by the theater department. I was dressed as a man of moderate wealth. My beard was trimmed to fit any prevailing fashion. My purse was filled with coins that would serve.

As I entered the sphere I turned and smiled at the white-suited technicians. A quick wave, I slipped inside, and the door was slammed into place. At last I was alone. I clasped the straps, and they tightened themselves. I relayed the readings of several instruments, listened to last minute instructions, and waited.

Tensing, I watched as the chronometer marked the last few seconds. The moments passed—

When the grand millisecond arrived I felt little more than a minor lurch. I had arrived.

My first impulse was to force open the door and run into the open air, to breathe the air the Bard was breathing, to share his world.

Instead, I took two deep breaths, paused, then went through the checklist.

But all the time I thought: 1615! Shakespeare had retired from the stage. Soon I would learn—what would I learn? The exact texts of the plays, perhaps the extent of the canon, answers to all the mysteries, details of his life; did all of these things wait for me?

When at last I completed the checklist I depressurized the cabin, opened the door, and stepped into the seventeenth century.

I also stepped into a pile of dung.

I spent a few moments hiding the machine in some bushes. One of my worries was that I might startle the highly superstitious natives, who, believing in the supernatural, might attempt to do me harm. This caused me to wonder: would the Bard himself believe that he was in the presence of a devil or an angel? Nay, surely *he* could accept the truth.

I sang as I tramped—one mile, two miles . . . Stratford was proving to be farther than I thought . . . three, four, hmmmm . . . six, seven, gasp . . . eight, wheeze . . . was that—? Yes—I could see—I had arrived at—

Stratford.

I hurried, guided by a map prepared by the history department.

It was not long before I reached what could only be New Place, the residence of Master Will. More than a little excited, I approached the gate, passed through it, and stepped forward towards the door. I briefly noted that the actual house was quite different, more—modern, if that's the word, than I had imagined. It mattered little to me at the moment, however. My heart skipped a beat as I read the name on the plate: Mast. Wm. Shakespeare. I had arrived.

I knocked firmly on the door, determined not to disgrace my century. A woman (no doubt the former Anne Hathaway) came to answer. Looking me over with what I thought might be amusement (was there something wrong with my costume?!) she said, "What ho! Stand and present yourself!"

"I have come," I said, "upon a matter of momentous importance. Is Master Shakespeare at home?!"

Hesitating not a moment, she shouted over her shoulder, "Hey nonny, ho nonny, another nonny ninny, Will!"

Mystified, I followed her beyond the door, puzzling over her remark. Leading me down a murky corridor, she at last brought me to a small study, which she indicated I should enter. I did so with much emotion.

There he sat!

Head down, pen racing across paper, the books filling the dim shelves, light streaming through the window to illumine the words divine: Shakespeare, messenger of the gods! What unknown work was he penning, what sonnet unimagined; with what phrase unguessed was he gracing paper as no product of coarse wood deserved to be? In that instant I wished wildly that I was the paper, the ink, the instrument by which the Immortal Bard—

He lifted his head and spoke.

"Sit down, won't you?" he said. "I'll be with you in a moment."

Something strange there.

But his voice . . . and his words! "I'll be with you in a moment." Who else? Who else could have spoken those words? I resolved at my earliest opportunity to travel further back into time, to the days when a younger Shakespeare graced the stage.

He blew his nose on his sleeve.

Of course, I thought hurriedly, I mustn't judge him by *my* standards. Besides, a deeper problem weighed on my mind. How could I possibly convey, without shocking, my mission to this most excellent member of the human race?

I reached for my camera, determined to save for all time a true portrait of the man who transcended ages. I brought the device to my face, glanced through the view-finder, and prepared to press the button when I noticed that a hand was obscuring the vision of the lens.

The hand belonged to none other than Will himself. I lowered the camera. But of course, how stupid of me, the strange instrument frightened him. I would explain its function and—

"Please," he was saying. "No pictures, please. You'll have to clear it with my agent."

Shock. What was I hearing? I was deluding myself, I hadn't heard anything of the sort. I was—

"Listen," I was saying, "I know you'll find this hard to believe, but you must try to understand. Listen carefully. I am—"

"—a man from the future, I know," he finished. "Come now," he continued, "you don't really think you're the first man who's ever—is something the matter?"

"How—"

"Oh! I understand. You must be one of the first. Imagine, I'm in the presence of one of the first time travelers. I'm so very sorry for the shock."

Sorry for the—wasn't that my line?

Suddenly I knew what had bothered me about the way he spoke.

"But you speak perfect English! I mean contemporary! I mean—and your wife!"

"Pretty good, don't you think? I love to get the chance to practice it. It's like a second language. But of course I had to learn it, don't you know, what with all the time travelers from all the different centuries coming and going willy-nilly as they pleased. Come to think of it, it *has* been a pretty quiet day. I think you're one of the first this morning."

I remained speechless, as the implications began to sink in.

He was eyeing my bag.

"What have you got for me?" he asked.

"Got for you?"

"Yes, all of the early time travelers brought me gifts, books, pocket dictionaries, histories, certificates, plaques, that sort of thing. What did *you* bring?"

I emptied the contents of my bag. He quickly glanced at the titles. The books of criticism he threw in a rubbish heap in the corner, along with an expletive.

"Bloody useless things, those, as if I'd written the plays to be read."

The collected works brought a small chuckle. The history he placed in a pile on his desk with the comment, ''Might be able to sell this one.''

Thinking it over, however, he withdrew it from the stack and threw it in the corner with the criticism.

''Not for much, though.''

Finally, he perused the volume of poetry. It had a special dedication to the Bard, praising him for his work, laying before his feet these humble trifles, etc. He harumphed, closed it, and looked at me.

''Is this the best you could do?''

I replied, ''It was selected by our English Department.''

''Figures,'' he said. ''Next time you come, bring some Zelazny.''

Zelazny? Who was—He must have read my face.

''Haven't you ever heard of him?'' he asked. ''And while you're at it send some Asimov too. Can't get enough through channels. I've got almost all of Heinlein's books, but let me see if there's something you . . .''

Tapering off, he turned to face a list stapled—stapled!— below his bookshelf, which I could now see very clearly. The bindings were decidedly un-seventeenth century.

''I remember now!'' he brightened. ''See if you can find me that issue of *Galaxy* from the summer of 1973. I've been dying to read the end of that Clarke novel.''

''Who are all these people?''

''Science fiction writers,'' he said with reverence. ''You fool,'' he added with derision.

''You *like* science fiction?''

One would have thought I'd cursed the Queen and spit on the Bible by the look he gave me.

''Of course I do. It reminds me of my work.''

''I'm afraid I don't understand.''

''Well, it's honest, for one thing. I wrote plays, and was looked down upon by my contemporaries for doing so. I didn't write what was considered literature. I wrote to entertain *and* to make a little money. The same thing was true for SF. But what happened centuries after its birth? Let me see if I can find my copy of that variorum edition of *The Martian*

Chronicles. Now you've got me sounding like a Heinlein character."

I said nothing.

"Something the matter?" he asked.

"Yes, something's the matter. Speak Elizabethan."

"Maybe later, if you behave. And don't forget, James is on the throne. You should have asked me to speak Jacobean."

"What's going on here?" I shouted. "I'm the first person to travel back in time!"

"But you're certainly not the first to get here!"

I shook my head as he continued.

"I've been getting visitors from the future as far back as I can remember. My mother, being a good Christian woman, had the hardest time giving me suck, because the documentary team from the thirty-third century wanted to film it all. I barely survived childhood. Fortunately my father was a shrewd businessman. He managed to capitalize off the circumstances. Of course he spent so much time in negotiations that he couldn't attend council meetings so, you know, he was thrown out, but—say, don't tell me you're surprised by all this. Why do you think I died only fifty years after I was born? I spent forty years in countless different centuries."

"What did you do?"

"Oh, the usual: dedicated hospitals, opened restaurants, christened spaceships, spoke at ladies' luncheons, appeared on talk shows, lectured on what you might call the chicken-and-peas circuit, that sort of thing."

I think I must have been shaking visibly, for he said, "Calm down, have a drink." He reached for a bottle and poured something strong. I sputtered as I downed it in one gulp.

"What *was* that?" I asked, remembering that the bottle and the seventeenth century—

"I'm not sure. Someone from the twenty-eighth century left it here. Well now, feel better? You know, Jesus once told me that to stay calm one should always practice—"

"Jesus?"

"Yes, of course. Some clowns from the thirtieth century thought it'd be a gas for me to meet him. Really nice fellow, don't you know, sort of intense; but he could take a joke. He never forgave me for the character of Shylock, though. Rather petty, don't you think? But then, you have to consider his point of view, and he *was* under a lot of pressure. If you think I've time-travelers in my hair you should've seen him!''

I must have looked forlorn.

''Tell you what, just to show there's no hard feelings, I'll sell you a copy of my complete works, and my autobiography as well.'' He reached behind and pulled two plastic-bound volumes from two different stacks. One was imposingly thick.

''Here they are, treasure of the ages, all the plays I ever wrote, approved text, cast lists, year of composition, sources, random bits of poetry, and a previously unpublished novel, *Go-Captains in Norstrilia*. And this here is the complete autobiography, with all the important facts that led to my becoming the Immortal Bard. Did you live before the twenty-sixth century?''

''Yes.''

''Dollars, credits, or muffins?''

''All I've got are these gold pieces.''

He looked them over.

''I guess I'll trust you. How many did you bring?''

''Twelve.''

''You're in luck. The price just happens to be twelve gold pieces.''

''But I'm the first Time Traveler!''

''Eleven. It's my final offer.''

I accepted.

''Have Anne give you a receipt at the door. Oh, and don't let her sell you my copy of Holinshed. They all fall for that.''

''Please,'' I begged, ''will you return with me to the twenty-first century?''

''Sorry, never travel before the twenty-fourth if I can help it.''

I could see there was nothing left for me to do. I turned to leave, a broken shell.

POP! Wha—!?

A man stepped out of nothing, holding what appeared to be an annoyed octopus. He stuck a tentacle in my face.

''That's right, look into the trivid, that's a good Timey.

Pevlik, System News Syndic, twenty-third century. Would you mind answering a few—"

POP!

"Here he is. My, you've given me a chase. Astor, *Galactic Globe*. Tell me, what is your impression of—"

POP!

"Stanik, *Centauri Sentinel*—"

POP! POP!

"Hey! You!"

POP! POP! POP!

"Stilgrin, *Filbert Studge Stationer!*"

POP! POP! POP! POP! POP!

Ten, fifteen, twenty assorted humanoids suddenly surrounded me. I felt faint, dizzy, dazed. I could hardly breathe.

"Let me out of here! What's going on?"

"Don't you know?" asked someone with purple hair.

"Know what?"

In unison: "You're the first Time Traveler!"

Everything began to fade as I sank to my knees. No, I thought, don't let it end this way.

"Zounds!" shouted a familiar voice. "By Gis and by Saint Charity, give the man air."

"Aw, come on, Will, give us a break," said one of the reporters.

"That I will. Doubt that the stars are fire, but never doubt that old Shaxpur would ever forget the people that made him famous. I know you want exclusives on the first Time Traveler, and I promise you, speaking as the lad's business manager—"

"My what?" I shouted. "A second ago you were ushering—"

"In the words of another Immortal Bard, 'It's raining soup, grab a bucket!' You want to make a little cash on this thing? These guys'll steal you blind if you let them."

"And you?"

He tried unsuccessfully to look hurt.

"I'd only take forty percent, no more than my fair share. It's only fitting I take care of you as my father took care of me."

"How much did he take?"

"Eighty percent till my twenty-first year."

"Good friend," I sighed, "For Jesus' sake waste no more time convincing me. Talk to them," I said, pointing at the mob, "and soon," I added. "I think they're getting hungry."

"Right away, boss. Who'll start the bidding for the interview. The man in the front offers three Asimovs and an Ellison. Who'll add a Brunner?"

ONE REJECTION
TOO MANY

Patricia Nurse

How much difference can a rejection from a science fiction magazine make? Usually, not a hell of a lot—but every once in a while it can change the entire universe, as this correspondence from Patricia Nurse ably demonstrates.

Dear Dr. Asimov:

Imagine my delight when I spotted your new science fiction magazine on the newsstands. I have been a fan of yours for many, many years and I naturally wasted no time in buying a copy. I wish you every success in this new venture.

In your second issue I read with interest your plea for stories from new authors. While no writer myself, I have had a time traveler living with me for the past two weeks (he materialized in the bathtub without clothes or money, so I felt obliged to offer him shelter), and he has written a story of life on earth as it will be in the year 5000.

Before he leaves this time frame, it would give him great pleasure to see his story in print—I

43

hope you will feel able to make this wish come true.

Yours sincerely,
NANCY MORRISON (Miss)

Dear Miss Morrison:

Thank you for your kind letter and good wishes.

It is always refreshing to hear from a new author. You have included some most imaginative material in your story; however, it is a little short on plot and human interest—perhaps you could rewrite it with this thought in mind.

Yours sincerely,
ISAAC ASIMOV

Dear Dr. Asimov:

I was sorry that you were unable to print the story I sent you. Vahl (the time traveler who wrote it) was quite hurt as he tells me he is an author of some note in his own time. He has, however, rewritten the story and this time has included plenty of plot and some rather interesting mating rituals which he has borrowed from the year 3000. In his own time (the year 5015) sex is no longer practiced, so you can see that it is perfectly respectable having him in my house. I do wish, though, that he could adapt himself to our custom of wearing clothes—my neighbors are starting to talk!

Anything that you can do to expedite the publishing of Vahl's story would be most appreciated, so that he will feel free to return to his own time.

Yours sincerely,
NANCY MORRISON (Miss)

Dear Miss Morrison:

Thank you for your rewritten short story.

I don't want to discourage you but I'm afraid you followed my suggestions with a little too much enthusiasm—however, I can understand that having an imaginary nude visitor from another time is a rather heady experience. I'm afraid that your story now rather resembles a far-future episode of *Mary Hartman, Mary Hartman* or *Soap*.

Could you tone it down a bit and omit the more bizarre sex rituals of the year 3000—we must remember that *Isaac Asimov's Science Fiction Magazine* is intended to be a family publication.

Perhaps a little humor would improve the tale too.

Yours sincerely,
ISAAC ASIMOV

Dear Dr. Asimov:

Vahl was extremely offended by your second rejection—he said he has never received a rejection slip before, and your referring to him as "imaginary" didn't help matters at all. I'm afraid he rather lost his temper and stormed out into the garden—it was at this unfortunate moment that the vicar happened to pass by.

Anyway, I managed to get Vahl calmed down and he has rewritten the story and added plenty of humor. I'm afraid my subsequent meeting with the vicar was not blessed with such success! I'm quite sure Vahl would not understand another rejection.

Yours truly,
NANCY MORRISON (Miss)

Dear Miss Morrison:

I really admire your persistence in rewriting your story yet another time. Please don't give up hope—you can became a fairly competent writer in time, I feel sure.

I'm afraid the humor you added was not the kind of thing I had in mind at all—you're not collaborating with Henny Youngman by any chance are you? I really had a more sophisticated type of humor in mind.

Yours truly,
ISAAC ASIMOV

P.S. Have you considered reading your story, as it is, on *The Gong Show?*

Dear Dr. Asimov:

It really was very distressing to receive the return of my manuscript once again—Vahl was quite speechless with anger.

It was only with the greatest difficulty that I prevailed upon him to refine the humor you found so distasteful, and I am submitting his latest rewrite herewith.

In his disappointment, Vahl has decided to return to his own time right away. I shall be sorry to see him leave as I was getting very fond of him—a pity he wasn't from the year 3000, though. Still, he wouldn't have made a very satisfactory husband; I'd have never known where (or when) he was. It rather looks as though my plans to marry the vicar have suffered a severe setback too. Are you married, Dr. Asimov?

I must close this letter now as I have to say goodbye to Vahl. He says he has just finished making some long overdue improvements to our time frame as a parting gift—isn't that kind of him?

> Yours sincerely,
> NANCY MORRISON (Miss)

Dear Miss Morrison:

I am very confused by your letter. Who is Isaac Asimov? I have checked with several publishers and none of them has heard of *Isaac Asimov's Science Fiction Magazine,* although the address on the envelope was correct for *this* magazine.

However, I was very impressed with your story and will be pleased to accept it for our next issue. Seldom do we receive a story combining such virtues as a well-conceived plot, plenty of human interest, and a delightfully subtle brand of humor.

> Yours truly,
> GEORGE H. SCITHERS, Editor,
> Arthur C. Clarke's Science Fiction Magazine

THE PINCH HITTERS

George Alec Effinger

Winner of both the Hugo and Nebula Awards, George Alec Effinger is most famous these days for his brilliant tales of Marid, the protagonist of When Gravity Fails *and* A Fire in the Sun. *But George's most enduring hero is Sandor Courane, science fiction writer/editor/slush-pile reader, who frequently dies at the end of a story—but like all good stock characters, keeps coming back to life in the sequel.*

THE TELEPHONE RANG, and the noise woke me up. I reached across the bed to pick up the receiver. I was still half asleep, and something about the dimly lit hotel room disturbed me. I couldn't identify the trouble, though. "Hello?" I said into the phone.

"Hello? Is this Sandor Courane?" said an unfamiliar voice.

I didn't say anything for a second or two. I was looking across the room at the other twin bed. There was someone sleeping in it.

"Is this Sandor Courane?" asked the voice.

"It often is," I said.

"Well, if it is now, this is Norris."

I was silent again. Someone was claiming to be a very good friend of mine, using a voice that didn't belong to Norris. "Uh huh," was all that I said. I remembered that I hadn't been alone the night before. I was at a rather large science fiction convention, and I had met a rather nice young woman.

The person in the other bed, still asleep, was a large man I had never seen before.

"Where are you?" asked the person who claimed to be Norris.

"In my room," I said. "What time is it? Who is this?"

"This is Norris Page! Have you looked outside?"

"Norris," I said, "I can't think of a single reason why I would waste the effort to walk across the room. And I don't know how to say this, but, uh, you don't sound at all like Norris, if you know what I mean. My clock says it's eight-thirty, and that's a rotten time to wake somebody up at a convention. So I think I'll just hang—"

"Wait a minute!" The voice was suddenly very urgent. Much more urgent than a voice generally gets at a science fiction convention. I waited. The voice went on. "Look out the window," it said.

"Okay," I said. I'm moderately obliging. I got up. I was wearing thin green pajamas, something I have never owned in my entire life. I didn't like that discovery at all. I walked quietly by the stranger on the other bed and peered through the slats of the venetian blinds. I stared for a moment or two, then went back to the telephone. "Hello?" I said.

"What did you see?" asked the voice.

"A bunch of buildings I've never seen before."

"It's not Washington, is it?"

"No," I said. "Who is this?"

"Norris. It's Norris. I'm in New York."

"Last night you were in Washington," I said. "I mean, Norris was here in Washington. Why don't you sound like Norris?"

There was a short, exasperated sound from the voice. "You know, you don't sound like you either. You're in Boston."

"Boston?"

"Yeah. And Jim is in Detroit. And Larry is in Chicago. And Dick is in Cleveland."

"I feel sorry for Dick," I said. I was born in Cleveland.

"I feel sorry for all of us," said Norris. "We're not us anymore. Look at yourself."

I did. Beneath the pajamas, my body had become large and hairy. My tattoo—I have an Athenian owl tattooed on my left forearm—was gone, and in its place was a skull with a dagger through its eye and a naked lady with an anchor and a snake. There were certain other pertinent revisions in the body. "Wow," I said.

"I've been up since six o'clock running this down," said Norris. "The five of us have been hijacked or something."

"Who did it?" I was feeling very unhappy about the situation.

"I don't know," said Norris.

"Why?" I was starting to feel very frightened about the situation.

"I don't know."

"How?"

"I don't know."

I was beginning to feel annoyed. "Since six o'clock, huh?" I said. "What *have* you found out?"

Norris sounded hurt. "I found you, didn't I? And Jim and Larry and Dick."

I got the same cold feeling at the base of my spine that I get when I have to have blood taken. "We're scattered all over the United States of America. Last night we were all in the same lousy hotel. What happened?"

"Take it easy." When Norris said that, I knew we were all in trouble. "It seems as though we've been, uh, transported back in time too."

I screamed, "What?"

"It's 1954 out there," said Norris.

I gave up. I wasn't going to say another word. When I started the day, I was sleeping very nicely. Every time I opened my mouth, it only encouraged Norris to tell me something else I didn't want to hear. I decided to clam up.

"Did you hear me?" he asked.

I didn't say anything.

"It's 1954 out there. You've been transported back and put in the body of, uh, wait a minute, I wrote it down, uh, Ellard MacIver. Do you know who that is?"

I felt cold again. "Yes," I said, "he was a utility infielder for the Red Sox. In the fifties."

"Right. You have a game today against the Athletics. Lots of luck."

"What am I supposed to do?"

Norris laughed, I don't know why. "Play ball," he said.

"How do we get back?" I shouted. The man in the other bed grumbled and woke up.

"I haven't figured that out yet," said Norris. "I have to go. This is long distance. Anyway, this week you play the Tigers, and you can talk it over with Jim. He's in the body of, uh, this guy Charlie Quinn. Second base."

"Wonderful," I said. "Terrific."

"Don't worry," said Norris. "I have to go. I'll talk with you later." He hung up.

I looked at the phone. "Terrific," I muttered.

The other guy propped himself up in the other bed and said, "Shut up, Mac, will you?" I just stared at him.

I realized that I should have asked Norris whose body he was in. I shrugged. Maybe Jim would know.

A few days later we had the situation completely sorted out. It still didn't bring us any closer to solving the problem, but at least it was sorted out. This is the way it looked:

Famous Science Fiction Writer	In the Body of	Team	Position	Batting Average
Sandor Courane (me)	Ellard MacIver	Boston Red Sox	Inf.	.221
Norris Page	Don Di Mauro	Chicago White Sox	Left Field	.288
Larry Shrader	Gerhardt 'Dutch' Ruhl	New York Yankees	1B	.334
Dick Shrader	Marv Croxton	Cleveland Indians	Center Field	.291
Jim Benedetti	Charlie Quinn	Detroit Tigers	2B	.254

I didn't like it at all. Not batting .221 and being thirty-six years old (I'm not thirty-six, but MacIver was, and he was in danger of losing his job next spring, and if we didn't get home soon, I'd have to become a broadcaster or something).

That morning I went to the ballpark with my roommate. His name was Tony Lloyd, and he was a huge first baseman. Everyone on the team called him "Money." His most memorable attribute was explaining how Jackie Robinson wouldn't survive the walk from the clubhouse to the dugout if the National League had any men with guts over there. I didn't listen to him much. Anyway, we had a game scheduled for two o'clock, but the Red Sox were headed for a mediocre finish to the season and that meant that everybody was taking all kinds of extra practice and hustling around and pretending that they cared a hill of beans about the outcome of every game.

I, for one, was excited. I was scared out of my skin too, but I was excited. I followed Lloyd into Fenway Park—the gate guard gave me a nod, recognizing my borrowed body— and stood for a while in the dressing room, just staring at things. I'd always wanted to be a ballplayer when I was a kid, of course, and now . . .

And now I *was* a ballplayer. Sort of. A sort of ballplayer, a bench-warming antique of a ballplayer who was hitting just well enough to prove he was still alive. I wondered why, if I were going to be transmiggled through time and space, I couldn't have ended up in the body of, oh, Ted Williams, say, whose locker wasn't far from mine. I stared at him; I stared at everybody else; I stared at the towels; I stared at the soap; I stared at the contents of my locker. *My* locker. My locker as a member of a professional baseball team. There were pictures of beautiful women taped to the inside of the door. There were parts of the uniform that I couldn't even identify. I had to watch a couple of other guys getting dressed to see how they worked. I think the guys noticed me watching.

After I got dressed I walked through the long, cool tunnel under the stands and emerged in the dugout. Before me was a vast, green, utterly beautiful world. Fenway Park. And they were going to let me go out there and run around on their grass.

I took my fielder's glove and trotted out toward second base. I know how to trot. I was in a little trouble once I reached where I was going. I said hello to men I didn't recognize. Someone else was hitting ground balls to us and we were lazily scooping them up. Well, anyway, *they* were; I was letting them hit me on the elbow, the knee, and twice on the chin.

"Hey, look at the old man," said some kid, backhanding a hot rocket of a grounder. "You going to be around next year, old man?"

I felt angry. I wanted to show that kid, but there wasn't anything I could show him, with the possible exception of sentence structure.

"He'll be around," said another kid. "They're going to bury him out under center field." Another grounder came my way and it zipped between my feet and out onto the grass. The kids laughed.

Later I took some batting practice. This was 1954, of course, and the batting practice was pitched by a venerable old ballplayer whose name had been a legend when I was a boy. I told him that I wasn't feeling very well, and he took some of the stuff off his pitches. They were nice and easy, right over the plate every time, and I hit some liners around the stadium. I pretended that they would have been base hits in a real game. It felt great. After I finished, Ted Williams stepped in and demolished the bleachers.

And then the fun began. The game started. I vaguely remembered hearing a kind of pep talk from Lou Boudreau, the manager. I guess they played the "Star Spangled Banner," but I don't remember that. And then, before I was even aware of what was happening, I was sitting in a corner of the dugout, watching, and we were in the third inning of the game. Frank Sullivan was pitching for us, and Arnie Portocarrero was pitching for Philadelphia.

Right then, if someone had asked me, I might have declined to go back to the seventies, back to typing up fantasies to pay my rent. Why should I? I could stay in 1954 and get paid to play baseball! Eisenhower was President. The space race wasn't even to the starting gate yet. Ernie Kovacs and

Buddy Holly were still alive. I could win a fortune betting on things and waiting for Polaroid to split.

But no. I had a responsibility to the science fiction world. After all, science fiction might well do without me (just let it try), but Norris and Jim and Dick and Larry were here too, and I had to help my friends, if I could. But could I? Why were we here, what had zapped us more than twenty years into the past?

And then I had a terrifying thought. What all this meant was that more than twenty years in the future, in New Orleans, some man named Ellard MacIver, a failure of a baseball player with very little to recommend him, was sitting down at my typewriter and continuing my writing career. No! I couldn't bear it! If anyone was going to ruin my career, I wanted it to be me.

On Sunday night we rode the train out to Detroit. It was a rotten trip. I hadn't gotten into any of the three weekend games with Philadelphia, which was just as well. I was extra baggage to the Red Sox, carried along in case a hole opened up and swallowed four-fifths of the team down into the bowels of the earth. I was looking forward to talking with Jim. Sure, 1954 had its good points—I think I counted about six of them—but, all in all, I had decided that we had to get out of the mess somehow, and as soon as possible. I had a contract outstanding with Doubleday, and I didn't want Ellard MacIver writing that novel. If he did and it won a Hugo, well, I'd have to join the Navy or something.

Fortunately, Jim was in the same frame of mind. Jim is a great guy normally, but his situation was driving him crazy. He was supposed to be a second baseman, a starting second baseman, and he had fallen on his face three times trying to pivot on double-play balls. Also, his batting had gone into a slump (understandably enough), and he didn't like the body he had been put into. "You think the old one gave me trouble," he said; "this one complains if I eat Wheaties."

We had lunch at my hotel on the afternoon of the first game of the Detroit series, Tuesday. "Have you had any ideas about who's doing this to us?" I asked him.

"Is somebody doing this to us?" he asked.

I looked at him blankly for a moment. It hadn't occurred

to me that all of this might be a function of the Universe, instead of an evil plot. That made me feel even worse. "Look," I said, "we have to believe that we can get out of this somehow."

Jim ate some more oatmeal. "Fine," he said, "we'll believe that. What next?"

"The next logical step is to assume that if this is being done to us, that *someone* is doing it."

Jim looked at me like he suddenly realized that I was just a bit dangerous. "That's not the most spectacular reasoning in the world," he said.

"Well, we have to make that assumption. It doesn't make any difference who it is. The main thing is that we flip things around the right way."

"Boy, do I hate this oatmeal," he said. "Wait. What if we flip things, and we end up somewhere else? I mean, like in the bodies of apple salesmen in the thirties. Don't do anything we'll regret."

"I won't," I said, because as yet I couldn't think of anything at all. "If anyone can figure this out, Larry can."

"Right," said Jim, smiling suddenly. "We'll let Larry figure it out. You and I write sort of surreal fantasies. Larry is the real nuts and bolts science fiction type. He'll know what to do."

"Right," I said. We finished eating and went out to the ballpark. I sat in the corner of the dugout during the game and watched Jim muffling around second base.

The next series was in Cleveland, my hometown. I thought about visiting my parents and seeing myself at seven years old, but the idea was vaguely repellent. I reminded myself that I'd have to see my younger brother at five years old, and that settled the matter. I went to a movie instead.

I talked with Dick several times, and he said that he'd heard from his brother, Larry. Larry is a good old rocketship and ray-gun kind of thinker, and we were counting on him to help us out of the predicament. "What do you think?" I asked Dick Shrader.

"Well," said Dick, doing something I'd never seen him do before—take a handful of chewing tobacco, mix it with bubble gum, and stuff it all in one cheek—"unless I have a bad slump the last few weeks, I stand a good chance of finishing over .300. I'm going to ask for thirty thousand next season.''

"Dick," I said loudly, "you're not paying attention."

"Okay. Thirty-five thousand."

Clearly there would be no progress at all until the series in New York, when Larry and I could go over the matter in great detail. I guess, then, that I can skip the next several days. Not much happened, really, other than a series with the Orioles during which I got to bat (a weak ground-out), and I had an interview with a newspaperman who thought I was Jimmy Piersall.

Following the first game with the Yankees, Larry and I went to a small restaurant where he wouldn't be recognized. We ordered dinner, and while we waited we talked. "How do you feel about this guy Dutch Ruhl taking over your writing career?" I asked.

"Doesn't bother me," said Larry, gulping some beer, Larry breathes beer.

"Why not?" My hopes rose. I thought he had found a solution.

"Well, if we get out of this, there won't be any problem, right?" he said, swallowing some more beer.

"Right," I said.

"And if we don't get out of it, well, I'll just wait around and come up behind him and take my career back."

"That's twenty years from now!" I said.

Larry didn't look disturbed. "Think of all the ideas I'll have by then," he said. "I'll do 'Star Trek' in 1960, and *2001* in 1961, and *Star Wars* in 1962, and—"

"What are you going to do with Dutch Ruhl?"

Larry knocked back the last of the beer. "Was there a Dutch Ruhl writing science fiction when we left?"

"No."

"Then there won't be."

"But there was somebody in the body of Larry Shrader, maybe you, maybe not. How are you going to prove *you're* Larry Shrader?"

Larry looked at me as though I were in some way tragic. "All I need are my driver's license and my Master Charge."

"Got those with you?"

Now Larry looked tragic. "No," he said.

"Who could stand to gain from this?" I wondered, as Larry signaled for several more beers.

"Who?" he said, in a hollow voice.

"Who?" I said.

There was a slight pause, and then we looked at each other.

"Who could stand to gain from the sudden disappearance of, well, if I do say so myself, the cream of the newer generation, the hope and future of science fiction?" he said, a little smile on his lips.

"Well," I said, "apart from the Dean of Science Fiction . . ."

"In conjunction with the Most Honored Writer of Science Fiction," said Larry, laughing a little.

"Acting in concert with the Acknowledged Master of Science Fiction," I said.

"With the aid of two or three others we might name," said Larry.

"Why would they do this to us?" I asked.

"Why, indeed? It's the natural reaction of the old dinosaurs when they spot the first strange mammals bounding through their jungle. But it's a futile action."

"How did they do it?" I was still bewildered.

Larry was not. These things were always marvelously simple to his agile mind. That was why he was hitting .334 for the Yankees and I was chewing gum for the Red Sox. Larry was on his way to becoming a dinosaur in his own right. "They accomplished it easily enough," he said. "They got us here the same way we're going home. By typewriter."

"You mean—" I said, my eyes wide with astonishment.

"Yes," said Larry, "what *is* reality, anyway?"

Before the veal marsala came, we had the solution to our problem. We weren't vengeful, though, because we have to set the tone of the future. That's a heavy burden, but we carry it gladly.

"Now what?" said Larry, drinking some beer for dessert.

"Now we go home. We can go now, or we can wait around here in 1954 for a while, for a kind of vacation."

"We'll take a vote," said Larry, because he's a four-square kind of guy.

Well, we did take a vote, and we decided to go right home, because some of us had library books overdue. Getting home was simple. It was like Dorothy's Ruby Slippers—it was there all the time. We all gathered in Washington, because that's where we had last been together. We all sat together in a large suite in the same hotel where so many years in the future there would be a science fiction convention. We had Cokes and beer and pretzels and potato chips. We had the television on ("The Stu Erwin Show"), and we messed the room up some. "Remember," said Norris, "not one word about baseball. Only science fiction."

"Just science fiction," said Dick Shrader.

We started talking about money, of course. We talked about who was paying what, and that led to a discussion of editors. When we realized how violent our passions were growing we changed the subject to "The Future of Science Fiction," and then "Science Fiction and the Media," and then "Academia and Science Fiction." Just about then a short, heavy man came into the suite with a camera and took Larry's picture. The man sat down and listened. We offered him some pretzels. We talked about "The Short Fiction Market," and two wild young women dressed like characters from a trilogy of novels came in to fill the bathtub with some viscous fluid. We didn't offer them pretzels. We talked about "Science Fiction as a Revolutionary Weapon," and two writers and an agent and four more fans came in, and it was getting noisy, and Jim called down for some ice, and I went into the hall, and more fans and more pros were coming toward the room, so I went to the elevator and went up to my room. I opened the door carefully. The light was on and I saw that there was someone else in the room. I was ready to turn away, but I saw that it was the same young woman who had been with me at the start of the adventure. I looked down, and of course I was in my old body (it's not *that* old, really, and it's a little worn, but it's mine) and everything was all right for the moment. We were victorious.

MUTE INGLORIOUS TAM

Frederik Pohl and
C. M. Kornbluth

*Frederik Pohl and the late Cyril M. Kornbluth are one
of the truly great collaborative teams in the history of
science fiction. Their novel,* The Space Merchants, *is
probably one of the four or five best-selling titles,
worldwide, of the past half-century. This sensitive tale
deals with, as Pohl says, "a science fiction writer who
couldn't be a science fiction writer because he was born
in a time when that art was not possible."*

ON A LATE Saturday afternoon in summer, just before the
ringing of Angelus, Tam of the Wealdway straightened from
the furrows in his plowed strip of Oldfield and stretched his
cracking joints.

He was a small and dark man of almost pure Saxon blood.
Properly speaking, his name was only Tam. There was no
need for further identification. He would never go a mile
from a neighbor who had known him from birth. But sometimes he called himself by a surname—it was one of many
small conceits that complicated his proper and straightforward life—and he would be soundly whipped for it if his
Norman masters ever caught him at it.

He had been breaking clods in the field for fifteen hours,
interrupted only by the ringing of the canonical hours from
the squat, tiny church, and a mouthful of bread and soft
cheese at noon. It was not easy for him to stand straight. It

59

was also not particularly wise. A man could lose his strip for poor tilth, and Tam had come close enough, often enough. But there were times when the thoughts that chased themselves around his head made him forget the steady chop of the wooden hoe, and he would stand entranced, staring toward Lymeford Castle, or the river, or toward nothing at all, while he invented fanciful encounters and impossible prosperings. It was another of Tam's conceits, and a most dangerous one, if it were known. The least it might get him was a cuff from a man-at-arms. The most was a particularly unpleasing death.

Since Salisbury, in Sussex, was flat ground, its great houses were not perched dramatically on crags, like the keeps of robber barons along the Rhine or the grim fortresses of the Scottish lairds. They were the least they could be to do the job they had to do, in an age which had not yet imagined the palace or the cathedral.

In the year 1303 Lymeford Castle was a dingy pile of stone. It housed Sir and Lady Robert Bowen (sometimes they spelled it Bohun, or Beauhun, or Beauhaunt) and their household servants and men-at-arms in very great discomfort. It did not seem so to them particularly. They had before them the housing of their Saxon subjects to show what misery could be. The castle was intended to guard a bridge across the Lyme River: a key point on the high road from Portsmouth to London. It did this most effectively. William of Normandy, who had taken England by storm a couple of centuries earlier, did not mean for himself or his descendants to be taken in the same way on another day. So Lymeford Castle had been awarded to Sir Robert's great-great-great-grandfather on the condition that he defend it and thereby defend London as well against invasion on that particular route from the sea.

That first Bowen had owned more than stones. A castle must be fed. The castellan and his lady, their household servants and their armed men could not be expected to till the field and milk the cows. The founder of Sir Robert's line had solved the problem of feeding the castle by rounding up a hundred of the defeated Saxon soldiers, clamping iron rings around their necks and setting them to work at the great task of clearing the untidy woods which surrounded the castle. After cleaning and plowing from sunup to sunset the slaves were free to gather twigs and mud, with which they made themselves kennels to sleep in. And in that first year, to celebrate the harvest and to insure a continuing supply of slaves, the castellan led his men-at-arms on a raid into Salisbury town itself. They drove back to Lymeford, with whips, about a hundred Saxon girls and women. After taking their pick, they gave the rest to the slaves, and the chaplain read a single perfunctory marriage service over the filthy, ring-necked slaves and the weeping Salisbury women. Since the male slaves happened to be from Northumbria, while the women were Sussex bred, they could not understand each other's dialects. It did not matter. The huts were enlarged, and next midsummer there was another crop, this time of babies.

The passage of two centuries had changed things remarkably little. A Bowen (or Beauhaunt) still guarded the Portsmouth-London high road. He still took pride in his Norman blood. Saxons still tilled the soil for him and if they no longer had the iron collar, or the name of slaves, they still would dangle from the gallows in the castle courtyard for any of a very large number of possible offenses against his authority. At Runnymede, many years before, King John had signed the Great Charter conferring some sort of rule of law to protect his barons against arbitrary acts, but no one had thought of extending those rights to the serfs. They could die for almost anything or for nothing at all: for trying to quit their master's soil for greener fields; for failing to deliver to the castle their bushels of grain, as well as their choicest lambs, calves and girl-children; for daring in any way to flout the divine law that made one kind of man ruler and another kind ruled. It was this offense to which Tam was prone, and one day, as his father had told him the day before he died, it would cost him the price that no man can afford to pay, though all do.

* * *

Though Tam had never even heard of the Magna Carta, he sometimes thought that a world might sometime come to be in which a man like himself might own the things he owned as a matter of right and not because a man with a sword had not decided to take them from him. Take Alys, his wife. He did not mind in any real sense that the men-at-arms had bedded her before he had. She was none the worse for it in any way that Tam could measure; but he had slept badly that night, pondering why it was that no one needed to consult him about the woman the priest had sworn to him that day, and whether it might not be more—more—he grappled for a word ("fair" did not occur to him) and caught at "right"— more right that he should say whose pleasures his property served.

Mostly he thought of sweeter and more fanciful things. When the falconers were by, he sometimes stole a look at the hawk stooping on a pigeon and thought that a man might fly if only he had the wings and the wit to move them. Pressed into driving the castellan's crops into the granary, he swore at the dumb oxen and imagined a cart that could turn its wheels by itself. If the Lyme in flood could carry a tree bigger than a house faster than a man could run, why could that power not pull a plow? Why did a man have to plant five kernels of corn to see one come up? Why could not all five come up and make him five times as fat?

He even looked at the village that was his home, and wondered why it had to be so poor, so filthy and so small; and that thought had hardly occurred even to Sir Robert himself.

In the year 1303 Lymeford looked like this:

The Lyme River, crossed by the new stone structure that was the fourth Lymeford Bridge, ran south to the English Channel. Its west bank was overgrown with the old English oak forest. Its right bank was the edge of the great clearing. Lymeford Castle, hard by the bridge, covered the road that curved northeast to London. For the length of the clearing, the road was not only the king's highway, it was also the Lymeford village street. At a discreet distance from the castle it began to be edged with huts, larger or smaller as their tenants were rich or fecund. The road widened a bit halfway to the edge of the clearing, and there on its right side sat the village church.

The church was made of stone, but that was about all you could say for it. All the wealth it owned it had to draw from the village, and there was not much wealth there to draw.

Still, silver pennies had to be sent regularly to the bishop, who in turn would send them on to Rome. The parish priest of Lymeford was an Italian who had never seen the bishop, to whom it had never occurred to try to speak the language and who had been awarded the living of Lymeford by a cardinal who was likewise Italian and likewise could not have described its location within fifty miles. There was nothing unusual in that, and the Italian collected the silver pennies while his largely Norman, but Saxon speaking, *locum tenens* scraped along on donations of beer, dried fish and the odd occasional calf. He was a dour man who would have been a dreadful one if he had had a field of action that was larger than Lymeford.

Across the street from the church was the Green, a cheerless trampled field where the compulsory archery practice and pike drill were undergone by every physically able male of Lymeford, each four weeks, except in the worst of winter and when plowing or harvest was larger in Sir Robert's mind than the defense of his castle. His serfs would fight when he told them to, and he would squander their lives with the joy a man feels in exercising the one extravagance he permits himself on occasion. But that was only at need, and the fields and the crops were forever. He saw to the crops with some considerable skill. A three-field system prevailed in Lymeford. There was Oldfield, east of the road, and the first land brought under cultivation by the slaves two hundred years ago. There was Newfield, straddling the road and marked off from Oldfield by a path into the woods called the Wealdway, running southeast from the Green into the oak forest at the edge of the clearing. There was Fallowfield, last to be cleared and planted, which for the most part lay south of the road and the castle. From the left side of the road to the river, the Mead spread its green acres. The Mead was held in common by all the villagers. Any man might turn his cows or sheep to graze on it anywhere. The farmed fields, however, were divided into long, narrow strips, each held by a villager who would defend it with his fists or his sickle against the encroachment of a single inch. In the year 1303 Oldfield and Newfield were under cultivation, and Fallowfield was being rested. Next year it would be Newfield and Fallowfield farmed, and Oldfield would rest.

While Angelus clanged on the cracked church bell, Tam stood with his head downcast. He was supposed to be praying. In a way he was, the impenetrable rote-learned Latin slipping through his brain like the reiteration of a mantra, but he was also pleasantly occupied in speculating how plump his daughter might become if they could farm all three fields each year without destroying the soil, and at the same time thinking of the pot of fennel-spiced beer that should be waiting in his hut.

As the Angelus ceased to ring, his neighbor's hail dispelled both dreams.

Irritated, Tam shouldered his wooden-bladed hoe and trudged along the Wealdway, worn deep by two hundred years of bare peasant feet.

His neighbor, Hud, fell in with him. In the bastard Midland-Sussex hybrid that was the Lymeford dialect, Hud said, "Man, that was a long day."

"All the days are long in the summer."

"You were dreaming again, man. Saw you."

Tam did not reply. He was careful of Hud. Hud was as small and dark as himself, but thin and nervous rather than blocky. Tam knew he got that from his father Robin, who had got it from his mother Joan—who had got it from some man-at-arms on her wedding night spent in the castle. Hud was always asking, always talking, always seeking new things. But when Tam, years younger, had dared to try to open his untamable thoughts to him, Hud had run straight to the priest.

"Won't the players be coming by this time of year, man?" he pestered.

"They might."

"Ah, wouldn't it be a great thing if they came by tomorrow? And then after Mass they'd make their pitch in the Green, and out would come the King of England and Captain Slasher and the Turkish Champion in their clothes colored like the sunset, and St. George in his silver armor!"

Tam grunted. " 'Tisn't silver. Couldn't be. If it was silver the robbers in the Weald would never let them get this far."

The nervous little man said, "I didn't mean it *was* silver. I meant it *looked* like silver."

Tam could feel anger welling up in him, drowning the good aftertaste of his reverie and the foretaste of his fennel beer. He said angrily, "You talk like a fool."

"Like a fool, is it? And who is always dreaming the sun away, man?"

"God's guts, leave off!" shouted Tam, and clamped his teeth on his words too late. He seldom swore. He could have bitten his tongue out after he uttered the words. Now there would be confession of blasphemy to make, and Father Bloughram, who had been looking lean and starved of late, would demand a penance in grain instead of any beggarly saying of prayers. Hud cowered back, staring. Tam snarled something at him, he could not himself have said what, and turned off the deep-trodden path into his own hut.

The hut was cramped and murky with wood smoke from its open hearth. There was a smoke hole in the roof that let some of it out. Tam leaned his hoe against the wattled wall, flopped down onto the bundle of rags in the corner that was the bed for all three of the members of his family and growled at Alys his wife: "Beer." His mind was full of Hud and anger, but slowly the rage cooled and the good thoughts crept back in: Why not a softer bed, a larger hut? Why not a fire that did not smoke, as his returning grandfather, who wore a scar from the Holy Land to his grave, had told him the Saracens had? And with the thought of a different kind of life came the thought of beer; he could taste the stuff now, sluicing the dust from his throat; the bitterness of the roasted barley, the sweetness of the fennel. "Beer," he called again, and became aware that his wife had been tiptoeing about the hut.

"Tam," she said apprehensively, "Joanie Brewer's got the flux."

His brows drew together like thunderclouds. "No beer?" he asked.

"She's got the flux, and not for all the barley in Oldfield could she brew beer. I tried to borrow from Hud's wife, and she had only enough for him, she showed me—"

Tam got up and knocked her spinning into a corner with

one backhanded blow. "Was there no beer yesterday?" he shouted. "God forgive you for being the useless slut you are! May the Horned Man and all his brood fly away with a miserable wretch that won't brew beer for the husband that sweats his guts out from sunup to sunset!"

She got up cringing, and he knocked her into the corner again.

The next moment there was a solid crack across his back, and he crashed to the dirt floor. Another blow took him on the legs as he rolled over, and he looked up and saw the raging face of his daughter Kate and the wooden-bladed hoe upraised in her hands.

She did not strike him a third time, but stood there menacingly. "Will you leave her alone?" she demanded.

"Yes, you devil's get!" Tam shouted from the floor, and then, "You'd like me to say no, wouldn't you? And then you'd beat in the brains of the old fool that gave you a name and a home."

Weeping, Alys protested, "Don't say that, husband. She's your child, I'm a good woman, I have nothing black on my soul."

Tam got to his feet and brushed dirt from his leather breeches and shirt. "We'll say no more about it," he said. "But it's hard when a man can't have his beer."

"You wild boar," said Kate, not lowering the hoe. "If I hadn't come back from the Mead with the cow, you might have killed her."

"No, child," Tam said uneasily. He knew his temper. "Let's talk of other things." Contemptuously she put down the hoe, while Alys got up, sniffling, and began to stir the peaseporridge on the hearth. Suddenly the smoke and heat inside the hut was more than Tam could bear, and muttering something, he stumbled outside and breathed in the cool air of the night.

It was full dark now and, for a wonder, stars were out. Tam's Crusader grandfather had told him of the great bright nights in the mountains beyond Acre, with such stars that a man could spy friend's face from foe's at a bowshot. England had nothing like that, but Tam could make out the Plow, fading toward the sunset, and Cassiopeia pursing it from the east. His grandfather had tried to teach him the Arabic names for some of the brighter stars, but the man had died when Tam was ten and the memories were gone. What were those two, now, so bright and so close together? Something about twin peacocks? Twins at least, thought Tam, staring at Gemini, but a thought of peacocks lingered. He wished he had paid closer attention to the old man, who had been a Saracen's slave for nine years until a lucky raid had captured his caravan and set him free.

A distant sound of yelping caught his ear. Tam read the sound easily enough; a vixen and her half-grown young, by the shrillness. The birds came into the plowed fields at night to steal the seed, and the foxes came to catch the birds, and this night they had found something big enough to try to catch them—wolf, perhaps, Tam thought, though it was not like them to come so near to men's huts in good weather. There were a plenty of them in Sir Robert's forest, with fat deer and birds and fish beyond counting in the streams; but it was what a man's life was worth to take them. He stood there, musing on the curious chance that put venison on Sir Robert's table and peaseporridge on his, and on the lights in the sky, until he realized Alys had progressed from abject to angry and must by now be eating without him.

After the evening meal Alys scurried over to Hud's wife with her tale of beastly husbands, and Kate sat on a billet of wood, picking knots out of her hair.

Tam squatted on the rags and studied her. At fifteen years, or whatever she was, she was a wild one. How had it happened that the babe who cooed and grasped at the grass whistle her father made her had turned into this stranger? She was not biddable. Edwy's strip adjoined Tam's in Fallowfield, and Edwy had a marriageable son. What was more reasonable than that Kate should marry him? But she had talked about his looks. True, the boy was no beauty. What did that matter? When, as a father should, he had brushed that aside, she had threatened plainly to run away, bringing ruin and the rope on all of them. Nor would she let herself be beaten into good sense, but instead kicked—with painful accuracy—and bit and scratched like a fiend from hell's pit.

He felt a pang at that thought. Oh, Alys was an honest woman. But there were other ways the child of another could be fobbed off on you. A moment of carelessness when you didn't watch the cradle—it was too awful to think of, but sometimes you had to think of it. Everybody knew that Old People liked nothing better than to steal somebody's baby and slip one of their own into the cradle. He and Alys had duly left bowls of milk out during the child's infancy, and on feast days bowls of beer. They had always kept a bit of iron by Kate, because the Old People hated iron. But still . . .

Tam lighted a rushlight soaked in mutton fat at what was left of the fire. Alys would have something to say about his extravagance, but a mood for talking was on him, and he wanted to see Kate's face "Child," he said, "one Sunday now the players will come by and pitch on the Green. And we'll all go after Mass and see them play. Why, St. George looks as if he wears armor all of silver!"

She tugged at her hair and would not speak or look at him.

He squirmed uncomfortably on the ragged bed. "I'll tell you a story, child," he offered.

Contemptuously, "Tell your drunken friend. I've heard the two of you, Hud and yourself, lying away at each other with the beer working in you."

"Not that sort of story, Kate. A story no one has ever told."

No answer, but at least her face was turned toward him. Emboldened, he began.

" 'Tis a story of a man who owned a great strong wain that could move without oxen, and in it he—"

"What pulled it, then? Goats?"

"Nothing pulled it, child. It moved by itself. It—" he fumbled, and found inspiration—"it was a gift from the Old People, and the man put on it meal and dried fish and casks of water, and he rode in it to one of those bright stars you see just over church. Many days he traveled, child. When he got there—"

"What road goes to a star, man?"

"No road, Kate. This wain rode in the air, like a cloud. And then—"

"Clouds can't carry casks of water," she announced. "You talk like Edwy's mad son that thinks he saw the Devil in a turnip."

"Listen now, Kate!" he snapped. "It is only a story. When the man came to—"

"Story! It's a great silly lie."

"Neither lie nor truth," he roared. "It is a story I am telling you."

"Stories should be sense," she said positively. "Leave off your dreaming, father. All Lymeford talks of it, man. Even in the castle they speak of mad Tam the dreamer."

"Mad, I am?" he shouted, reaching for the hoe. But she was too quick for him. She had it in her hands; he tried to take it from her, and they wrestled, rock against flame, until he heard his wife's caterwauling from the entrance, where she'd come running, called by the noise; and when he looked round, Kate had the hoe from him and space to use it and this time she got him firmly atop the skull—and he knew no more that night.

In the morning he was well enough, and Kate was wisely nowhere in sight. By the time the long day was through he had lost the anger.

Alys made sure there was beer that night, and the nights that followed. The dreams that came from the brew were not the same as the dreams he had tried so hard to put into words. For the rest of his life, sometimes he dreamed those dreams again, immense dreams, dreams that—had he had the words, and the skill, and above all the audience—a hundred generations might have remembered. But he didn't have any of those things. Only the beer.

THE CURSE OF
THE MHONDORO NKABELE

by Eric Norden

This is easily the strangest story in the entire book. It may also be the funniest. It may even be the scariest. Eric Norden, the author, has moved on to conducting Playboy *interviews and writing for similar markets, and I'm sure you'll agree long before you finish "The Curse of Mhondoro Nkabele" that it's science fiction's loss.*

329 East 8th Street
New York, New York 10009
May 10, 1980

Mr. Edward L. Ferman
Magazine of Fantasy & Science Fiction
Cornwall, Connecticut 06753

Esteemed Editor Ferman:

As one who peruses your illustrious periodical with great admiration and enjoyment, please permit me to submit for your attention one of my own humble literary efforts.

Hoping to hear from you forthwith, I remain
Your obedient servant,
O. T. Nkabele, Esq.

Cornwall, Connecticut 06753
May 23, 1980

Mr. O. T. Nkabele
329 East 8th Street
New York, New York 10009

Dear Mr. Nkabele:

Thank you for letting us see "Astrid of the Asteroids." I'm afraid it does not meet our current editorial requirements.

Sincerely,
Edward L. Ferman

329 East 8th Street
New York, New York 10009
May 25, 1980

Mr. Edward L. Ferman
Magazine of Fantasy & Science Fiction
Cornwall, Connecticut 06753

PERSONAL & CONFIDENTIAL

Esteemed Editor Ferman:

I'm afraid, as is sometimes unavoidable in all great publishing enterprises, that there has been a clerical error on the part of your staff. I have just received a letter, bearing what can only be a facsimile of your signature, returning my manuscript "Astrid of the Asteroids," which I know you will be most anxious to publish. At first I was sorely troubled by this misunderstanding, but I soon realized that one of your overzealous underlings, as yet unfamiliar with my name, took it upon himself to reject my work unread. Thus I am resubmitting "Astrid," as well as two more of my latest stories, with instructions that they are for your eyes only. Do not be too harsh on the unwitting culprit, dear Editor Ferman, as such debacles are not unknown in literary history. The initial reception of James Joyce's *Ulysses* is but one case in point. . . .

I should appreciate your check to be made out to cash, as I have not as yet opened a banking account in this city.

Hoping to hear from you forthwith, I remain
Your obedient servant,
O. T. Nkabele, Esq.

Cornwall, Connecticut 06753
June 12, 1980

Mr. O. T. Nkabele
329 East 8th Street
New York, New York 10009

Dear Mr. Nkabele:

Thank you for letting us see "Slime Slaves of G'harn" and "Ursula of Uranus." I'm sorry to say that, as was the case with your original story, neither piece meets our present needs.

If you are contemplating further submissions, I should point out to you that as a matter of editorial policy we require all manuscripts to be *typed*, perferably on white, unlined paper, and on only one side of the page. Manuscripts should also be accompanied by a stamped, self-addressed return envelope.

Sincerely,
Edward L. Ferman

329 East 8th Street
New York, New York 10009
June 19, 1980

Mr. Edward L. Ferman
Magazine of Fantasy & Science Fiction
Cornwall, Connecticut 06753

Esteemed Editor Ferman:

How clumsy I have been! Please excuse my unforgivable ignorance of publishing requirements in your great country, and my thoughtlessness in inflicting on you my, let us be frank, less than decipherable calligraphy. With considerable good fortune I have found an accomplished typist, Ms. Rachel Markowitz, a fellow student at New York University's Washington Square Campus where I am matriculating, who has most graciously consented to prepare my manuscripts in the prescribed manner, and at most reasonable rates. Ms. Markowitz, a most gracious and charming young lady, has also, if it is not immodest to say so, developed a great admiration for my *oeuvre*, and has volunteered to assist me in the intricacies of American publishing, with particular emphasis on what she refers to as subsidiary rights. If you have any questions on such matters, I suggest you address them directly to her. (She may be reached, for the time being, at the above address.)

In any case, I am happy to resubmit, in the desired format, "Astrid of the Asteroids," "Slime Slaves of G'harn" and "Ursala of Uranus." If you should wish to make one check payable for all three works, that would be quite satisfactory.

Hope to hear from you forthwith, and with abject apologies for my execrable scrawl, I remain

Your obedient servant,
O. T. Nkabele, Esq.

P.S. I am enclosing Ms. Markowitz's typing bill, as well as a receipt for the unlined white paper you specified.

Cornwall, Connecticut 06753
June 25, 1980

Mr. O. T. Nkabele
329 East 8th Street
New York, New York 10009

Dear Mr. Nkabele:

I'm afraid I'm somewhat at a loss for words. I had hoped my previous letter made it clear that I *had* read all three of your stories, despite their being handwritten, and could not use any of them. The fault, I'm afraid, lies least of all in format.

Sheer pressure of time normally precludes editorial evaluation of unsolicited manuscripts, but in this case I would strongly suggest you study the more recent work in the field, particularly Harlan Ellison's two *Dangerous Visions* anthologies and the annual collection of Nebula Award stories. Your own work, frankly, is unpublishable as it now stands, although I will admit you have rather neatly captured the tone and texture of 1940s "space opera." There have been vast changes in the field since the heyday of the pulps, however, and there is no longer a market for such material, even in juveniles. If you were aiming at parody, that fails too—why flog a long-dead b.e.m.? And I'm afraid your treatment is so relentlessly serious it might evoke the worst kind of literary laughter—the unintended.

I hope you won't be too discouraged by these comments. You display a flair for vivid action prose, and your plots, though hackneyed, are tightly structured. There does, however, seem to be a language problem on occasion. *"Zut alors!"*, *"sacre bleu"* and *"nom d'un chien"* are, so far as I know, no longer in common parlance, even in France. I am not sure of the etymological derivation of *"Zounds!"* but it, too, is an uncommon expletive in contemporary English-language s-f.

Am I correct in assuming that French is your native language? If so, any problems in translation could be ameliorated by the wider reading in modern s-f I suggested earlier.

I would also caution you to beware the pitfalls of conceptual, as well as linguistic, anachronism. I.e., it is unlikely that the *Mary Tyler Moore Show* would be a weekly staple on the vidscreens of the humanoid colony on 31st Century Venus which you describe in "Slime Slaves of G'harn," "particularly after widespread intermarriage with the amphibious Mottled Marsh Marsupials and the attendant changes in sexuality and sensibility. In a different vein, but equally jarring, the Gargons of Ganymede you depict in "Ursula of Uranus" are, so far as I can gather, no more than oversized purple lobsters, and it's unlikely they would have the capability, much less the desire, to ravish Ursula and her friends. (Avoid euphemism as well as anachronism, as in "Ursula's mammoth mammary proturberances heaved in horror as she watched the slimy giant crustacean approach. . . .")

I could go on, but I hope these criticisms have been both constructive and helpful. I'll be happy to see your future work, but remember: *study the market.* That is really the best advice I can give any aspiring writer.

Sincerely,
Edward L. Ferman

329 East 8th Street
New York, New York 10009
June 29, 1980

Mr. Edward L. Ferman
Magazine of Fantasy & Science Fiction
Cornwall, Connecticut 06753

My dear Mr. Ferman:

I am in receipt of your missive of 25th June, and, in all honesty, *I* am the one at a loss for words. I find it both shocking and profoundly disturbing that you have so totally misunderstood my work. My sole remaining hope at this stage of our relationship is that a frank and forthright discussion of our differences may dissuade you from the creatively suicidal course you are pursuing. I am thinking not only of your own reputation, Mr. Ferman, but of your periodical's; I should certainly regret being forced by your blindness (a temporary condition, I trust) to take my work to your competitors. Therefore, in a spirit of openness and good will that hopefully will lead to dialogue and understanding, let me confront the major issues you raise in your communication.

Yes, you are correct in surmising that English is not my native language, but neither is French. I was born twenty-nine years ago in the town of Kaolak, in the eastern recesses of Senegal, by the Falémé River. My "first" language was Diola, the tongue of my people, although under the colonial administration French was the official language of the country, and useful in that it allowed the main tribes—Diolas, Fulas and Mandingos—to communicate with one another. (You may have remarked that our illustrious President, His Excellency Léopold Senghor, the great poet and philosopher who first conceived "negritude" as a literary and cultural belief system, wrote in

French so that he could be understood by all his people.) My father, Sikhalo, was paramount chief of our people and my uncle, Nbulamauti, was the *mganga*, or spiritual counselor of our tribe, and a learned master of *uchawi*, our indigenous religion. The Diolas are traditionally animist, but my father sent me at the age of nine to the mission school in Mbawne Province run by the Holy Ghost Fathers, a predominantly French and Belgian order. There I mastered not only French but, through the good offices of Father Devlin, the one Irish priest, English as well.

I originally had some doubts about the missionaries, but my father approved the doctrine of transubstantiation, viewing it as an affirmation of our own ancient practices. He himself, as a very young child, had once tasted a priest, of the Franciscan order I believe, and he felt that consuming the blood and flesh of Christ would be a salutary experience for me. You and I, Mr. Ferman, would of course interpret this as poetic allegory, as Mr. Melville did so evocatively in his great fish story, but my father is close to the earth. In any case, I was soon quite content at the school, due mainly to the blessed Father Devlin, a good and gentle man who took me, so to speak, under his wing. It was also due to Father Devlin that I had my first exposure to science fiction, at the age of eleven.

This brings me to your contention (the word "criticism" would unduly dignify what can most generously be adjudged a misapprehension) that I am not *au courant* with the science fiction field. It is to laugh! Due to Father Devlin, who had become a devotee while a parish priest in Newark, New Jersey, U.S.A., I was nurtured on science fiction as on my mother's milk. When Father Devlin arrived in Senegal in 1953 he had with him *three* steamer trunks packed with his lifetime collection of s-f, over five hundred magazines, ranging from the marvelous *Thrilling Wonder Stories, Famous Fantastic Mysteries, Super Science Stories* and *Planet* to the more intellectual journals such as

Startling and *Amazing Stories,* and dating from
1936 to 1952. Under his diligent tutelage I pored
over these treasure troves of the imagination, star-
borne through their pages to the nethermost
reaches of the cosmos. By the age of fourteen I had
memorized many stories by heart, and was a particular fan of Robert Moore Williams, E. E. "Doc"
Smith, Nelson Bond, Ray Cummings, Eric Frank
Russell, P. Schuyler Miller, Raymond Z. Gallun,
the revered Stanley G. Weinbaum, L. Ron Hubbard and the magnificent Richard Shaver, so bril-
liantly discovered by my favorite editor, Ray A.
Palmer of *Amazing Stories.* ("Dear Rap," where
are you now? *Où sont les neiges d'antan?*) Study
the market, Mr. Ferman? I dare say I know the
market as well as any living fan. It is true that I
have only been in the United States under my exchange scholarship for two months now, and have
not yet read a great many of the more recent magazines and books, but what better apprenticeship
could I have! Ever since I was a day-dreaming boy,
Mr. Ferman, sometimes misunderstood by the
other children because of my stocky build (which
Ms. Markowitz, who is typing this, singularly ad-
mires, being similarly well-endowed herself), I
have immersed myself in s-f, lived s-f, dreamed s-
f, eaten s-f as my daily millet. How often were the
times as an adolescent that I would slip away from
school, clutching a treasured copy of *Amazing Stories,* and sit under a tamarind or baobab tree, mute
in joy and wonder at the magical universes into
which I was transported, oblivious to all around
me. Even as the other lads stole into the bush with
giggling young maidens to play hide-the-snake, I
was riding the asteroid belts, or battling the
dreaded deros in their eldritch caverns beneath
the earth, or winning the hand of a Martian princess. And you suggest *I* am ignorant of this field?
The mind boggles, Mr. Ferman. The mind positively boggles.

But let us return to our muttons. I will not deign
to comment on your specific references to my work

(others, less charitably inclined, might employ the word "nit-picking") or on the somewhat condescending tone of your letter. That, Mr. Fermen, is something better left to you and your conscience. I am, however, for the third and *final* time, submitting to you "Astrid of the Asteroids," "Slime Slaves of G'harn" and "Ursula of Uranus." I hope and trust you will read them with a fresh insight and a new spirit, untainted by whatever animus perverted your initial perusal. (Could it be that you, like Father Devlin, are plagued by "the bottle sickness," and the distortions of mood and perception it engenders? This would explain much.) In any case, Mr. Ferman, I wish you well, and can only hope that the blinders will be struck from your eyes, and my work revealed to you as what it truly is—the most significant contribution to the corpus of science fiction since Stanley G. Weinbaum. If not, I am afraid I will be forced to consider alternative markets.

Yours,

O. T. Nkabele, Esq.

P.S. Ms. Markowitz, who is conversant with such matters, points out that the only prominent black writer in s-f today is Samuel "Chip" Delany, and wonders if your obtuseness could be motivated by racialism. I will reserve judgment on this matter.

P.P.S. If my earlier surmise was correct, I commend to your attention a morning-after concoction I used to prepare for Father Devlin, and which appreciably improved both his health and temper: a calabash containing the juice of three paw-paws and two limes, leavened with the slightest *soupçon* of fresh palm oil and a dash of Tabasco. Ideally, this should be followed by a light repast of manioc, mealies and wild figs, the latter consumed in moderation.

Cornwall, Connecticut 06753
July 7, 1980

Mr. O. T. Nkabele
329 East 8th Street
New York, New York 10009

Dear Mr. Nkabele:

Mr. Ferman has asked me to return the enclosed manuscripts to you. Thank you for
thinking of F&SF.

Sincerely,
James T. Leasor
Assistant to the Editor

329 East 8th Street
New York, New York 10009
July 10, 1980

Mr. Edward L. Ferman
Magazine of Fantasy & Science Fiction
Cornwall, Connecticut 06753

My dear Mr. Ferman:

I am dismayed at the evident breakdown in
communication between us. I urgently suggest
a face-to-face meeting to iron out the misun-
derstandings that have arisen, either
in Connecticut or here in New York City. Please
ring me any time of the day or night at area
code 212, 675-4709. (Feel free to reverse the
charges.) My calendar is free for the next two
weeks, and I am completely at your disposal.

Dear Mr. Ferman, we must end this petty
bickering and get down to a serious evaluation
of my work. I am sure that if we sat together
over a sundowner and discussed the situation,
your attitude would soon change. We owe this

not only to each other, but to the field of science fiction we both love so dearly.

> With warmest affection,
> O. T. Nkabele, Esq.

Cornwall, Connecticut 06753
July 19, 1980

Mr. O. T. Nkabele
329 East 8th Street
New York, New York 10009

Dear Mr. Nkabele:

I must admit that my irritation over your earlier letter has taken some time to subside. I was particularly put off by your veiled accusation of racism, which was really a cheap shot. There are relatively few black s-f writers for the same reason there are still relatively few blacks prominent in other areas of American life and literature: a 300-year-old legacy of oppression and exclusion does not die easily. There is, however, no conspiracy to exclude blacks from s-f; just the opposite, in fact. Furthermore, it would be the rankest kind of paternalistic condescension, if not reverse racism, for me to treat your work any differently, or to qualify my criticism, simply because of your skin color. So let's bury that red herring once and for all. You are obviously as defensive about your work as any fledgling writer, but I must warn you that your overly touchy attitude will only serve to antagonize other editors in the field.

Which brings me to the reason I am, after all, resuming our correspondence. I must admit that, after my initial annoyance had worn off, I was rather intrigued, and even touched, by your description of growing up on a diet of pulp

s-f in the heart of Africa. One problem in our
field, due both to parochialism and translation
difficulties, is that we know regrettably little
about s-f outside the English-speaking world.
There have, of course, been some good volumes
of Russian and Eastern European s-f published
here (Stanislaw Lem, obviously), and we occasionally see some French work, while Judith
Merrill has just begun translating Japanese
s-f into English. There are also several foreign-
language editions of F&SF, and we receive some
feedback from writers and readers in the countries where they appear. But otherwise we are
relatively ignorant of what is (or is not) being
written in vast areas of the world. Africa, of
course, is a case in point. I have heard there is
some s-f being published in Nigeria, but this
has only reached my attention because it's in
English, which is still the *lingua franca* there.
So the whole subject of African s-f fascinates
me, as does your own story of your childhood
addiction to the vintage pulps. This is obviously the root of your current literary problems, of course; you are still writing in a style
that was out of date twenty years ago. But before you bridle, let me suggest that your background also holds the germs of an intriguing
article idea.

I would like you to write up your childhood
experiences for us, a personal memoir telling
how you first came into contact with Western
s-f and fell in love with it, and how it affected
your life. What was it like to be a teen-ager
from tribal Africa immersed in the alien world
of American s-f? How did your family and fellow students react? How did it color your view
of the United States when you first came here?
Did you ever feel excluded by the technologically advanced, all-white societies depicted in

most of the stories of that time? How did science fiction change your view of yourself, your village, your tribe? How did you translate the work into an African cultural matrix? I think the answers to all these questions would be fascinating to our readers, and provide them with a totally fresh perspective on s-f. We rarely run articles, with the exception of Dr. Asimov's monthly science column, but perhaps we could carry it as an extended book review section, or maybe, who knows, as part of a general symposium on Third World s-f. I obviously can't use your fiction, as I've tried so unavailingly to make clear, but this could break you into print at the same time you're updating your knowledge of contemporary s-f. (Believe me, my advice in that area is *not* condescending; it is vital.)

Now to the less pleasant side of this assignment. You would have to tone down your florid style, and avoid rhetorical overkill. Bear in mind Hemingway's wise adage: kill your darlings. And I'd have to exact a promise in advance that you won't quibble over my editorial blue pencil. Don't take this the wrong way, please; you have a talent, but it's not only anachronistic in content but stylistically undisciplined. The first may be more easily corrected than the second, but I'm willing to have a go.

Finally, let me add that I appreciate the conciliatory tone of your last letter. I hope it won't sound pompous if I say that I rarely enter into prolonged correspondence with unknown authors. I simply don't have the time; nor, to be frank, in most cases the inclination. But I was moved by your childhood experiences and I think our readers could be too. Think about it.

Best,
Edward L. Ferman

329 East 8th Street
New York, New York 10009
July 23, 1980

Mr. Edward L. Ferman
Magazine of Fantasy & Science Fiction
Cornwall, Connecticut 06753

Esteemed Editor Ferman:

I welcome your letter, as it reveals a distinct
thaw in our relationship. I always knew that, on
reflection, you would realize the futility, if not self-
destructiveness, of your earlier attitude.

As to your suggestion, I am afraid it poses
certain problems. I have always intended to
write my autobiography, but I do not think the
time is yet ripe. First my work must be accepted by a large audience in America and
abroad, which is why publication of my short
stories is a vital prerequisite. I would also publish initially in hard-cover, so that the book
clubs and Hollywood could bid on the rights.
Ms. Markowitz assures me this is most important. I would, of course, be happy for F&SF to
serialize it in whole or part, subject, of course,
to mutually satisfactory financial terms.

We are, however, getting a bit ahead of ourselves on this. Thus, I am enclosing a revised
version of "Slime Slaves of G'harn," tailored to
meet your objection about the sexual prefer-
ences of the Gargons of Ganymede. They are no
longer giant crustaceans but giant gerbils
which, being mammalian, should have no difficulty consummating their lustful desires for
Ursula. I hope this will prove a token of my
willingness to meet you halfway.

I must reiterate my desire for a personal

meeting, and as soon as possible. These matters should be ideally considered on what Ms. Markowitz so aptly terms a one-to-one basis. I would be more than happy to visit you in Connecticut at your convenience.

With warmest affection,
O. T. Nkabele, Esq.

Cornwall, Connecticut 06753
July 29, 1980

Mr. O. T. Nkabele
329 East 8th Street
New York, New York 10009

Dear Mr. Nkabele:

Mr. Ferman has asked me to return "Slime Slaves of G'harn" to you. He does not believe further correspondence on the matter would prove productive.

Sincerely,
James T. Leasor
Assistant to the Editor

Cornwall, Connecticut 06753
August 8, 1980

Mr. O. T. Nkabele
329 East 8th Street
New York, New York 10009

Dear Oginga:

Once again, I want to thank you for your most gracious gifts. The silver-chased *assegai* is hanging above the fireplace as I write this, and the beautiful carved wood fertility statue has a place of honor in my study. I really shouldn't have accepted such magnificent, and obviously valuable, presents from you; it must have been that last "sundowner" you prepared that undermined my resistance. (The next morning it seemed as if the sun *had* set, and permanently!) But be assured that I am grateful.

I am, in retrospect, very glad you came up. After my initial surprise wore off at encountering you in my local barber shop, of all places, I was relieved that you had reconsidered your earlier attitudes and were willing to make a serious effort to improve and update your work. I'm afraid I had rather given up on you after that last letter, which I hope explains my initial coolness when we met, but I am pleased my words had some impact, however belated. Anyway, that's all water under the bridge, and I anxiously await the first draft of your autobiographical article, "Safari to Wonder: the Pulps and I." (I think we should discuss that title further, but it will do for now.) I also hope the books I loaned you will be of some help in modernizing your knowledge of s-f.

By the way, my memories of the latter part of the evening are rather dim, but by any chance did you leave a small pouch of animal skin behind at my place? I found it under my pillow the next morning, and I assumed it was another of your generous gifts, perhaps a good-luck fetish. It is filled with bits of bone, feathers, dirt, hair, beads, cowrie shells, scraps of cloth, lumps of iron and a tiny clay figurine pinned down with wooden pegs and pierced with thorns in the head and heart. If it was a present, thanks once again, but if you lost it just let me know and I'll mail it off to you.

Good luck on the article!

Best regards,
Ed

P.S. You mentioned that your major at N.Y.U. is physiotherapy. Would you recommend massage as a cure for persistent headaches that are unresponsive to medication? I've had the granddaddy of them all for the past few days now, and nothing seems to work. (Or maybe I *do* need that recipe you concocted for your Irish mentor!) Seriously, if you have any suggestions let me know, as it's beginning to affect my concentration.

329 East 8th Street
New York, New York 10009
August 12, 1980

Mr. Edward L. Ferman
Cornwall, Connecticut 06753

My dear friend Ed:

Thank you so much for your gracious letter. I too shall treasure the delightful evening at your home, rendered doubly poignant by the turbulent course of our prior relationship. But, like the famous journalist Stanley and the intrepid explorer Livingstone, our reunion was memorable precisely because of those obstacles of mutual misunderstanding that preceded and impeded it. Now, however, our collaboration has begun! Let it be both creatively fruitful and financially remunerative. (The latter is the least of my considerations, of course, but, as a saying of my people has it, "The man without mealie does not sing songs.")

The pouch you refer to is, as you surmise, a good-luck charm or *ju-ju*, a small token of my affection for you. It may be worn around the neck or simply kept within the hut as a ward against malign spirits. And, yes, therapeutic massage is *very* good for headache.

I also want to thank you for the novels and collections of short stories. I have not as yet read them all, but I must confess I am shocked and depressed at the profound deterioration in our field since my apprenticeship in Africa. It is obvious that I was blessed with exposure to the Golden Age of science fiction, and that the downward spiral towards decadence and decay has accelerated horrendously since the mid-fifties. Writers like Theodore Sturgeon, whom I remember from an earlier, healthier stage in his career, particularly disturb me, as they must know the birthright they are betraying. (If I may be permitted a note of levity, the eggs Sturgeon lays are far from caviar!) Certainly, his current stories would never have been accepted by *Thrilling Wonder Stories* in the glorious days gone by. And this Barry Malzberg you suggested I read—my word, dear Edward, surely he is afflicted of the Gods! The man is a veritable pustulence on the face of the universe, a yellow dog barking in the night. We have another saying in my tribe, "The jackal dreams lions' dreams." How true! How tragically true. And how a creature such as Malzberg would cringe and whimper if ever confronted with the shade of Stanley G. Weinbaum, the Great Master himself. And these women, Ursula LeGuin and Joanna Russ, they should be beaten with stout sticks! I would not give one hamstrung goat for the pair of them. (It is apposite here to reflect on the words of the good Dr. Johnson, who pointed out that "A woman's preaching is like a dog walking on his hind legs; it is not done well, but you are surprised to find it done at all.") Of all the stories I have read recently, only Kilgore Trout's *Venus on the Half Shell* is worthy to bear the mantle of the giants of yesteryear. Truly, my good friend, the field we love is facing terrible times, and it is indeed providential that I have arrived on the scene to arrest the rot. Perhaps, in fact, there was a Larger Purpose of Father Devlin's introducing me to science fiction. We shall see.

I have not yet got around to Mr. Ellison's books, but I am glad you told me he experiments with new work in his *Dangerous Visions* series. I have sent him several of my stories, and expect a prompt and enthusiastic reply. And thank you once again for providing me with his home address and unlisted phone number. Perhaps the three of us, united, can yet cleanse the science fiction temple of this babbling *canaille!*

Once more, thank you for a delightful weekend. Looking out my window at the squalor of what the natives call the East Village, I can only wish I were back with you in Connecticut. Your Cornwall is so green and beautiful, I can understand why the game hens flourish. I hope on my next trip you will introduce me to Daphne du Maurier, an old favorite of mine, and we can find time to visit some of your picturesque tin mines and smugglers' coves.

Hoping to see you again soon, I remain

Your devoted pal,
Oginga
(You may call me Oggy)

Cornwall, Connecticut 06753
August 16, 1980

Mr. Harlan Ellison
Villa Van Vogt
9263 Easton Drive
Beverly Hills, California 90210

Dear Harlan:

I'm afraid I owe you something of an apology. It's a long story, but I'm being pursued by a young African exchange student who fancies himself another Heinlein—or, God save us all, another Stanley G. Weinbaum. It's an interesting story, actually. He was brought up in a remote area of Senegal on a diet of 1940s pulp s-f, and he writes and thinks like a reincarnated ha' penny-a-word hack. (I thought I'd partially converted him, but after his last letter I have some doubts.) Anyway, after an exchange of letters that you wouldn't believe he showed up in Cornwall and collared me, all 300 pounds of him. (Wrapped in a *dashiki* that would blind you at forty paces.) I couldn't help feeling sorry for the kid, he's like a big fat puppy, so I took him back to the house for a talk and a few drinks. He seemed contrite, said he recognized the problems with his writing, and we worked up an article on how he grew up in the jungle on a diet of space opera. Could be quite good, really, though God knows I'll have a hell of a rewrite job on my hands. But the point of all this is that I got royally plastered, for the first time in years—funny too, I don't remember drinking that much—and apparently gave him your address and phone number in a fit of alcoholic fugue. Your *home* number.

Now I know what you're going to say, Harlan, but have pity. Every Ellison has his Brutus, and you can always change your number and/or move. If you think I'm joking, wait till the phone calls start. I know my man. Actually, I hope he doesn't give you too hard a time, but he's a persistent cuss and I suggest you let him down gently. Otherwise, he's liable to turn up in *your* barber shop!

I haven't had a chance to read your new piece yet, the work is piling up and I haven't been too well lately. I've got the damndest headache, I can't seem to shake it, and I'm a little worried about my hearing. There's a kind of constant, staccato beating in my inner ear, it sounds almost like drums. I guess I'll have to go to an ee&t man if it keeps up.

Ah, well, time's winged chariot hovers on all our heels.

Once again, I'm sincerely sorry for inadvertently violating your privacy. I hope we'll still be on speaking terms after this, and you'll let me buy you dinner at the Worldcon in atonement. Sans booze!

Best,
Ed

P.S. Could you ask one of your Japanese gardeners what, if anything, can be done about rose blight? All our roses just died overnight, I found the bushes shriveled and black in the morning. And the weather was perfect, too. I really can't understand it, and after all the work I put in it's a bit depressing. Christ, I moved to Connecticut in the first place to tend my garden and avoid the badgering of hot-eyed young geniuses fresh from the Famous Writers' School. Seems I'm not doing too well on either front.

ELLISON ENTERPRISES UNIVERSAL
"Heute gehörten Hollywood,
morgen die ganze welt"
9640 Sunset Boulevard
Los Angeles, California 90069
CABLE ADDRESS: ENEMU   ORDERS TO GO

August 21, 1980

Edward My Son:

You are forgiven, though reluctantly. Yes, your protege has been pursuing me, like a hound out of hell. I got a batch of his drek in the mail last week, and then the phone calls began. I was polite to the schmuck the first few calls because I hadn't got around to his stuff,

and because he said you two were collaborating
on some magnum opus or other. It was only
because of that I finally sat down and waded
through the crap. Jesus, it was godawful, so lu-
dicrously so that I thought the whole thing was a
put-on at first. But nobody, I mean *nobody,* could
write that consistently, humorlessly bad without
sincerity. Shit, I haven't read such wondrously lo-
botomized prose in years, it was a real nostalgia
trip. He kept calling up pestering me for a reaction
and I tried to fob him off, but when he rang at two
in the morning last Friday, and me making the
beast with two backs on the casting couch, I really
told him what I thought of the garbage. He hung
up in a tiff and so far, Yahweh be praised, he hasn't
called back, either here at the office or at home. It
did get a bit hairy for a while though, calls every
hour of the night and day. I got to wandering
around muttering, "Who will free me from this
turbulent scribe?" Well, so far so good.

The thing is, Ed, you weren't helping the poor
turd by encouraging him. To lumber toward a pun,
this guy is not the *crème* of the *Senégalèse.* I mean,
look, I'm as sympathetic as you are to all the no-
talent hacks out there, but you don't do the schle-
miels any good by feeding their delusions of gran-
deur; sometimes, to coin a phrase, you've gotta be
cruel to be kind. I will admit that after I got your
letter with all that stuff about growing up on the
pulps out in Tarzan-land I felt a wee bit guilty
about the way I'd dressed him down, but the
putz's gotta find out someday that his stuff's un-
readable, not to mention unpublishable. And
without getting shirty with you, *cher maitre,* who
needs it anyway? I mean, you should see the shit
I'm getting from the *heavies* for *Last Dangerous
Visions.* I sure don't need to comb the boondocks
for something even worse. Christ, I've gotta tell
writers I like and respect I can't use their pieces,
and then you inflict this *merde* on me! No more,

Edward. Peace, calm, I beg you. Beco... drinker, and spare your friends. The ... manage on their own, God knows there a... of them out there. In fact, one of them le... leather bag full of what looks like chicke... and graveyard dirt on my doorstep the other ... Jesus, L.A. is really one huge out-patient c... Don't recruit *more* crazies for me!

About your roses, tough titty. My gardeners a... at a loss, they say only a sudden frost could kil... 'em off all at once, and that's hardly likely in August. Not in your part of the world anyway. But you think you've got problems? My fuckin' hair is falling out! Started yesterday, and it's going as fast as your roses. Jesus, I'm gonna need a friggin' rug soon. Cry your hearts out, ladies. Oh, well, this is the summer of our discontent.

You've got a date for the Worldcon, and it's gonna cost you.

Peace,
Harlan of the Bald Pate

Cornwall, Connecticut 06753
August 24, 1980

Mr. Harlan Ellison
Villa Van Vogt
9263 Easton Drive
Beverly Hills, California 90210

Dear Harlan:

This will sound silly, but could you please describe, in detail, the contents of that pouch you mentioned? I have my reasons, and I would appreciate a quick response. I've tried to call you, but there is no answer.

Our golden retriever, Jenny, is dead. Something seems to have eaten her. Our neighb...

swears he saw a leopard slinking
the night. Ridiculous, of course.
phone or wire me that information
ouch? If you call, speak loudly. I can't
o well over these goddamned drums.

Best regards,
Ed

9263 Easton Drive
Beverly Hills, Calif. 90210
August 27, 1980

Mr. Edward L. Ferman
Magazine of Fantasy & Science Fiction
Cornwall, Connecticut 06753

Edward me darlin':

Sorry you couldn't reach me on the phone,. but
I've turned the damned thing off for a few days.
Oddly enough, I've got a lousy headache myself,
and nothing seems to help. Probably overwork.
I've been batting my brains out on "The Sound of
Screaming," that TV musical comedy of mine
about the Moors Murder Trial in England. Some
asshole producer cast Julie Andrews as Myra Hin-
dley, and she's breaking my chops with script revisions. It's my first score, too, and the bitch is
ruining the title song. ("And the moors echo now/
With the sound of screaminggg. . . .") I'm not too
happy with their choice of Donny Osmond for Ian
Brady, either.

Anyway, that's my problem. As to the pouch,
I threw it away a couple of days ago. Why? Did
you get one too? Maybe we're being hexed by
hat African pal of yours! God, to die so young,
like Alexander, with the world in my grasp. . . .
Listen, *mon vieux*, I don't have to go outside
he field for my enemies; I can name a half-
ozen Hugo winners who are probably fashion-

ing wax images of me right now! But if I get
another, I'll send it off to you. Hokay?

Be good, and don't send me any more Stanley
Weinbaums, even in blackface.

Love and Kisses,
Harlan

P.S. Hey, seriously, were you playing straight
about your dog? If so, I'm really sorry, that's
a real bummer. Maybe it was a pack of wild
dogs; I hear a lot of abandoned summer pets
have gone feral. My sympathies.

329 East 8th Street
New York, New York 10009
August 28, 1980

Mr. Edward L. Ferman
Magazine of Fantasy & Science Fiction
Cornwall, Connecticut 06753

My dear friend Edward:

It was good talking to you last night. I'm sorry
you'd been ringing for the past two days, but I was
out of town on business, and Ms. Markowitz was
visiting her parents in a place called Great Neck.
(How one relishes these exotic, and evocative,
American place names!) In fact, when you phoned
I had just returned from the airport.

I am most desolate to hear of your troubles.
First the headaches, then your roses, and now
your poor dog. It is said that these things tend
to run in threes, but that is scant consolation
for you. I was surprised, I must admit, at your
inclination to suspect a supernatural agency
behind these sad events. Surely, dear Edward,
we are living in the fourth quarter of the twentieth century, not in some primitive backwater

of medieval times. I will grant you that among my own people such calamities would be ascribed to the intervention of malign spirits, or possibly to one's own guilt rebounding on one in punishment of a sin or grievous error of judgment, and thereby unleashing self-destructive psychic manifestations. In my land it is believed that when one of royal blood is wronged and unable to redress that wrong himself a *mhondoro*, or "mouthpiece of the spirit," will appear to avenge him. It has been known for the spirit of a great warrior or medicine man to materialize on earth and enter into the body of a wild animal in order to torment and ultimately devour those ignorant or malicious humans who prey like insolent jackals on his hapless descendants. Only the intercession of the original victim, it is said, can break the curse and banish the avenging shades to eternal darkness. But whom have you wronged so deeply, whom have you misunderstood so profoundly, whom have you hurt so callously, as to bring down on your head the wrath of the victim's ancestral spirits? All such conjecture is, in any case, rank superstition, and I am surprised to find a man of your knowledge and sophistication succumbing to it. There must be a perfectly logical explanation for your travails. Must there not?

Without appearing overly sensitive I must also confess that I was troubled by your insinuation that my humble gifts were somehow related to your recent misfortunes. My dear Edward, must our friendship, so recently sealed, now be sundered by hysterical suspicion and paranoid allegation? Permit me to say, as gently as possible, that you are overwrought, and need a good rest. You mention that the noise in your head, which you fancifully describe as drums, is keeping you from sleep. Perhaps that is the root of your problem, and you should consult an alienist of good repute. But always feel free to call on your friend Oginga for advice or consolation.

I am afraid we can dismiss Harlan Ellison as an ally in our crusade to redeem science fiction. I have been in touch with him recently, and he was most crudely abusive and insensitive; in fact, at one point he went so far as to threaten legal action if I continued to contact him! I regret to say he is no gentleman, and can be written off as a force for progress in the field. I am afraid, my friend, that the struggle to wrest s-f from the hands of the obfuscators and pornographers is ours alone. It will be a lonely battle, but victory will be all the more sweet for that reason. And remember the tocsin sounded by Edmund Burke, which Father Devlin prophetically taught me so many years ago: "The triumph of evil is insured when good men do nothing."

I have a feeling that you are finally in a receptive mood for "Slime Slaves of G'harn," "Astrid of the Asteroids" and "Ursula of Uranus," which I am enclosing. Though I hesitate to say so, my friend, it is not impossible that your failure to as yet fully appreciate these works is at the root of your present troubles. Your subconscious may be warring with you, urging you to reconsider and reevaluate my stories, and thus creating severe psychic stress which manifests itself in headaches and auditory hallucinations. Nothing, dear Edward, is impossible. I counsel you to remember that.

With warmest affection,
Your pal,
Oggy

Cornwall, Connecticut 06753
September 1, 1980

Dr. Isaac Asimov
Asimov Hall
Asimov State University
Asimovia, New York 14603

Dear Isaac:

God, is it really true about Harlan? I couldn't believe the first press reports, but Fritz Lieber called me from L.A. a little while ago and confirmed it all. The poor devil. I knew it had to come some day, but I always thought it would be at the hands of a fellow writer. Not like this.

I know I was a little incoherent on the phone last night, but I swear that this ties in with what's happening to me. Ellison rebuffed the African too, and look what happened to him. Christ, I may be next! The drums are getting louder every day, and I've developed sharp, stabbing pains in my chest and joints. This morning I found my parakeet dead in his cage, his little neck snapped like a twig. And the cage was *locked*, Isaac, I had the only key. I know you're a confirmed rationalist but I swear to you, I am being hexed! Or voodooed, or hoodooed or whatever the right African name for it is. I don't know whether the bastard intends to kill me too or just terrify me to the point where I'll agree to publish his abominable stories. God, psychic blackmail! But I can't go on like this, I haven't slept for three days, and the pain is getting unbearable. You've got to help me, Isaac, use your encyclopedic knowledge, find an antidote to the curse. Remember M. R. James' *The Casting of the Runes?* Maybe there's some way I can hit back, make his damned magic boomerang on him! But I know nothing about these matters, I used to be as thoroughgoing a sceptic as you are. I tried to ask Fritz about it, he's an expert on the occult and the whole thing is so bloody reminiscent of *Conjure Wife*, but the minute I described the *ju-ju* bag and its contents he got all stuttery, made some excuse about having to leave for a trip to Mexico, and hung up. Some friend.

Listen, Isaac, I'm not crazy, no matter how it sounds. You and I have both read about these things actually working in Haiti; well, now they're working in Connecticut. For the love of God, help me!!!! I'm enclosing the ju-ju bag: examine it, tell me what I can do. Should we burn it? Or would that just make things worse? My life and my sanity are in your hands, Isaac. Don't let me down.

Desperately,
Ed

ASIMOV STATE UNIVERSITY
"The Intelligent Have A Right Over The Ignorant, The Right of Instructing Them."
—Ralph Waldo Emerson

September 6, 1980

Mr. Edward L. Ferman
Cornwall, Connecticut 06753

Dear Ed:

Yes, it was a great tragedy about Harlan. (Not in the Aristotelian sense that great tragedy requires the fall of a great man, of course, but on the human level; after all, even Harlan had a mother who will mourn him, and remember when Harlie was one.) When the first, fragmen-

tary reports came over the news I suspected
Harlan had perished by his own hand; he had
toiled too long in the literary abattoir of locust-
land, and I knew it was exacting a heavy toll.
The last time I saw him I quoted Fred Allen's
line that "You can take all the sincerity in Hollywood, place it in the navel of a fruit fly and
still have room enough for three caraway seeds
and a producer's heart." He said nothing, just
smiled wanly and twitched several times. Poor
Harlan. There will not be another like him.

I've just come back from the funeral in Los Angeles, which is why I'm a little late in responding
to your letter. A senior police officer was there and
I spoke to him in private, since I'm thinking of
doing a mystery based on the case, in the vein of
my *Murder at the A.B.A.* The cops still haven't
located the zoo or circus from which the giant python escaped, but they are scouring the state. Apparently Harlan was attacked and devoured
beside the swimming pool of the Beverly Hills Hotel, on his way to a ceremony in the Polo Lounge
where he was to have received his fourth Atilla
award from the Screen Writers' Guild West. What
bitter irony! The police shot the snake shortly af-
terwards, when it attempted to consume an el-
derly lady walking her dog on Mulholland Drive.
Apparently it was still hungry.

I was really glad I attended the funeral. There
should have been someone there besides his ac-
countant, whom I suspect showed up only to
make sure. (Harlan was already partially digested
when they autopsied the python, so the coffin was
closed and he went away a bit disappointed.) It
was a bittersweet occasion for all of us in s-f.

Now to address myself to the subject of your
letter and phone call. Frankly, Ed, you put me
in a difficult position. You know I have both
respect and affection for you, but it would be
dereliction of our friendship to encourage you

in this delusion. I'm afraid you've been driving yourself too hard in recent years, far too hard, and this *idée fixe* is obviously the result. You know that I do not have a closed mind; in fact, I fully subscribe to Haldane's Law that the universe is not only queerer than we imagine, it is queerer than we *can* imagine. But that does not mean I have to swallow a lot of nonsensical mumbo-jumbo about hexes and curses and drums and leopards in the night. I'm sorry, Ed, but I'm afraid the problem is all in your troubled mind. Sure, people in Haiti can die of a voodoo hex, *if they believe totally and fanatically in the power of voodoo.* Psychosomatic medicine is still in its infancy, but we do know that individuals can *will* themselves to serious illness and even death. My fear is that this is precisely what is happening to you. I urgently suggest that you contact Dr. Joseph Rauschbusch in New York City, a highly qualified psychoanalyst who worked wonders for Malzberg. His number is 676-4350, and I've already spoken to him, so he's expecting your call.

Before a cure can be effective, Ed, you must grasp the fact that a logical, rational explanation is, in this case as in all others, the *only* explanation. Remember Sherlock Holmes' dictum, as true in science as in criminology: "When you have eliminated the impossible, whatever remains, *however improbable,* must be the truth." To you, old friend, the improbable truth is that you are having a nervous breakdown; rather than face that, you have taken refuge in consoling impossibilities. And do not quote back to me Aristotle's claim that "plausible impossibilities should be preferred to unconvincing possibilities"; I have succinctly demolished that position in my recent book, *Isaac Asimov's Guide to the Wit and Wisdom of All Human History* (Afflatua Press, N.Y., 1976). Of course, whenever they're challenged, the camp followers of irrationality will resort to Hegel's rejoinder when told that the facts contradicted his theories: "All the worse for the facts." Do not join them, Ed. The facts dictate that you seek expert medical advice, and as quickly as possible.

If it will help put your mind at rest, I have examined your pouch, and although I can't identify all the ingredients as yet, they appear thoroughly non-toxic and, believe it or not, nonmagical. The shells are cowrie and the hair does seem to be human, and of European texture, but that means nothing in and of itself; your meeting the African in the barber shop was obviously nothing more than a coincidence. This little grab-bag of junk can hurt *no one,* Ed. Only you can hurt yourself. I hope I have been of some help in making that clear.

On a lighter note, my latest book, *Isaac Asimov's Guide to Health, Happiness and Regularity through Self-Negation,* is doing very well, and will soon be out in paperback. (So far, it's even outselling my *Isaac Asimov's Guide to Guides.*) At a recent autograph party in Poughkeepsie, several nubile young ladies, obviously enamored of both my charm and talent, inquired if I had a hobby. I replied, with a bow to Oliver St. John Gogarty: "Converting lesbians." Well, I can tell you, Edward, I couldn't get rid of them after that. In fact, later that night . . . [Deleted for reasons of taste, and space—The Editor]

. . . Well, Edward, I must get back to the grindstone, I've got another book to turn out this afternoon. (My first venture into political porn, *Sex Slaves of the Judiciary Committee,* based loosely on Watergate.) Hope you'll soon free yourself of the Black Dog, and we can get together for lunch.

Cordially,
Isaac

WU014 PD

CORNWALL CONN SEP 12 345 AEDT

O T NKABELE
329 E 8
NYC

CANNOT GO ON LIKE THIS STATE YOUR TERMS
EDWARD FERMAN
3240 RIDGEDALE AVE
CORNWALL CONN

329 East 8th Street
New York, New York 10009
September 13, 1980

Mr. Edward L. Ferman
Magazine of Fantasy & Science Fiction
Cornwall, Connecticut 06753

My dear friend Ed:

I have received your wire and am most sympathetic to your plight, although I cannot countenance the idea that *multi*, or witchpower, is at the root of your difficulties. Nevertheless, inasmuch as your welfare and happiness are so important to me, I have swallowed my doubts and performed certain *uchawi* rituals of cleansing or, in Western parlance, exorcism, that were handed down to me by my uncle, the *Mganga* of our people. If a vindictive *mhondoro* is indeed pursuing you, he is now banished to the Eternal Night from whence he came. Thaumaturgically speaking, however, there is no assurance that he will not rematerialize in the future, if the situation which triggered his initial manifestation should recur.

Thus, eternal vigilance on my part would be required in order to prevent another psychic onslaught on your mind and body, this time possibly fatal. Needless to say, dear Edward, I cannot intellectually justify your supernatural hypothesis, but I hope my actions will reassure you and soothe your troubled thoughts.

I also trust that following your recuperation you will return to my stories with a fresh and positive perspective. I am currently working on a new piece, "The Hell Pits of R'ghanna," which I will dispatch to you shortly. It is of novella length, and should elicit much favorable comment among the cognoscenti.

With warmest fraternal feelings,
Your buddy.
Oggy

Cornwall, Connecticut 06753
September 20, 1980

Mr. O. T. Nkabele
329 East 8th Street
New York, New York 10009

Dear Oginga:

Yes, the headaches and chest pains have stopped, and I am slowly returning to normal. If anything in my life can ever be normal again. I understand your letter fully. Let us leave it at that.

Enclosed is a check for "Astrid of the Asteroids," "Slime Slaves of G'harn" and "Ursula of Uranus."

Yours,
Edward L. Ferman

329 East 8th Street
New York, New York 10009
October 27, 1980

Mr. Edward L. Ferman
Magazine of Fantasy & Science Fiction
Cornwall, Connecticut 06753

Dear Ed:

Thank you for your check for "Hell Pits of
R'ghanna." I am enclosing a rough sketch of
the cover illustration, which you will kindly
have your own artist follow explicitly.

Your friend,
Oggy

Cornwall, Connecticut 06753
March 23, 1981

Mr. O. T. Nkabele
329 East 8th Street
New York, New York 10009

Dear Oginga:

Enclosed is a check for "Selena of Sirius" and
"Space Pirates of Saturn." I am sorry the
amount is smaller this time, but we have had
grave circulation problems from the day we began running your stories. I understand that
since the elephant got Ben Bova you have been
writing for *Omni* as well. I hope their finances
are in better shape than ours.

Would you please provide us with an 8" by
10" glossy photograph of yourself (head and
shoulders) for the artist working on the cover
of our Oginga Nkabele Special Issue. He needs
it as soon as possible.

Yours,
Ed

P.S. I'm enclosing a list of the members of Science Fiction Writers of America, and most of their addresses. Under separate cover I've sent you a convention folio which has many of the photographs of individual writers you requested. They should be voting on the Nebula Awards in mid-April. I'm afraid I don't know where any of them have their hair cut, but I'm sure you'll find out.

> 329 East 8th Street
> New York, New York 10009
> May 10, 1981

Mr. Edward L. Ferman
Magazine of Fantasy & Science Fiction
Cornwall, Connecticut 06753

My dear Ed:

Thank you for your most gracious telegram of congratulations on my Nebula. I sincerely believe it is the field itself, rather than your humble servant, that is the true beneficiary. Who, precisely, votes on the Hugos at the World Convention? How may I get in touch with them? I am still, alas, regrettably innocent of the inner machinations of American fandom.

> With warmest regards,
> Your pal,
> Oggy

> Cornwall, Connecticut 06753
> January 12, 1982

Mr. O. T. Nkabele
23 Sutton Place
New York, New York 10023

Dear Oggy:

It was good seeing you and Rachel on the

weekend. I hope you'll come up again on your return from Hollywood.

No, I don't personally know anyone on the Nobel Prize Committee, but I have visited the Swedish Embassy and they inform me the judges are comprised of members of the Swedish and Norwegian Parliaments. The Embassy is mailing me their names and addresses, and I will forward them to you.

Thank you for sending us "Visitation of the Vrill." I'm glad you still find time to think of your old friends at F&SF, particularly now that we've gone mimeo. Let me know what you have in mind for the cover.

Best wishes,
Ed

P.S. Could you send me that hangover recipe you once mentioned? The B-12 shots no longer seem to do the job. I'll be tapering off soon, though. Really.

THE PRO

Edmond Hamilton

Edmond Hamilton wrote swashbuckling, star-spanning space operas for the better part of fifty years . . . but every now and then, just to prove that he could do it, he would turn in a superlative short story that could have been written by any of our so-called Modern Masters, stories like "The Inn Outside the World," and even more personal stories such as this one.

THE ROCKET STOOD tall and splendid, held for now in the nurse-arms of its gantry, but waiting, looking up and waiting . . .

And why the hell, thought Burnett, do I have to think fiction phrases even when I'm looking at the real thing?

"Must give you kind of a creepy feeling, at that," Dan said.

"God, yes," Burnett moved his shoulders, half grinning. "Creepy, and proud. I invented that thing. Thirty years ago come August, in my *Stardream* novel, I designed her and built her and launched her and landed her on Mars, and got a cent a word for her from the old *Wonder Stories.*"

"Too bad you didn't take out a patent."

"Be glad I didn't," Burnett said. "You're going to fly her. My Stardream was prettier than this one, but only had two short paragraphs of innards." He paused, nodding slowly. "It's kind of fitting, though, at that. It was the *Stardream* check, all four hundred dollars of it, that gave me the brass to ask your mother to marry me."

He looked at his son, the slim kid with the young-old face and the quiet smile. He could admit to himself now that he had been disappointed that Dan took after his mother in the matter of build. Burnett was a big man himself, with a large head and large hands and heavy shoulders, and Dan had always seemed small and almost frail to him. And now here was Dan in his sun-faded khakis blooming like a rose after all the pressure tests and the vertigo tests and the altitude tests and the various tortures of steel chambers and centrifuges, tests that Burnett doubted he could have stood up to even in his best days. He was filled with an unaccustomed and embarrassing warmth.

"You won't get to Mars in her, anyway," he said.

Dan laughed. "Not this trip. We'll be happy to settle for the Moon."

They walked on across the sun-blistered apron, turning their backs on the rocket. Burnett felt strangely as though all his sensory nerve-ends had been sandpapered raw so that the slightest stimulus set them to quivering. Never had the sun been so hot, never had he been so conscious of his own prickling skin, the intimate smell of clean cotton cloth dampening with sweat, the grit of blown sand under his feet, the nearness of his son, walking close behind him . . .

Not close enough. Not ever close enough.

It was odd, Burnett thought, that he had never until this moment been aware of any lack in their relationship.

Why? Why not then, and why now?

They walked companionably together in the sun, and Burnett's mind worked, the writer's mind trained and sharpened by thirty-odd years of beating a typewriter for an always precarious living, the mind that could never any more be wholly engulfed in any personal situation but must stand always in some measure apart, analytical and cool, Burnett the writer looking at Burnett the man as though he were a character in a story. Motivation, man. An emotion is unreal unless it's motivated, and this is not only unmotivated, it's inconsistent. It's not in character. People often seem to be inconsistent but they're not, they always have a reason for everything even if they don't know it, even if nobody knows it, and so what's yours, Burnett? Be honest, now. If you're not honest the whole thing, man and/or character, goes down the drain.

Why this sudden aching sense of incompletion, of not having done so many things, unspecified, for, by, and with this apparently perfectly happy and contented young man?

Because, thought Burnett. Because . . .

The heat waves shook and shimmered and the whitenesses of sand and blockhouse and distant buildings were unbearably painful to the eye.

"What's the matter, Dad?" asked Dan, sharp and far away.

"Nothing. Just the light—dazzling . . ." And now the sweat was cold on his big hard body and there was a cold evil inside him, and he thought, Well, hell, yes, of course. I'm scared. I'm thinking . . . Go ahead and drag it out, it won't be any the better for hiding away there inside in the dark. I'm thinking that this boy of mine is going to climb into that beautiful horror back there, not very many hours from now, and men are going to fasten the hatch on him and go away, and other men will push buttons and light the fires of hell in the creature's tail, and that it could be, it might be.

There's always the escape tower.

Sure there is.

Anyway, there you have it, the simplest motivation in the world. The sense of incompletion is not for the past, but for the future.

"Sun's pretty brutal here sometimes," Dan was saying. "Maybe you should have a hat on."

Burnett laughed and took off his sunglasses and wiped the sweat-damp out of his eyes. "Don't sell the old man short just yet. I can still break you in two." He put the glasses on again and strode strongly, cleanly, beside Dan. Behind them the rocket stood with its head in the sky.

In the common room of the astronauts' quarters they found some of the others, Shontz who was going with Dan, and Crider who was back-up man, and three or four more of the team. Others had already left for the global tracking stations where they would sweat out the flight with Dan and Shontz. They were all stamped out of much the same mold as Dan, and that wasn't a bad one, Burnett thought, not bad at all. Most of them had visited in his house. Three of them had even read his stories before they ever met either him or Dan. Now, of course, they all had. It seemed to delight them that they had on their team a top boy whose father was a writer of science fiction. He had no doubt that they had many a private joke about that, but all the same they greeted him with pleasure, and he was glad of them, because he needed some distraction to forget the coldness that was in him.

"Hey!" they said. "Here's the old expert himself. Hi, Jim, how goes it?"

"I came down," he told them, "to make sure you were doing everything according to the way we wrote it."

They grinned. "Well, how does it look to an old pro?" asked Crider.

Burnett pulled his mouth down and looked judicial. "Pretty good, except for one small detail."

"What's that?"

"The markings on the rocket. You ought to paint them up brighter, good strong reds and yellows so they'll show up against that deep, black, velvety, starshot space."

Shontz said, "I had a better idea, I wanted the top brass to paint the rocket black velvet and star-shot so Them Out There couldn't see us going by. But the generals only looked at us kind of funny."

"Illiterates," said a tall solemn-faced young man named Martin. He was one of the three who had read Burnett's stories. "Cut my teeth on them," he had said, making Burnett feel more ancient than overjoyed.

"Right," said Crider. "I doubt if they ever even watched Captain Marvel."

"That's the trouble," said Fisher, "with a lot of people in Washington." Fisher was round-faced and sunburned and cheerful, and he too had cut his teeth on Burnett's stories. "When they were kids they never read anything but Captain Billy's Whiz Bang, and that's why they keep coming out with questions like, 'Why put a man on the Moon?' "

"Oh, well," said Burnett, "that's nothing new. People said that to Columbus. Fortunately, there's always some idiot who won't listen to reason."

Crider held up his right hand. "Fellow idiots, I salute you."

Burnett laughed. He felt better now. Because they were so relaxed and unworried he could loosen up too.

"Don't get smart with me," he said. "I wrote the lot of you. When you were drooling in your cribs I was making you up out of ink and sweat and the necessity to pay the bills. And what did you do, you ungrateful little bastards? You all came true."

"What are you working on now?" asked Martin. "You going to do that sequel to *Child of a Thousand Suns?* That was a great story."

"Depends," said Burnett. "If you'll promise to keep the hell out of the Hercules Cluster just long enough for me to get the book written . . ." He counted on his fingers. "Serialization, hard-cover, soft-cover . . . Three years at a minimum. Can you do that?"

"For you, Jim," said Fisher, "we'll hold ourselves back."

"Okay, then. But I tell you, it isn't funny. These probes peering around Mars and Venus and blabbing everything they know, and some smart-assed scientist coming up every day with a new breakthrough in psionics or cryogenics or see-tee or FTL drives . . . it's getting tough. Nowadays I have to know what I'm talking about, instead of just elaborating on a theory or making something up out of my own head. And now my own kid is going to the Moon so he can come back and tell me what it's really like, and there will go a dozen more stories I can't write."

Talking, just talking, but the talk and the hearty, grinning young faces did him good and the coldness in him was gone . . .

"Have faith, Dad," said Dan. "I'll find you something down in the caverns. A dead city. Or at the least an abandoned galactic outpost."

"Well, why not?" said Burnett. "Everything else has happened."

He grinned back at them. "I'll tell you one thing, science fiction is a tough living but I'm glad it all came true while I was around to see it, and to see how the people who laughed at such childish nonsense took it. The look of blank shock on their little faces when Sputnik first went up, and the lovely horror that crept over them as they gradually began to realize that Out There is a really big place . . .''

He was not just talking now, he felt a throb of excitement and pride that his own flesh and blood was a part of this future that had so suddenly become the present.

They talked some more and then it was time to go, and he said goodbye to Dan as casually as though the boy was taking a shuttle hop between Cleveland and Pittsburgh, and he went away. Only once, when he looked back at the rocket, very distant now like a white finger pointing skyward, did the fear wrench at his guts again.

He flew home that night to Cartersburg, in central Ohio. He sat up very late talking to his wife, telling her about Dan, how he had looked and what he had said and how he, Jim, thought Dan was really feeling.

"Happy as a clam at high tide," he told her. "You should have come with me, Sally. I told you that."

"No," she said. "I didn't want to go."

Her face was as calm and relaxed as Dan's had been, but there was a note in her voice that made him put his arms around her and kiss her.

"Quit worrying, honey. Dan's not worried, and he's the one that's doing it."

"That's just it," she said. "He's doing it."

Burnett had an extra drink or two to sleep on. Even so he did not sleep well. And in the morning there were the reporters.

Burnett was beginning to not like reporters. Some of them were friendly guys, and some were just guys doing a job, but there were others . . . especially those who thought it intriguing that a science fiction writer should have fathered an astronaut.

"Tell me, Mr. Burnett, when you first started to write science fiction, did you really believe it would all happen?"

"That question's a little sloppy, isn't it?" said Burnett. "If you mean, did I think space-travel would happen . . . yes, I did."

"I've been reading some of your early stories. Managed to get hold of some of the old magazines . . .''

"Good for you. Some of them are selling for nearly as much as I got for the stories. Go ahead."

"Well, Mr. Burnett, not only in your stories but in almost all the others, I was struck by the faith in space-travel they showed. Tell me, do you think the science fiction you chaps wrote helped make space-travel come true?"

Burnett snorted. "Let's be realistic. The big reason why rockets are going out now, instead of a century from now, is because two great nations are each afraid the other will get an advantage."

"But you feel that science fiction did *something* to bring it about, don't you?"

"Well," said Burnett. "You could say that it encouraged unorthodox thinking and sort of prepared the mental climate a little for what was coming."

The reporter had finally made his point and seized triumphantly upon it. "So that one might say that the stories you wrote years ago are partly responsible for the fact that your son is going to the Moon?"

The coldness came back into Burnett. He said flatly, "One might say that if one wanted some soppy human interest angle to add to the coverage of the moonflight, but there's not any truth in it."

The reporter smiled. "Come now, Mr. Burnett, your stories surely had some influence on Dan in making his choice of a career. I mean, having been exposed to these stories all his life, reading them, listening to you talk . . . wouldn't all that sort of urge him into it?"

"It would not and it did not," said Burnett. He opened the door. "And now if you'll excuse me, I've got a lot of work to do."

When he shut the door, he locked it. Sally had gone off somewhere to avoid the whole thing and the house was quiet. He walked through it to the back garden and stood there staring hard at some red flowers and smoking until he could hold his hand steady again.

"Oh, well," he said aloud, "forget it."

He went back into the house, to his own room, his work-room—he had never called it a study because he didn't study in it, he only worked—and shut the door and sat down in front of his typewriter. There was a half-written page in it, and six pages of copy beside it, the groping and much x'ed-out unfinished first chapter to the sequel of *Child of a Thousand Suns*. He read the last page, and then the page in the typewriter, and he put his hands on the keyboard.

A very long time later he sighed and began almost mechanically to type.

Later still Sally came in and found him sitting. He had taken that page out of the typewriter but he had not put another one in, and he was just sitting there.

"Troubles?" asked Sally.

"Can't seem to get the thing going, is all."

She shook him gently by the shoulder. "Come and have a drink, and then let's get the hell out of this house for a while."

She did not often talk like that. He nodded, getting up. "Drive in the country might do us good. And maybe a movie tonight." Anything at all to get our minds off the fact that tomorrow morning is lift-off if the weather is right. Already Dan has slipped out of our grasp into the strange seclusions of the final briefing.

"Did I urge him?" he said suddenly. "Did I, Sally? Ever?"

She looked at him startled, and then she shook her head decisively. "No, Jim, you never did. He just naturally had to go and do this. So forget it."

Sure. Forget it.

But Dan did get his horizons stretched young. And who's to say what minute seed dropped so carelessly along the way, a single word perhaps, written for two cents or one cent or half a cent, and long forgotten, may by devious ways have led the boy to that little steel room atop a skyrocket?

You might as well forget it, for there's nothing you can do.

They had the drive in the country, and they ate something, and they went to the movie, and then there was nothing to do but go home and go to bed. Sally went to bed, anyway. He did not know if she slept. He himself stayed up, sitting in his workroom alone with his typewriter and a bottle.

All around him on the walls were the framed originals of

cover paintings and interior illustrations from his stories. There was one from *Stardream,* written long before Dan was born, showing a beautiful white rocket in space, with Mars in the background. Underneath the pictures were rows of shelves filled with the end results of more than thirty years of writing, marching battalions of yellowing pulps a little frayed at the corners, paperbacks, the respectable hardcovers with their shiny jackets. This room was himself, an outer carapace compounded from his needs and his dreams, the full times when his mind flowered ideas like a spring river and the times of drought when nothing came at all, and always the work which he loved and without which he would cease to be Jim Burnett.

He looked at the empty typewriter and the pages beside it and he thought that if he was going to sit up all night, he ought to go on with the story. What was it that Henry had said, years ago . . . "A professional is a writer who can tell a story when he doesn't feel like telling a story." That was true, but even for an old pro, there were times . . .

At some time during the dark hours Burnett fell asleep on the couch and dreamed that he was standing outside the closed hatch of the capsule, pounding on it and calling Dan's name. He couldn't get it open, and he walked angrily around until he could look in through the port and see Dan lying there in the recoil chair, a suited dummy with a glittering plastic head, his gloved hands flicking at rows of toggles and colored levers with a cool unhurried efficiency that was unpleasantly robotlike. "Dan," he shouted. "Dan, let me in, you can't go off without me." Inside the plastic helmet he saw Dan's head turn briefly, though his hands never stopped from arranging the toggles and levers. He saw Dan's face smiling at him, a fond but somehow detached smile, and he saw the head shake just a shade impatiently. And he heard Dan answer, "I'm sorry, Dad, I can't stop now, I've got a deadline." A shield or curtain, or perhaps a cloud of vapor from the liquid hydrogen moved across the port and he couldn't see Dan any more, and when he hammered on the hatch again he was unable to strike it hard enough to make the slightest sound.

Without warning, then, he was a long distance away and

the rocket was going up, and he was still shouting, "Dan, Dan, let me in!" His voice was swallowed up in thunder. He began to cry with rage and frustration and the sound of his tears was like rain falling.

He woke to find that it was morning and a small thunderstorm was moving through, one of those little indecisive ones that change nothing. He got up rustily, wondering what the hell that dream was all about, and then looked at his watch. A little less than two hours to launch.

He had one quick one to untie the knots in his stomach and then put the bottle away. Whatever happened, he would watch it sober.

Damned queer dream, though. He hadn't been worried at all, only angry.

Sally was already up and had the coffee on. There were dark smudges under her eyes and the age-lines seemed to stand out clearer this morning than they usually did, not that Sally was old but she wasn't twenty any more either, and this morning it showed.

"Cheer up," he said, kissing her. "They've done this before, you know. Like eight times, and they haven't lost anybody yet." Immediately, superstitiously, he was sorry he had said it. He began to laugh rather too loudly. "If I know Dan," he said, "if I know that kid, he's sitting in that capsule cooler than a polar bear's nose in January, the only man in the country that isn't . . ."

He shut up too abruptly, and the phone rang. *The* phone. They had long ago shut off the regular one, silencing the impossible number of relatives and friends and wellwishers and reporters and plain pests, and this one that rang was a private thing between them and the Cape. He picked it up and listened, watching Sally standing frozen in mid-floor with a cup in her hands, and then he said, Thank you, and put it down.

"That was Major Quidley. Everything's Go except the weather. But they think the cloud-cover will pass. Dan's fine. He sends his love."

Sally nodded.

"We'll know right away if they call off the shot."

"I hope they don't," Sally said flatly. "I don't think I could start this all over again."

They took their coffee and went into the living room and turned on the television and there it was, alone and splendid in the midst of the deserted field, the white flanks gleaming softly, touched around with little nervous spurts of vapor, and high above, so high, so small atop that looming shaft, the capsule thrust impatiently toward the clouds.

And Dan was in there, suited, helmeted, locked away now from man and parent earth, waiting, watching the sky and listening for the word that would send him riding the thunder, bridling the lightning with sure hands out into the still black immensity where the stars . . .

Oh, Christ. Word stuff, paper stuff, and that's neither words nor paper in that goddam little coffin, that's my son, my kid, my little dirty gap-toothed boy with the torn britches and the scabs on his knees, and he wasn't ever intended to ride thunder and bridle lightning, no man is. Pulp heroes were all made of wood and they could do it, but Dan's human and soft and easily broken. He hasn't any business there, no man has.

And yet in that fool dream I was mad because I couldn't go too.

T-minus forty and holding. Perhaps they'll call it off . . .

Announcers' faces, saying this and that, stalling, filling up time, making ponderous statements. Personages making ponderous statements. Faces of people, mobs of people with kids and lunches and bottles of pop and deck chairs and field glasses and tight capri pants and crazy hats that wanted to blow off in the wind, all watching.

"They make me sick at my stomach," he snarled. "What the hell do they think this is, a picnic?"

"They're all with us, Jim. They're pulling for him. And for Shontz."

Burnett subsided, ashamed. "Okay," he grumbled, "but do they have to drink orange soda?"

The announcer pushed his headphone closer to his ear and listened. "The count is on again, ladies and gentlemen, T-minus thirty-nine now and counting. All systems are Go, the cloud-cover is beginning to break up, and there comes the sun . . ."

The announcer vanished and the rocket was there again. The sun struck hard on the white flanks, the sharp uplifted nose.

Dan would feel that striking of the sun.

T-minus thirty and counting.

I wish I could write this instead of watching it, Burnett thought. I've written it a hundred, two hundred, times. The ship rising up on the hammering flames, rising steady, rising strong, a white arrow shafting on a tail of fire, and you know when you write it that it's going to do just that because you say so, and plunge on into the free wide darkness of space and go where you damned well tell her to without any trouble.

T-minus twenty and counting.

I wish, thought Burnett, I wish . . .

He did not know what he wished. He sat and stared at the screen, and was only dimly aware when Sally got up from beside him and left the room.

Ten. Nine. And that's science fiction too, that countdown going backwards, somebody did it in a movie or a story decades ago because he thought it would be a nice touch. And here they are doing it.

With my kid.

Three, two, one, ignition, the white smoke bursting in mushrooming clouds from beneath the rocket, but nothing happening, nothing at all happening. But it is, the whole thing's starting to rise, only why does it seem so much slower than the others I watched, what's wrong, what the hell is wrong . . .

Nothing. Nothing's wrong, yet. It's still going up, and maybe it only seems slower than the other times. But where are all the emotions I was sure I was going to feel, after writing it so many times? Why do I just sit here with my eyes bugging and the palms of my hands sweating, shaking a little, not very much but a little . . .

Through the static roar and the chatter, Dan's voice cutting in, calm and quick. "All systems Go, it looks good, how does it look down there? Good, that's good . . ."

Burnett felt an unreasonable flash of pure resentment. How can he be so calm about it when we're sweating our hearts out down here? Doesn't he give a damn?

"Separation okay . . . second-stage ignition okay . . . all okay . . ." the level voice went on.

And Burnett suddenly knew the answer to his resentful wonder. He's calm because he's doing the job he's trained for. Dan's the pro, not me. All we writers who daydreamed and babbled and wrote about space, we were just amateurs, but now the real pros have come, the tanned, placid young men who don't babble about space but who go up and take hold of it . . .

And the white arrow went on upward, and the voices talked about it, and it was out of sight.

Sally came back into the room.

"It was a perfect shot," he said. And added, for no reason he could think of, "He's gone."

Sally sat down in a chair, not saying anything, and Burnett thought, What kind of dialogue is that for a man who's just seen his son shot into space?

The voices went on, but the tension was going out of them now, it looks good, it looks very good, it *is* good, they're on their way . . .

Burnett reached out and snapped off the television. As though it had been waiting for the silence, the phone rang again.

"You take it, honey," he said, getting up. "Everything's okay for now, at least. . . . I might as well get back to work."

Sally gave him a smile, the kind of a smile a wife gives her husband when she sees all through his pretenses but wants to tell him, It's all right, go on pretending, it's all right with me.

Burnett went into his workroom and closed the door. He took up the bottle in his hands and sat down in his padded chair in front of the typewriter with the empty roller and the neat stack of clean yellow sheets on one side and the thin pile of manuscript on the other. He looked at it, and he turned and looked at the shelves where thirty years of magazines and books and dreams and love and sweat and black disappointment were lined up stiff and still like paper corpses.

"Your stories surely had some influence on Dan in making the choice of his career?"

"No," said Burnett loudly, and drank.

"Wouldn't all that sort of urge him into it . . . your son . . . going to the Moon . . ."

He put the cork in the bottle and set it aside. He stood up and walked to the shelves and stood by them, looking, picking out one thing and then another, the bright covers with the spaceships and the men and girls in their suits and helmets, and the painted stars and planets.

He put them back neatly into their places. His shoulders sagged a little, and then he beat his fist softly against the shelves of silent paper.

"Damn you," he whispered. "Damn you, damn you . . ."

THE REUNION AT THE MILE-HIGH

Frederik Pohl

For those of you who haven't heard of the Futurians, they were a group of rather precocious teenagers who banded together half a century ago with delusions of making a mark in the science fiction field—and except for Isaac Asimov, Frederik Pohl, Cyril M. Kornbluth, James Blish, Judith Merrill, Robert A.W. Lowndes, Donald A. Wollheim, Damon Knight, Virginia Kidd, and perhaps a dozen others, we've hardly heard anything from them since.

Frederik Pohl, looking back over the years, wrote this story about what might have happened had fate taken a slightly different turn.

IN THOSE LONG and long-ago days—it's been half a century!—we were not only young, we were mostly poor. We were all pretty skinny, too, though you wouldn't think that to look at us now. I know this, because I have a picture of the twelve of us that was taken right around 1939. I dug it out to loan it to my publisher's public relations people just the other day, and I looked at it for a long time before I put it in the overnight mail. We didn't look like much, all grinning into the camera with our hairless, hopeful teenage faces. If you'd been given a couple of chances to guess, you might have thought we were a dozen Western Union boys on our day off (remember Western Union boys?), or maybe the senior debating club at some big-city all-boy high school. We weren't any of those things, though. What we actually were was a club of red-hot science fiction fans, and we called ourselves the Futurians.

That old photograph didn't lie. It just didn't tell the whole truth. The camera couldn't capture the things that kept us together, because they were all inside our heads. For one thing, we were pretty smart—we knew it ourselves, and we were *very* willing to tell you so. For another, we were all deeply addicted readers of science fiction—we called it stf in those days, but that's a whole other story. We thought stf was a lot of fun (all those jazzy rocket ships and zippy death rays, and big-chested Martians and squat, sinister monsters from Jupiter—oh, *wow!*) That wasn't all of it, though. We also thought stf was *important*. We were absolutely sure that it provided the best view anyone could have of T*H*E F*U*T*U*R*E—by which we meant the kind of technologically dazzling, socially utopian, and generally wonderful world which the rather frayed and frightening one we were stuck with living in might someday become. And, most of all, we were what our old Futurian buddy, Damon Knight, calls toads. We weren't very athletic. We didn't get along all that well with our peers—and not even as well as that with girls. And so we spent a lot of time driven in upon our own resources, which, mostly, meant reading. We all read a *lot*.

We even more or less agreed that we were toads. At least, we knew that girls didn't seem anxious to fall bedazzled by any of our charms. I'm not sure why. It wasn't that we were hopelessly ugly—well, not all of us, anyway. Dave Kyle and Dick Wylie and Dick Wilson were tall and actually pretty good-looking. Even the snapshot shows that. I think our problem was partly that we were scared of girls (they might laugh at us—some of them no doubt had), and partly a matter of our internal priorities. We were more into talking than tennis, and we put books ahead of jitterbugging.

That was half a century ago. In other words, *history*. My secretary, who is also my chief research assistant when I need a specific fact from the library, tells me that 62.8 percent of the people alive today weren't even born then, which undoubtedly means that that ancient year of 1939 seems as remote and strange to most people now as the Spanish-American War did to me.

I would like to point out, though, that 1939 didn't seem all that hot to us, either, even while we were living it. It wasn't a fun time. We were the generation caught between Hoover and Hitler. We had the breadlines of the Great Depression to remember in our recent past, and the Nazi armies looming worrisomely in our probable future. When we looked out at the real world we lived in we didn't much like what we saw.

So, instead, we looked inside the stf magazines we adored, and then we looked inside our own heads. We read a lot, and we tried to write. Because the other thing about us, you see, was that we were all pretty hardworking and ambitious. Since we weren't thrilled by our lives, we tried to change them. We had our meetings—we'd get together, once a month or so, in somebody's basement or somebody else's living room, and we'd talk about this and that; and then we'd go out for an ice-cream soda; and then we'd gradually splinter apart. Some of us would go home—especially the ones who had to get up in the morning, like Isaac Asimov. (He worked at his parents' candy store, and the commuters started coming in for their morning paper at five-thirty A.M.) Most of the rest of us would just wander, in twos and threes. I'd start out by walking Dirk and Johnny Michel to their subway station. But generally, by the time we got to it, we'd be in the middle of some really interesting discussion (did the General Motors Futurama at the World's Fair have the right idea about the World of Tomorrow, all twelve-lane superhighways and forty-story apartments? Were John Campbell's Arcot, Wade & Morey stories as good as Doc Smith's *Skylark?*)— so then they'd walk me back to my station . . . or around the block . . . or anywhere. Always talking. Talking mattered to us. Writing mattered, too, almost as much. We did a lot of it, on our battered second-hand portable typewriters, each on his own but always with the intention of showing what we had written to the others. *Words* mattered, and we particularly intended to make *our* words matter. Somehow. We didn't really know how, exactly, but when you think of it, I guess we succeeded. If we were toads, as Damon says, then sometime or other some wandering fairy princess must have come along and kissed us, and turned us into something different . . . or we wouldn't have been getting together at the top of the Mile-High Building for our Fiftieth Reunion, with reporters all over the place and our older, considerably more impressive faces staring out at the world on the *Six O'Clock News*.

You can't fly nonstop from Maui to New York, even on the sleeper, because they don't let flying boats operate over the continent. So I had to change planes in Los Angeles. Naturally I missed my connection, so when we finally landed at Idlewild I was late already.

The porter cut a taxi out of the snarl for me—it's wonderful what a five-dollar bill can do at an airport. As I got into the cab I stretched my neck to look toward the New York City skyline, and I could see the Mile-High Building poking far above everything else, looking like a long, long hunting horn sitting on its bell . . . if you can imagine a hunting horn with gaps along its length, held together (as it seemed at that distance) by nothing bigger than a couple of pencils. They say they need those wind gaps in the tower, because a hurricane just might push the whole thing over if they didn't allow spaces for the air to get through. Maybe so. I'm willing to believe that the gaps make the building safer, but they certainly aren't reassuring to look at.

Still, the Mile-High has managed to stay up for—let's see—it must be six or seven years now, and it's certainly an imposing sight. You can see it from anywhere within forty or fifty miles of New York. More than that. It's so immense that, even across most of Queens and part of Brooklyn, when I looked at it I was distinctly looking *up*. Then, when I got out of the cab at its base, it was more than big, it was scary. I couldn't help flinching a little. Whenever I look straight up at a tall building I get the feeling it's about to fall on me, and there's nothing taller than the Mile-High.

A limousine had pulled up behind me. The man who got out looked at me twice, and I looked at him thrice, and then we spoke simultaneously. "Hello, Fred," he said, and I said: "Doc, how are you? It's been a long time."

It had been—twenty years, anyway. We were obviously going to the same place, so Doc Lowndes waited for me while I paid off the taxi, even though it was gently drizzling on Sixth Avenue. When I turned away from the taxi driver, after a little argument about the tip, Doc was doing what I had been doing, staring up at the top of the Mile-High. "Do you know what it looks like?" he asked. "It looks like the space gun from *Things to Come*. Remember?"

I remembered. *Things to Come* had been our cult movie, back in the 1930s; most of us had seen it at least a dozen times. (My own record was thirty-two.) "Yeah, *space*," I said, grinning. "Rocket ships. People going to other planets. We'd believe almost anything in those days, wouldn't we?"

He gave me a considering look. "I still believe," he told me as we headed for the express elevators to the top.

The Mile-High Building isn't really a *Things to Come* kind of edifice. It's more like something from that even more ancient science fiction film, *Just Imagine*—silly futuristic spoof packed with autogyros and Mars rockets and young couples getting their babies out of vending machines. I first saw *Just Imagine* when I was ten years old. The heroine was a meltingly lovely teenager, just imported from Ireland to Hollywood, and that movie is why all my life I have been in love with Maureen O'Sullivan.

The Mile-High Building doesn't have any of those things, least of all (worse luck!) the still lovely Maureen, but it is definitely a skyscraper that puts even those old movie-makers to shame. To get to the top you go a measured mile straight up. Because the elevators are glass-walled, you get to see that whole incredible five thousand plus feet dropping away as you zoom upward, nearly a hundred miles an hour at peak velocity.

Doc swayed a little as we accelerated. "Pretty fast," he said. "*Real* fast," I agreed and began telling him all about the building. It's hollow inside, like an ice-cream cone, and I knew quite a lot about it because when I was still living in New York City, before I could afford the place on Maui, I used to know a man named Mike Terranova. Mike was a visualizer working for an architect's office—at another point in his career he did the drawings for the science fiction comic strip I wrote for a while, but that's another story, too. Mike really was better at doing machines and buildings than at drawing people, which is probably why our strip only ran one year, but he made up for it in enthusiasm. He was a big fan of the Mile-High. "Look at the wind gaps in it," he told me once, as we walked down Central Park West and saw the big thing looming even thirty blocks away. "That's to let the wind through, to reduce the force so it shouldn't sway. Of course, they've also got the mass dampers on the two hundredth and three hundredth and four hundredth floors, so it doesn't sway much anyway."

"It's just another skycraper, Mike," I told him, amused at his enthusiasm.

"It's a different *kind* of skycraper! They figured out the best offices are the ones with an outside view, so they just didn't build any offices inside! It's all hollow—except for the bracing struts and cables, and for the three main floor-through sections, where you change elevators and they have all the shops and things."

"It's brilliant," I said; and actually it was. And I was explaining all this to Doc, and all the time I was talking we were flashing past those vast central atria that are nearly a hundred stories high each, with their balconies, and flowers growing down from the railings, and lianas crisscrossing the central spaces; and Doc was looking at me with that patient expression New Yorkers reserve for out-of-towners.

But all he said was, "I know."

Then I was glad enough for the break when we walked across the hundredth-story level, between the soda fountains and the clothing shops, to the next bank of elevators, and then the next. Then you gct out at the top, five thousand and change feet above the corner of Fifty-second Street and Sixth Avenue, and you have to take an escalator up another flight to the club itself.

I don't like standing still, so I took the escalator steps two at a time. Doc followed gamely. He was puffing a little as we reached the door the doorman was already holding open for us.

"Put on a little weight, I see," I told him. "Too much

riding in limousines, I'd say. There must be big bucks in the poetry racket these days.''

I guess my tone must have sounded needling, because he gave me a sidelong look. But he also gave me a straightforward reply, which was more than I deserved. "I just don't like taxi drivers," he said. "Believe me, I'm not getting rich from my royalties. Publishing poetry doesn't pay enough to keep a pig in slop. What pays my bills is readings. I do get a lot of college dates."

I was rebuked. See, we Futurians had been pretty sharp-tongued kids, big on put-down jokes and getting laughs at each other's expense; just the thought of coming to the reunion seemed to get me back in that mood. I wasn't used to seeing Bob in his present gentler incarnation.

Then the white-haired woman took our coats, and even gentle Bob got a kind of smirk on his face as I handed over my trenchcoat. I knew what he was looking at, because I was wearing my usual at-home outfit: canary-yellow slacks, beach-boy shirt, and thongs. "I didn't have a chance to change," I said defensively.

"I was just thinking how nice it is for you folks that live in Hawaii," he told me seriously, and led the way into the big reception room where the party had already started.

There had certainly been changes. It wasn't like the old days. Maybe it was because they were talking about making Bob poet laureate for the United States. Or maybe it was just the difference between twenty and seventy. We didn't have to explain how special we were now, because the whole world was full of people willing to explain that to us.

There were at least a hundred people in the room, hanging around the waiters with the champagne bottles and studying the old pictures on the wall. It was easy to see which were the real Futurians: they were the ones with the bald spots or the white beards. The others were publicity people and media people. There were many more of them than of us, and their average age was right under thirty.

Right in the middle was Dr. Isaac Asimov, sparring good-naturedly with Cyril Kornbluth. They were the center of the biggest knot, because they were the really famous ones. Gen-

eral Kyle was there—in uniform, though he was long retired
by now—telling a young woman with a camera how he got
those ribbons at the battle of Pusan. Jack Robinson was
standing in the background, listening to him—no cameras
pointed at Jack, because the reporters didn't have much interest in schoolteachers, even when that one had been one of
Harvard's most distinguished professors emeritus. I saw Jack
Gillespie, with a gorgeous blonde six inches taller than he
was on his arm—she was the star of one of his plays—and
Hannes Bok, looking older and more content than he used to,
drinking Coca-Cola and munching on one of the open-faced
sandwiches. There wasn't any doubt they were pretty well
known by any normal standards. Jack had already won a Pulitzer, and Hannes's early black-and-whites were going for
three hundred thousand dollars apiece in the galleries on Fifty-
seventh Street. But there's a difference between say-didn't-I-
see-you-once-on-TV and *famous*. The media people knew
which ones to point their cameras at. Cyril didn't have one
Pulitzer, he had three of them, and the word was he'd have
had the Nobel Prize if only he'd had the sense to be born a
Bolivian or a Greek. And as to Isaac, of course—well, Isaac
was *Isaac*. Adviser to Presidents, confidant of the mighty,
celebrated steady guest of the Jack Paar show and star of a
hundred television commercials. He wasn't just *kind* of famous. He was the one of us who couldn't cross a city street
without being recognized, because he was known by features
to more people than any senator, governor, or cardinal of the
Church. He even did television commercials. I'd seen him in
Hawaii, touting the Pan American Clipper flights to Australia
. . . and he didn't even *fly*.

They'd blown up that old photograph twelve feet long, and
Damon Knight was staring mournfully up at it when Doc and
I came over to shake hands. "We were such kids," he said.
True enough. We'd ranged from sixteen—that was Cyril—to
Don Wollheim, the old man of the bunch: why, then he had
been at least twenty-three or twenty-four.

So much has been written about the Futurians these days
that sometimes I'm not sure myself what's true, and what's
just press-agent puffery. The newspaper stories make us sound

very special. Well, we certainly thought we were, but I doubt that many of our relatives shared our opinion. Isaac worked in his parents' candy store, Johnny Michel helped his father silk-screen signs for Woolworth's Five and Ten, Dirk Wylie pumped gas at a filling station in Queens, Dick Wilson shoved trolleys of women's dresses around the garment district on Seventh Avenue. Most of the rest of us didn't have real jobs at all. Remember, it was the tail end of the Great Depression. I know that for myself I considered I was lucky, now and then, to get work as a restaurant busboy or messenger for an insurance company.

A young woman came over to us. She was reading from a guest list, and when she looked at me she wonderfully got my name right. "I'm from *Saturday Evening Post Video,*" she explained. "You were one of the original Futurians, weren't you?"

"We all were. Well, Doc and I were. Damon came along later."

"And so you knew Dr. Asimov and Mr. Kornbluth from the very beginning?"

I sighed; I knew from experience just how the interview was going to go. It was not for my own minor-league fame that the woman wanted to talk to me, it was for a reminiscence about the superstars. So I told her three or four of the dozen stories I kept on tap for such purposes. I told her how Isaac lived at one end of Prospect Park, in Brooklyn, and I lived at the other. How the Futurians would have a meeting, any kind of a meeting, and then hate to break it up, and so we'd just walk around the empty streets all night long, talking, sometimes singing—Jack and I, before he finished his first play; Doc and I, reciting poetry, singing all the numbers out of our bottomless repertory of the popular songs of the day; Cyril and I, trying to trick each other with our show-off game of "Impossible Questions."

" 'Impossible Questions,' " she repeated.

"That was a sort of a quiz game we played," I explained. "We invented it. It was a *hard* one. The questions were intended to be about things most people wouldn't know. Like, what's the rhyme scheme of a chant royal? Or what's the color of air?"

"You mean blue, like the sky?"

I grinned at her. "You just lost a round. Air doesn't have any color at all. It just *looks* blue, because of what they call Rayleigh scattering. But that's all right: these were *impossible* questions, and if anyone ever got the right answer to any of them he won and the game was over."

"So you and Dr. Asimov used to play this game—"

"No, no. *Cyril* and I played it. The only way Isaac came into it was sometimes we'd go over to see him. Early in the morning, when we'd been up all night; we'd start off across the park around sunrise, and we'd stop to climb a few trees— and Cyril would give the mating call of the plover-tailed teal, but we never had a teal respond to it—and along about the time Isaac's parents' candy store opened for business we'd drop in and his mother would give us each a free malted milk."

"A free malted milk," the woman repeated, beaming. It was just the kind of human-interest thing she'd been looking for. She tarried for one more question. "Did you know Dr. Asimov when he wrote his famous letter to President Franklin Roosevelt, that started the Pasadena Project?"

I opened my mouth to answer, but Doc Lowndes got in there ahead of me. "Oh, damn it, woman," he exploded. "*Isaac* didn't write that letter. Alexis Carrel did. Isaac came in much later."

The woman looked at her notes, then back at us. Her look wasn't surprised. Mostly it was—what's the word I want? Yes: pitying. She looked at us as though she were sorry for us. "Oh, I don't think so," she said, politely enough. "I have it all here."

"You have it wrong," Doc told her, and began to try to set her straight.

I wouldn't have bothered, though the facts were simple enough. Albert Einstein had written to the President claiming that Hitler's people were on the verge of inventing what he called "an atomic bomb," and he wanted FDR to start a project so the U.S.A. could build one first. Dr. Alexis Carrel heard about it. He was a biochemist and he didn't want to see America wasting its time on some atomic-power will-o'-the-wisp. So he persuaded his friend Colonel Charles A.

Lindbergh to take a quite different letter to President Roosevelt.

It wasn't that easy for Lindbergh, because there was a political problem. Lindbergh was certainly a famous man. He was the celebrated Lone Eagle, the man who had flown the Atlantic in nineteen twenty-something all by himself, first man ever to do it. But a decade and a bit later things had changed for Lindbergh. He had unfortunately got a reputation for being soft on the Nazis, and besides he was deeply involved in some right-wing Republican organizations—the America First Committee, the Liberty League, things like that—which had as their principal objective in life leaving Hitler alone and kicking that satanic Democrat Franklin D. Roosevelt out of the White House.

All the same, Lindbergh had a lot of powerful friends. It took two months of pulling hard on a lot of strings to arrange it, but he finally got an appointment for five minutes of the President's time on a slow Thursday morning in Warm Springs, Georgia. And the President actually read Carrel's letter.

Roosevelt wasn't a scientist and didn't even have any scientists near him—scientists weren't a big deal, back in the thirties. So FDR didn't really know the difference between a fissioning atomic nucleus and a disease organism, except that he could see that it was cheaper to culture germs in petri dishes than to build billion-dollar factories to make this funny-sounding, what-do-you-call-it, nuclear explosive stuff, plutonium. And FDR was a little sensitive about starting any new big-spending projects for a while. So Einstein was out, and Carrel was in.

By the time Isaac got drafted and assigned to the secret research facility it was called the Pasadena Project; but by the time Doc got to that point the *Saturday Evening Post* woman was beginning to fidget. "That's very interesting, Mr.—Lowndes?" she said, glancing at her notes. "But I think my editors would want me to get this sort of thing from Dr. Asimov himself. Excuse me," she finished, already turning away, with the stars of hero worship beginning to shine in her eyes.

Doc looked at me ruefully. "Reporters," he said.

I nodded. Then I couldn't resist the temptation any longer. "Let's listen to what he does tell her," I suggested, and we trailed after her.

It wasn't easy to get near Isaac. Apart from the reporters, there were all the public relations staffs of our various publishers and institutes—Don Wollheim's own publishing company, Cyril's publishers, Bob Lowndes's, the *New York Times,* because Damon was the editor of their *Book Review.* Even my own publisher had chipped in, as well as the galleries that sold Hannes Bok's paintings and Johnny Michel's weird silk screens of tomato cans and movie stars' faces. But it was the U.S. Information Agency that produced most of the muscle, because Isaac was their boy. What was surrounding Isaac was a *mob.* The reporter was a tough lady, though. An elbow here, a side-slither there, and she was in the front row with her hand up. "Dr. Asimov? Weren't you the one who wrote the letter to President Roosevelt that started the Pasadena Project?"

"Good lord, no!" Isaac said. "No, it was a famous biochemist of the time, Dr. Alexis Carrel. He was responding to a letter Albert Einstein had written, and—What is it?"

The man from the *Daily News* had his hand up. "Could you spell that, please, Dr. Asimov?"

"E-I-N-S-T-E-I-N. He was a physicist, very well known at the time. Anyway, the President accepted Dr. Carrel's proposal and they started the Pasadena Project. I happened to be drafted into it, as a very young biochemist, just out of school."

"But you got to be pretty important," the woman said loyally. Isaac shrugged. Someone from another videopaper asked him to say more about his experiences, and Isaac, giving us all a humorously apologetic look, did as requested.

"Well," he said, "I don't want to dwell on the weapons systems. Everybody knows that it was our typhus bomb that made the Japanese surrender, of course. But it was the peacetime uses that I think are really important. Look around at my old friends here." He swept a generous arm around the dais, including us all. "If it hadn't been for the Pasadena Project some of us wouldn't be here now—do you have any *idea* how much medicine advanced as a result of what we learned? Antibiotics in 1944, antivirals in 1948, the cancer cure in 1950, the cholesterol antagonist in 1953?''

A California woman got in: ''Are you sure the President made the right decision? There are some people who still think that atomic power is a real possibility.''

''Ah, you're talking about old Eddy Teller.'' Isaac grinned. ''He's all right. It's just that he's hipped on this one subject. It's really too bad. He could have done important work, I think, if he'd gone in for real science in 1940, instead of fooling around with all that nuclear stuff.''

There wasn't any question that Isaac was the superstar, with Cyril getting at least serious second-banana attention, but it wasn't all the superstars. Quite. Each one of the rest of us got a couple of minutes before the cameras, saying how much each of us had influenced each other and how happy we all were to be seeing each other again. I was pretty sure that most of us would wind up as faces on the cutting-room floor, but what we said, funnily enough, was all pretty true.

And then it was over. People began to leave.

I saw Isaac coming out of the men's room as I was looking for the woman with my coat. He paused at the window, gazing out at the darkling sky. A big TWA eight-engined plane was coming in, nonstop, probably from someplace like Havana. It was heading toward Idlewild, hardly higher than we were, as I tapped him on the shoulder.

''I didn't know celebrities went to the toilet,'' I told him.

He looked at me tolerantly. ''Matter of fact, I was just calling Janet,'' he said. ''Anyway, how are things going with you, Fred? You've been publishing a lot of books. How many, exactly?''

I gave him an honest answer. ''I don't exactly know. I used to keep a list. I'd write the name and date and publisher for each new book on the wall of my office—but then my wife painted over the wall and I lost my list.''

''Approximately how many?''

''Over a hundred, anyway. Depends what you count. The novels, the short-story collections, the nonfiction books—''

''Over a hundred,'' he said. ''And some of them have been

dramatized, and book-clubbed, and translated into foreign languages?'' He pursed his lips and thought for a moment. ''I guess you're happy about the way your life has gone?''

''Well, sure,'' I said. ''Why wouldn't I be?'' And then I gave him another look, because there was something about his tone that startled me. ''What are you saying, Eye? Aren't *you?*''

''Of course I am!'' he said quickly. ''Only—well, to tell you the truth, there's just one thing. Every once in a while I find myself thinking that if things had gone a different way, I might've been a pretty successful writer.''

THE WORLD SCIENCE FICTION CONVENTION OF 2080

Ian Watson

Worldcon—the World Science Fiction Convention—has long been a favorite topic of science fiction writers. At last count, five novels had been set at various Worldcons (and, strangely, four of them were murder mysteries).

British author Ian Watson is less concerned with who will get killed at the 2080 Worldcon than he is with who will be left to celebrate.

WHAT A GATHERING! Four hundred people—writers, fans and both magazine editors—have made their way successfully to these sailcloth marquees outside the village of New Boston.

We know of another three people who didn't make it, and the opening ceremony included a brief "In Memoriam" tribute to each of them, followed by one minute's silence for all. For Kurt Rossini, master of heroic fantasy—slain by an Indian arrow on his way from far California. For Suzie McIntosh, whose amusing woodcuts (sent down by trade caravan from Moose Jaw last summer season) adorn the program booklet—killed by a wolf pack outside of Winnipeg. And for our worst loss, lovely Charmian Jones, acclaimed Queen of Titan in the masquerade at the last Worldcon three years ago in Tampa, whose miniature is worn close to many a fan's heart from the Yukon to Florida Bay—murdered by Moslem pirates during a kidnap raid on Charleston while she was passing through. (Could she have survived seraglio life in North Africa, and even become a bit of a queen there? No! Cut off from the slow percolation of fandom's lifeblood? Never! She defended her honor bravely with a short sword, and died.)

Some dozen others with attending memberships haven't arrived, either. We hope that they're just late—held up by contrary winds or a broken wagon axle. No doubt we will learn in six months or so when their personalzines travel the trade routes.

In the bar tent, around the still, at the ox roast, and in the art tent with its fine embroideries and batiks based on the Old Masters Delany, Heinlein, Le Guin, we greet old friends and colleagues and swap our travel tales. And I thought that my own journey from South Scotland on foot, on horseback, by canal longboat, and finally for five weeks by sailship across the stormy Atlantic (our mortars loaded against raiders) was eventful enough! But compared to some of the others' experiences, mine was a cake run: Indians, Badlands, outlaw bands, mercenaries, pietist communities that close around one like a Venus's-flytrap, Army Induction Centers, plague zones, technophile citadels! I was even two and a half weeks early and managed to arrive with the manuscript of a new novel in my knapsack, penned on the sailship in between working my passage, all ready for bartering to "Monk" Lewiston, head of Solaris Press of Little New York.

The new novel is called *The Aldebaran Experience* and is about a starship journey from the Luna Colony through metaspace to an alien planet orbiting Aldebaran. It is, though I say it myself, an ambitious exercise in what the critic Suvin once called "cognitive estrangement"—but one can't really convey the breadth of the book in a couple of lines; besides, here isn't the place—though I did appear on a foreign writers' panel to discuss my own by now well-known earlier novel *The Film-Maker's Guide to Alien Actors* (Neogollancz Press, Edinburgh) dating from only four years ago. (Ah, the speed of publication and distribution in our SF world!)

On this panel, along with me, were the Frenchman Henri Guillaume, whose tale of mighty computerized bureaucracy and subjective time distortions, *The Ides of Venus*, is still winning acclaim for its originality—a definite step beyond the Old French Masters, Curval and Jeury; and the Mexican Gabriel Somosa—an exciting encounter; and my fellow islander Jeremy Symons, whom I last met in the flesh at our biennial thrash Gypsycon '77 all the way in Devon—his *The Artificial Man* has been a hot contender for this year's Hugo award ever since the nominations started trickling along the trade routes and over the ocean two years ago.

But I should describe the highlights of this wonderful get-together under cloth in New Boston. Frankly, that panel was rather ho-hum. Poor Jeremy had come down with some allergy workings in the bilges, which affected his throat, and his voice would hardly carry to the back of the marquee. . . .

Highlights, then: *The Film*. Yes, indeed, as advertised in the flyer a year ago, a film had been found! And what a film. Craftsmen built a hand-cranked projector whose light source was the sun itself, focused by an ingenious system of lenses and mirrors from outside the marquee; and six times during the Boskon week we stared, enthralled, at the flickerings of an original print of *Silent Running*, praying that rainclouds would not dim the light too much. Let me not hear any sarcasm about the appropriateness of the title, since no way could anyone activate a soundtrack. We were all enchanted.

The Auction: oh, this was an experience. There was an Ace Double on sale! And an original SF Book Club edition of a Larry Niven collection. *And,* yellow and brittle with age, issues 250 to 260 inclusive of *Locus*. As well as much interesting and historic stuff from our own early post-Collapse era, such as a copy of a handwritten scroll novel (from just before we got hand presses cranking again) by the great Tessa Brien—part of her Jacthar series. The copies of *Locus* went in exchange for a fine Pinto pony—the Alabaman who bid his mount for them was quite happy to walk all the way home. But the Ace Double (Phil Dick's *Dr. Futurity* backed by *The Unteleported Man*) went for a slim bar of gold.

Then there was the Solaris Press party where Henri Guillaume, high on Boston applejack, attempted to dance the can-

can, endearing himself to everyone—a few quick sketches
were "snapped" of this, and there was even a watercolor for
barter by the next morning.

And *The Banquet,* of spiced rabbit stew, followed by . . .
The Hugo Awards: the carved beechwood rocketships for the
best work in our field over the three years '75 to '78. First,
for the best fanzine, scooped by Alice Turtle's *Call of the
Wild* from New Chicago; then for the best story in either of
the bi-annual magazines *Jupiter* or *Fantasy,* won by Harmony
Friedlander for her moving "Touchdown" in *Jupiter* four
years ago; and finally the long-awaited novel Hugo, going to
Boskon's Guest of Honor, Jerry Meltzer (as expected, by
everyone except Jeremy Symons!), for his cosmos-spanning
Whither, Starman?

But I think it is Jerry Meltzer's Guest of Honor speech that
I shall most treasure the memory of. The speech was entitled,
"Some Things Do Not Pass." From the very beginning of it
I was riveted, reinvigorated, and felt my life reaffirmed.

Jerry is pushing sixty now, which is quite a miracle now
that the average life-expectancy is down to forty or so. He
has lost an ear to frostbite and wears a coonskin cap at all
times to cover his mutilation. He's a raftsman on the Mis-
souri.

Surveying the marquee full of four hundred faces, he
smiled—wisely, confidently. He spoke slowly.

"Some things do not pass. Some things *increase* in truth
and beauty. Science Fiction is one of these. I say this because
Science Fiction is a fiction: it is a *making,* a forging of the
legends of our tribe, and the best legends of all humanity.
Now that *research* and *probing* have ceased—he grinned dis-
missivley—"we can indeed freshly and freely invent our science and our worlds. SF was always being spoilt, having her
hands tied and the whip cracked over her head by scientific
facts. They've gone now—most of those blessed facts, about
quarks and quasars and I don't know what!—and there won't
be any more! It's all mythology now, friends. SF has come
into her own, and we who are here today, we know this.
Friends, we're Homers and Lucians once again—because science is a myth, and we're its myth-makers. Mars is ours

again, and Saturn is, and Alpha C—and lovely Luna. We can read the Grand Masters of yore in a light that the poor folk of the Late Twentieth could never read them in! I say to you, Some Things Do Not Pass. Their loveliness increases. Now we can make that mythic loveliness wilder and headier and more fabulous than ever. This is the true meaning of my *Whither, Starman?''*

He spoke till the Con Committee lit the whale-oil flambeaux in the tent, and then he talked some more. At the end he was chaired shoulder-high out into the meadow underneath the stars. And just then, what must have been one of the very last dead satellites from the old days streaked across the sky like a comet tail, burning up as it plunged towards the Atlantic to drown fathoms deep. Maybe it was only an ordinary shooting star—but I don't think so. Nor did anyone else. Four hundred voices cheered its downfall, as Jerry threw back his head and laughed.

With a gesture he quietened the crowd. "My friends," he called out, "we really own the stars now. We really do. Never would have done, the other way. Dead suns, dead worlds the lot of them, I shouldn't be surprised—dead universe. Now Sirius is ours. Canopus is. The dense suns of the Hub are all ours. All." His hands grasped at the sky. It gripped the Milky Way, and we cheered again.

Two mornings later, after many perhaps overconfident goodbyes—"See you in '83!"—I walked down into New Boston to the harbor along with my compadre Jeremy—who was somewhat hung over and weaved about at times—to take ship next week or the week after for Liverpool. I wouldn't need to work my passage back, though. I'd bartered *The Aldebaran Experience* to "Monk" Lewiston for a bundle of furs, much in demand on our cold island.

In a year or so I'll receive my free copy, hand-printed in Solaris Press's characteristic heavy black type, by way of some sheep drove up through the Borders. If Monk is fast in getting it out and the trade routes are kind, who knows, it just might just get on the ballot for '83—to be voted at the fishing village of Santa Barbara, way across the Plains and Deserts and Badlands.

Can I possibly make it to Santa Barbara? Truth to tell, I can hardly wait. After this year's wonderful thrash, I'll be on the sailship—and I'll board those stagecoaches, come Hell or high water.

I nudged Jeremy in the ribs.

"We own the stars," I said. "You and I."

HIS AWARD-WINNING SCIENCE FICTION STORY

Mike Resnick

Sometimes, as I write my stories, I wonder just what my characters think of the various obstacle courses through which I run them, and what input they would like to have in the creation of my fiction. So when editor George Laskowski asked much the same question, I came up with the following.

Chapter 1

CALL ME ISHMAEL.

Chapter 2

Lance Stalwart and Conan Kinnison sat at the controls of their tiny two-man scout ship, a good dozen parsecs in advance of the main body of the Terran Fleet, debating their possible courses of action, reviewing all their options.

One moment they had been all alone in the Universe, or so it had seemed; then all space was filled with the Arcturian navy, millions upon millions of ships, some short and squat, a few saucer-shaped, a handful piercing the void like glowing silver needles, all made of an impenetrable titanium alloy, well over half of them equipped for hyperspatial jumps, all girded for warfare, each and every one mannered by a crew of malicious, malignant, hate-filled Arcs, each of whom had been schooled in spacial warfare since earliest infancy, each a precisely-functioning cog in the vast, seemingly impervious and unconquerable Arc war machine that had smashed its way to victory after victory against the undermanned Terrans and was even now plunging toward the Terran home system in a drive that was not to be denied unless Stalwart and Kinnison managed to pull a couple of magical rabbits out of their tactical hat.

"Jesus H. Christ!" muttered Stalwart disgustedly. "If I'd ever written a sentence like that they'd have thrown me out of school."

"I'd sure love to have the purple prose concession on this guy's word processor," agreed Kinnison.

"And here we are, risking our asses in the middle of God knows where, and we don't even know what a goddamned Arc looks like," complained Stalwart. "If *I* were writing this story, that's the very first thing I'd put in."

Chapter 2

It walked in the woods.

It was never born. It existed. Under the pine needles the fires burn, deep and smokeless in the mold. In heat and in darkness and decay there is growth. It grew, but it was not alive. It walked unbreathing through the woods, and thought and saw and was hideous and strong, and it was not born and it did not live. And—perhaps it could not be destroyed.

"No good!" snapped Kinnison. "It's not enough that you're going to get sued over my name. Now you've gone and swiped an entire opening from Theodore Sturgeon. You'd better go back right now and describe an Arc properly."

"Right," said Resnick.

Chapter 2

He walked in the woods.

He was never born. *He* existed. *He* grew, but *he* was not alive. *He* walked unbreathing through the woods, and thought and saw and was hideous and strong, and *he* was not born and *he* did not live. And—

"You are not exactly the swiftest learner I ever came across," said Kinnison.

"I've had it with this crap!" snapped Stalwart. "Screw you, Resnick! I'm going up to Chapter 20. Maybe things will get a little better by then."

He set off at a slow trot, vanishing into the distant haze.

"That's funny," mused Kinnison. "I always thought Chapter 20 was more to the left."

"Only if you're writing in Arabic," said his companion.

"Who the hell are you?" demanded Kinnison.

"Harvey Wallbanger," said Harvey Wallbanger.

"Should I know you?"

"I'm from the Space Opera Stock Character Replacement Center," said Wallbanger. He stretched vigorously. "Ah, it feels good to be back in harness! I've been sitting on the sidelines for years. I would have preferred a Hawk Carse reprint, but my agent says that the main thing for a Stock Character is to keep working."

"I suppose so," said Kinnison, eyeing him warily.

"By the way," said Wallbanger, "why are you eyeing me warily?"

"Oh, no reason," said Kinnison, averting his eyes.

"Go ahead, tell me," urged Wallbanger. "I won't be offended. Really I won't."

"You don't have any facial features," said Kinnison.

"I don't need them," answered Wallbanger. "I'm just here so you won't have to talk to yourself."

"This is crazy!" snapped Kinnison. "I don't know who I'm fighting, or why they're mad at me, or what they look like, and my shipmate is doing God knows what in Chapter 20, and now they've given me a faceless assistant, and I'm going on strike."

"What?" said Wallbanger, fulfilling his literary function to perfection.

"This just doesn't make any sense," said Kinnison, "and I'm not going back to work until I've got some motivation."

Suddenly a cloud of dust arose in the Altair sector. The sound of hoofbeats grew louder and louder until a magnificent coal-black stallion galloped into view, steam rising in little clouds from his heavily-lathered body.

The Great Masked Writer of the Planes dismounted and approached Kinnison and Wallbanger. He was tall, debonaire, handsome in a masculine, ruddy sort of way, incredibly erudite, and unquestionably the world's greatest lay. He

HA!

"What the hell was that?" asked Kinnison.

"Just my wife, dusting the computer keyboard," said Resnick. "It certainly shouldn't be construed as an editorial comment."

I REPEAT: HA!

"At least tell her to use lower-case letters," whined Kinnison. "She's giving me a headache." He paused. "What are you doing here, anyway? It's really most irregular."

Resnick patted the stallion's beautifully-arched neck. "Steady there, big fella," he said in tones that inspired instant confidence. He turned back to Kinnison. "He'll give you a half-mile in 47 seconds any time you ask for it. He performs best with blinkers and a run-out bit, and he doesn't like muddy tracks."

"Why are you telling me all this?" asked Kinnison.

"Because he's yours now," said Resnick, handing over the reins. "Take him."

"What's his name?"

"Motivation."

"But he's a horse!"

"Look—you asked for Motivation, I'm giving you Motivation. Now, do you want him or not?"

"I'm terribly confused," said Kinnison. "Maybe we ought to go back to the beginning and see if it works out any better this time."

Chapter 1

Call me Ishmael.

Chapter 2

"You've lost me already," complained Kinnison, scratching his shaggy head. "I mean, like, who the hell is Ishmael?"

"It's a sure-fire beginning," said Resnick, shoving Wallbanger into the murky background. "Every great American novel begins with 'Call me Ishmael'."

"How many novels is that, at a rough guess?" asked Kinnison.

"Well, the downstate returns aren't all in yet," replied Resnick, "but so far, rounded off, it comes to one."

"Hah!" snapped Kinnison. "And how the hell many Ishmaels do you know?"

"One," said Resnick, delighted at how neatly it was all working out.

"Who?"

"Ishmael Valenzuela," said Resnick, who may have overstated the case originally, but was unquestionably the greatest lay in the sovereign state of Ohio.

HA!

"Who the hell is Ishmael Valenzuela?" demanded Kinnison.

"A jockey," answered Resnick. "He rode Kelso and Tim Tam and Mister Gus."

"What's he got to do with this story?"

"I thought he might ride Motivation in the *Prix de l'Arc de Triomphe*," explained Resnick. "It's the biggest race in Europe. Then I'll have an Ishmael and an Arc all in the same place, and it'll make it much easier to tie up all the loose ends."

"It'll never work," said Kinnison. "What if they call it the Prix instead of the Arc?"

"They wouldn't dare! This is a G-rated story."

"Still, it would make me very happy if you'd go back to the beginning and get rid of Ishmael."

"Well, I don't know . . ."

"Come on," urged Kinnison. "After all, you got in your dirty pun, bad as it was."

"Yeah," said Resnick. "But that was six sentences ago. We could have used a little something right here."

Chapter 1

And call me Conrad.

Chapter 2

"I don't think I'm getting through to you at all," complained Kinnison. "Now you've ripped off a Roger Zelazny title."

"Boy, nothing pleases you!" muttered Resnick.

Chapter 1

Call me Ishmael.

Chapter 2

"You sure as hell haven't gotten very far," said Lance Stalwart, strolling in from the northeast.

"Are you back already?" asked Kinnison, startled.

"There's nothing much happening up ahead. Resnick makes it with Loni Anderson 30 or 40 times between Chapter 12 and Chapter 18, but that's about it. I'm still trying to figure out what she's doing in a science fiction story."

"I've always been a Goldie Hawn man myself," said Kinnison, appropros of nothing.

"No way," said Resnick. "Loni Anderson has two insurmountable advantages."

"You can't keep making filthy jokes like that!" roared Kinnison. "This is supposed to be a serious space opera, and here you are talking about Loni Anderson's boobs, for Christ's sake!"

"Yeah!" chimed in Stalwart. "You can't go around talking about her tits in print! Don't you know kids are going to be reading this, you stupid fucking bastard?"

"This chapter," said Kinnison, "is turning into an udder disaster."

Chapter 1

Call me Ishmael.

Chapter 2

Conan Kinnison, a retarded Albanian dwarf, hobbled over to Lance Stalwart, whose wrought-iron lung had stopped functioning. The ship's temperature had risen to 44 degrees Centigrade, the oxygen content was down to six percent, and all the toilets were backing up.

"Is it too late to apologize?" rasped Kinnison through his hideously deformed lips.

The most fantastic bed partner in Hamilton County, Ohio

HA!

nodded his acquiescence, mercy being one of his many unadvertised virtues.

Chapter 1

Call me Ishmael.

Chapter 2

"Ahh, that's better!" said Lance Stalwart, stretching his bronzed, muscular, six-foot seven-inch frame. "You know, I think the problem may be that you don't know where this story is going. It really hasn't got much direction."

"It's got Motivation, though," said Resnick sulkily.

"Maybe what it needs is a title," offered Kinnison. "Most of the stories I've read have had titles."

"Why bother?" said Resnick wearily. "The editors always change them anyway."

"Only if they make sense," said Kinnison.

Chapter 3: The Search for a Title

"The floor is now open for suggestions," said the most skillful lover living at 1409 Throop Street in Cincinnati, Ohio.

WHAT ABOUT THE GARDENER?

Chapter 3: The Search for a Title

"The floor is now open for suggestions," said the most skillful lover (possibly excepting the gardener) living at 1409 Throop Street in Cincinnati, Ohio.

BIG DEAL.

"It's got to sound science-fictional, grip the reader, and give me a little direction," continued Resnick. "I will now entertain recommendations."

"The Mote in God's Thigh," said Loni Anderson.

"Buckets of Gor," suggested John Norman.

"Call Me Ishmael," said Valenzuela.

"Tarzan Stripes Forever," said Harvey Wallbanger.

"I don't like any of them," said Kinnison.

"Me neither," agreed Stalwart. "It is my considered opinion that the title ought to be: *His Award-Winning Science Fiction Story.* That way, when Resnick's next collection comes out, the editor can put a blurb on the cover stating that the volume includes His Award-Winning Science Fiction Story."

"I *like* that idea!" said Resnick enthusiastically.

"Then it's settled," said Kinnison with a sigh of relief. "I feel like a new man."

"Me, too!" said Loni Anderson. "Where's the gardener?"

Chapter 2

"You know," said Kinnison wearily, "if you'd spend a little less time watching the Bengals' defense blow one lead after another and a little more time trying to write this goddamned story, I'd be willing to meet you halfway. But as things stand now, I don't have the energy for a whole novel. I keep getting this sense of *déjà vû.*"

"Me, too," said John Carter, who had wandered over from the Barsoom set. "Only it's spelled *Dejah vu.*"

"Why not make a short story out of it?" continued Kinnison.

"Well, it's not really an *Omni* or *Playboy* type of story," responded Resnick, "and no one else pays very well."

"How about selling it to Harlan Ellison for *The Last Dangerous Visions?*" suggested Kinnison. "Word has it that it'll be coming out in another ten years or so."

"Hah! Call that stuff dangerous visions?" snorted Stalwart contemptuously. "I've got an uncle who can't see a redwood tree at ten paces, and he drives a school bus. Now, *that's* dangerous vision!"

"Well, I was saving it for a smash ending," said Resnick, "but if we've all decided that this is a short story, I might as well bring it out now."

So saying, he produced a little gadget which could blow up approximately half the known universe. The patents on the various parts were held by Murray Leinster, Jack Williamson, Edmund Hamilton, and E. E. Smith (who also invented half of Conan Kinnison, but I can't say which half because this is a G-rated story.)

"I think I've seen one of those before," said Lance Stalwart. "What do you call it?"

"This," explained Resnick, "is a pocket frammistan, guaranteed to get you out of any jams you may get into, except for those requiring massive doses of penicillin."

"It's a nice idea," said Kinnison, "but we can't use it."

"Why not?" demanded Resnick.

"We can't use a pocket frammistan," explained Kinnison patiently, "because none of us has any pockets. In fact, until you insert a few descriptive paragraphs into this story, none of us is even wearing any pants."

"You'd better solve this one quick," warned Stalwart, "or you stand in considerable danger of having this damned thing turn into a novelette."

"Let's backtrack a little," suggested Resnick, "and see if there is anything we missed."

Chapter 1

Call me Ishmael.

Chapter 2

"Ah, here it is!" said Resnick, picking up a crumpled piece of paper off the floor.

"What is it?" asked Kinnison, peeking over his shoulder.

"Our salvation," said Resnick, uncrumpling the paper. On it was scribbled a single word: *Laskowski*.

"It's just an old piece of correspondence," said Kinnison despondently.

"Not any more," said Resnick.

"But what does it mean?" asked Stalwart.

"That's the beauty of it," said Resnick. "This is a science fiction story, so we can make it do or mean anything we want."

"Not quite anything," said Kinnison fussily. "Unless, of course, you want this to wind up as a fantasy story."

"I'll keep that in mind," said Resnick, who was anxious to get to Chapters 12 through 18.

"Give us an idea how it works," said Stalwart.

"Right," said Kinnison. "If we're going to have to depend on a laskowski, we at least deserve some say in its function."

"Fair enough," agreed Resnick, walking to the blackboard.

Chapter 3: The Creation of the Laskowski

Students will be allowed 40 minutes, no more and no less, and must mark their papers with a Number One Lead Pencil. Anyone disobeying the honor system will have bamboo splints driven under his fingernails, or maybe be forced to read *Dhalgren*.

What Laskowski Means To Me:

A). "Your Highness, may I present Arx Kreegah, the Grand Laskowski of the star system of . . ."

B). "Hey, Harry, get a load of the laskowskis on that babe, willya?"

C). Kinnison touched the button once, and the dread Laskowski Ray shot out, destroying all life in its path, except for one pathetic little flower . . .

D). "Ah, Earthman, just because I have two laskowskis

where Terran females have but one, does that make me any less a woman?''

E). "The rare eight-legged laskowski mosquito, though seemingly harmless, can, when engorged with the blood of a left-handed Turkish rabbi . . .''

F). "They're closing on us fast!'' cried Stalwart. "If we don't get the Laskowski Drive working in the next ten seconds, we're up Paddle Creek without a . . .''

G). "Chess is fine for children,'' said Pooorht Knish, waving a tentacle disdainfully, "but out here we play a *real* game: laskowski.''

H). "No, thanks,'' panted Kinnison. "I couldn't laskowski again for hours!''

I). None of the above.

Chapter 4

"Well, how did it come out?'' asked Stalwart.

"We've got six votes for None of the Above, two didn't understand the question, and seventeen voted for Harold Stassen,'' said Resnick grimly.

"Then we're back where we started?'' asked Kinnison, choking back a manly little sob.

"Not quite,'' said Resnick. "We got all the way up to Chapter 4 this time.''

"While you guys have been talking, I've been reading some market reports,'' said Wallbanger, "and I've come to the conclusion that a short story is just about the hardest thing to sell.''

"So what do you suggest?'' asked Resnick.

"A vignette.''

"A what?''

"You know—a short-short story,'' replied Wallbanger. "They get rejected much faster. Why, you could get a rejection every four days with a vignette, whereas a short story might not be bounced more than once a month. As for a novel''—he shrugged disdainfully—"hell, it could take ten years to get turned down by everyone.''

"I don't know,'' said Resnick unhappily. "I sort of had my heart set on a rip-roaring space opera, with about 35 chapters, glittering with wit and action and a subtle sense of poetic tragedy.''

''Couldn't you condense it all into a vignette?'' said Kinnison. ''I'm exhausted. I don't think I could go through all this again.''

''Or maybe even a poem,'' suggested Stalwart hopefully.

''Or a nasty book review,'' added Wallbanger. ''There's a huge market for them, especially if you misuse a lot of five syllable words.

''No,'' said Kinnison decisively. ''Let him stick with what he does best.''

''Right,'' said Resnick, sitting down at the word processor.

Chapter 1

Call me Ishmael.

(For George ''Lan'' Laskowski, long-suffering friend and editor)

THE MONKEY'S FINGER

Isaac Asimov

Isaac Asimov, arguably the most recognizable figure in science fiction—in fact, I can't imagine how you would argue against it—has his own idea of how science fiction gets written. I suppose it makes as much sense as any other explanation, and it's a lot more amusing than most.

"YES. YES. YES. Yes. Yes. Yes. Yes. Yes. Yes. Yes. Yes. Yes. Yes. Yes. Yes. Yes," said Marmie Tallinn, in sixteen different inflections and pitches, while the Adam's apple in his long neck bobbed convulsively. He was a science fiction writer.

"No," said Lemuel Hoskins, staring stonily through his steel-rimmed glasses. He was a science fiction editor.

"Then you won't accept a scientific test. You won't listen to me. I'm outvoted, eh?" Marmie lifted himself on his toes, dropped down, repeated the process a few times, and breathed heavily. His dark hair was matted into tufts, where fingers had clutched.

"One to sixteen," said Hoskins.

"Look," said Marmie, "what makes you always right? What makes me always wrong?"

"Marmie, face it. We're each judged in our own way. If magazine circulation were to drop, I'd be a flop. I'd be out on my ear. The president of Space Publishers would ask no questions, believe me. He would just look at the figures. But circulation doesn't go down; it's going up. That makes me a

154

good editor. And as for you—when editors accept you, you're a talent. When they reject you, you're a bum. At the moment, you are a bum.''

"There are other editors, you know. You're not the only one.'' Marmie held up his hands, fingers outspread. "Can you count? That's how many science fiction magazines on the market would gladly take a Tallinn yarn, sight unseen.''

"Gesundheit,'' said Hoskins.

"Look,'' Marmie's voice sweetened, "you wanted two changes, right? You wanted an introductory scene with the battle in space. Well, I gave that to you. It's right here.'' He waved the manuscript under Hoskin's nose and Hoskins moved away as though at a bad smell.

"But you also wanted the scene on the spaceship's hull cut into with a flashback into the interior,'' went on Marmie, "and that you can't get. If I make that change, I ruin an ending which, as it stands, has pathos and depth and feeling.''

Editor Hoskins sat back in his chair and appealed to his secretary, who throughout had been quietly typing. She was used to these scenes.

Hoskins said, "You hear that, Miss Kane? *He* talks of pathos, depth, and feeling. What does a writer know about such things? Look, if you insert the flashback, you increase the suspense; you tighten the story; you make it more valid.''

"*How* do I make it more valid?'' cried Marmie in anguish. "You mean to say that having a bunch of fellows in a spaceship start talking politics and sociology when they're liable to be blown up makes it more *valid?* Oh, my God.''

"There's nothing else you can do. If you wait till the climax is past and then discuss your politics and sociology, the reader will go to sleep on you.''

"But I'm trying to tell you that you're wrong and I can prove it. What's the use of talking when I've arranged a scientific experiment—''

"What scientific experiment?'' Hoskins appealed to his secretary again. "How do you like that, Miss Kane. He thinks he's one of his own characters.''

"It so happens I know a scientist.''

"Who?''

"Dr. Arndt Torgesson, professor of psychodynamics at Columbia."

"Never heard of him."

"I suppose that means a lot," said Marmie, with contempt. "*You* never heard of him. You never heard of Einstein until your writers started mentioning him in their stories."

"Very humorous. A yuk. What about this Torgesson?"

"He's worked out a system for determining scientifically the value of a piece of writing. It's a tremendous piece of work. It's—it's—"

"And it's secret?"

"Certainly it's secret. He's not a science fiction professor. In science fiction, when a man thinks up a theory, he announces it to the newspapers right away. In real life, that's not done. A scientist spends years on experimentation sometimes before going into print. Publishing is a serious thing."

"Then how do *you* know about it? Just a question."

"It so happens that Dr. Torgesson is a fan of mine. He happens to like my stories. He happens to think I'm the best fantasy writer in the business."

"And he shows you his work?"

"That's right. I was counting on you being stubborn about this yarn and I've asked him to run an experiment for us. He said he would do it if we don't talk about it. He said it would be an interesting experiment. He said—"

"What's so secret about it?"

"Well—" Marmie hesitated. "Look, suppose I told you he had a monkey that could type *Hamlet* out of its head."

Hoskins stared at Marmie in alarm. "What are you working up here, a practical joke?" He turned to Miss Kane. "When a writer writes science fiction for ten years he just isn't safe without a personal cage."

Miss Kane maintained a steady typing speed.

Marmie said, "You heard me; a common monkey, even funnier-looking than the average editor. I made an appointment for this afternoon. Are you coming with me or not?"

"Of course not. You think I'd abandon a stack of manuscripts this high"—and he indicated his larynx with a cutting motion of the hand—"for your stupid jokes? You think I'll play straight man for you?"

"If this is in any way a joke, Hoskins, I'll stand you dinner in any restaurant you name. Miss Kane's the witness."

Hoskins sat back in his chair. "You'll buy me dinner? You, Marmaduke Tallinn, New York's most widely known tapeworm-on-credit, are going to pick up a check?"

Marmie winced, not at the reference to his agility in overlooking a dinner check, but at the mention of his name in all its horrible trisyllabicity. He said, "I repeat. Dinner on me wherever you want and whatever you want. Steaks, mushrooms, breast of guinea hen, Martian alligator, anything."

Hoskins stood up and plucked his hat from the top of the filing cabinet.

"For a chance," he said, "to see you unfold some of the oldstyle, large-size dollar bills you've been keeping in the false heel of your left shoe since nineteen-two-eight, I'd walk to Boston. . . ."

Dr. Torgesson was honored. He shook Hoskin's hand warmly and said, "I've been reading *Space Yarns* ever since I came to this country, Mr. Hoskins. It is an excellent magazine. I am particularly fond of Mr. Tallinn's stories."

"You hear?" asked Marmie.

"I hear. Marmie says you have a monkey with talent, Professor."

"Yes," Torgesson said, "but of course this must be confidential. I am not yet ready to publish, and premature publicity could be my professional ruin."

"This is strictly under the editorial hat, Professor."

"Good, good. Sit down, gentlemen, sit down." He paced the floor before them. "What have you told Mr. Hoskins about my work, Marmie?"

"Not a thing, Professor."

"So. Well, Mr. Hoskins, as the editor of a science fiction magazine, I don't have to ask you if you know anything about cybernetics."

Hoskins allowed a glance of concentrated intellect to ooze out past his steel-rims. He said, "Ah, yes. Computing machines—M.I.T.—Norbert Weiner—'' He mumbled some more.

"Yes. Yes." Torgesson paced faster. "Then you must know that chess-playing computers have been constructed on cybernetic principles. The rules of chess moves and the object of the game are built into its circuits. Given any position on the chess board, the machine can then compute all possible moves together with their consequence and choose that one which offers the highest probability of winning the game. It can even be made to take the temperament of its opponent into account."

"Ah, yes," said Hoskins, stroking his chin profoundly.

Torgesson said, "Now imagine a similar situation in which a computing machine can be given a fragment of a literary work to which the computer can then add words from its stock of the entire vocabulary such that the greatest literary values are served. Naturally, the machine would have to be taught the significance of the various keys of a typewriter. Of course, such a computer would have to be much, much more complex than any chess player."

Hoskins stirred restlessly. "The monkey, Professor. Marmie mentioned a monkey."

"But that is what I am coming to," said Torgesson. "Naturally, no machine built is sufficiently complex. But the human brain—ah. The human brain is itself a computing machine. Of course, I couldn't use a human brain. The law, unfortunately, would not permit me. But even a monkey's brain, properly managed, can do more than any machine ever constructed by man. Wait! I'll go get little Rollo."

He left the room. Hoskins waited a moment, then looked cautiously at Marmie. He said, "Oh, brother!"

Marmie said, "What's the matter?"

"What's the matter? The man's a phony. Tell me, Marmie, where did you hire this faker?"

Marmie was outraged. "Faker? This is a genuine professor's office in Fayerweather Hall, Columbia. You recognize Columbia, I hope. You saw the statue of Alma Mater on 116th Street. I pointed out Eisenhower's office."

"Sure, but—"

"And this is Dr. Torgesson's office. Look at the dust."

He blew at a textbook and stirred up clouds of it. "The dust alone shows it's the real thing. And look at the title of the book: *Psychodynamics of Human Behavior,* by Professor Arndt Rolf Torgesson."

"Granted, Marmie, granted. There is a Torgesson and this is his office. How you knew the real guy was on vacation and how you managed to get the use of his office, I don't know. But are you trying to tell me that this comic with his monkeys and computers is the real thing? Hah!"

"With a suspicious nature like yours, I can only assume you had a very miserable, rejected type of childhood."

"Just the result of experience with writers, Marmie. I have my restaurant all picked out and this will cost you a pretty penny."

Marmie snorted, "This won't cost me even the ugliest penny you ever paid me. Quiet, he's coming back."

With the professor, and clinging to his neck, was a very melancholy capuchin monkey.

"This," said Torgesson, "is little Rollo. Say hello, Rollo."

The monkey tugged at his forelock.

The professor said, "He's tired, I'm afraid. Now, I have a piece of his manuscript right here."

He put the monkey down and let it cling to his finger while he brought out two sheets of paper from his jacket pocket and handed them to Hoskins.

Hoskins read, " 'To be or not to be; that is the question: Whether 'tis nobler in the mind to suffer the slings and arrows of outrageous fortune, or to take arms against a host of troubles, and by opposing end them? To dic: to sleep; No more: and, by a sleep to say we—' "

He looked up. "Little Rollo typed this?"

"Not exactly. It's a copy of what he typed."

"Oh, a copy. Well, little Rollo doesn't know his Shakespeare. It's 'to take arms against a sea of troubles.' "

Torgesson nodded. "You are quite correct, Mr. Hoskins. Shakespeare *did* write 'sea.' But you see that's a mixed metaphor. You don't fight a sea with arms. You fight a host or army with arms. Rollo chose the monosyllable and typed 'host.' It's one of Shakespeare's rare mistakes.''

Hoskins said, ''Let's see him type.''

''Surely.'' The professor trundled out a typewriter on a little table. A wire trailed from it. He explained, ''It is necessary to use an electric typewriter as otherwise the physical effort would be too great. It is also necessary to wire little Rollo to this transformer.''

He did so, using as leads two electrodes that protruded an eighth of an inch through the fur on the little creature's skull.

''Rollo,'' he said, ''was subjected to a very delicate brain operation in which a nest of wires were connected to various regions of his brain. We can short his voluntary activities and, in effect, use his brain simply as a computer. I'm afraid the details would be—''

''Let's see him type,'' said Hoskins.

''What would you like?''

Hoskins thought rapidly. ''Does he know Chesterton's 'Lepanto'?''

''He knows nothing by heart. His writing is purely computation. Now, you simply recite a little of the piece so that he will be able to estimate the mood and compute the consequences of the first words.''

Hoskins nodded, inflated his chest, and thundered, ''White founts falling in the courts of the sun, and the Soldan of Byzantium is smiling as they run. There is laughter like the fountains in that face of all men feared; it stirs the forest darkness, the darkness of his beard; it curls the blood-red crescent, the crescent of his lips; for the inmost sea of all the world is shaken by his ships—''

''That's enough,'' said Torgesson.

There was silence as they waited. The monkey regarded the typewriter solemnly.

Torgesson said, ''The process takes time, of course. Little Rollo has to take into account the romanticism of the poem, the slightly archaic flavor, the strong sing-song rhythm, and so on.''

And then a black little finger reached out and touched a key. It was a *t*.

''He doesn't capitalize,'' said the scientist, ''or punctuate, and his spacing isn't very reliable. That's why I usually re-type his work when he's finished."

Little Rollo touched an *h,* then an *e* and a *y*. Then, after a longish pause, he tapped the space bar.

"They," said Hoskins.

The words typed themselves out: "they have dared the-white repub lics upthe capes of italy they have dashed the adreeatic roundthe lion of the sea; and the popehas throw n his arms abroa dfor agoni and loss and called the kings of chrissndom for sords about the cross."

"My God!" said Hoskins.

"That's the way the piece goes then?" asked Torgesson.

"For the love of Pete!" said Hoskins.

"If it is, then Chesterton must have done a good, consistent job."

"Holy smokes!" said Hoskins.

"You see," said Marmie, massaging Hoskins's shoulder, "you see, you see, you see. You see," he added.

"I'll be damned," said Hoskins.

"Now look," said Marmie, rubbing his hair till it rose in clusters like a cockatoo's crest, "let's get to business. Let's tackle my story."

"Well, but—"

"It will not be beyond little Rollo's capacity," Torgesson assured him. "I frequently read little Rollo parts of some of the better science fiction, including many of Marmie's tales. It's amazing how some of the yarns are improved."

"It's not that," said Hoskins. "Any monkey can write better SF than some of the hacks we've got. But the Tallinn story is thirteen thousand words long. It'll take forever for the monk to type it."

"Not at all, Mr. Hoskins, not at all. I shall read the story to him, and at the crucial point we will let him continue."

Hoskins folded his arms. "Then shoot. I'm ready."

"I," said Marmie, "am more than ready." And he folded his arms.

Little Rollo sat there, a furry little bundle of cataleptic misery, while Dr. Torgesson's soft voice rose and fell in cadence with a spaceship battle and the subsequent struggles of Earthmen captives to recapture their lost ship.

One of the characters made his way out to the spaceship hull, and Dr. Torgesson followed the flamboyant events in mild rapture. He read:

". . . Stalny froze in the silence of the eternal stars. His aching knee tore at his consciousness as he waited for the monsters to hear the thud and—"

Marmie yanked desperately at Dr. Torgesson's sleeve. Torgesson looked up and disconnected little Rollo.

"That's it," said Marmie. "You see, Professor, it's just about here that Hoskins is getting his sticky little fingers into the works. I continue the scene outside the spaceship till Stalny wins out and the ship is back in Earth hands. Then I go into explanations. Hoskins wants me to break that outside scene, get back inside, halt the action for two thousand words, then get back out again. Ever hear such crud?"

"Suppose we let the monk decide," said Hoskins.

Dr. Torgesson turned little Rollo on, and a black shriveled finger reached hesitantly out to the typewriter. Hoskins and Marmie leaned forward simultaneously, their heads coming softly together just over little Rollo's brooding body. The typewriter punched out the letter t.

"T," encouraged Marmie, nodding.

"T," agreed Hoskins.

The typewriter made an a, then went on at a more rapid rate: "take action stalnee waited in helpless hor ror forair locks toyawn and suited laroos to emerge relentlessly—"

"Word for word," said Marmie in raptures.

"He certainly has your gooey style."

"The readers like it."

"They wouldn't if their average mental age wasn't—" Hoskins stopped.

"Go on," said Marmie, "say it. Say it. Say their IQ is that of a twelve-year-old child and I'll quote you in every fan magazine in the country."

"Gentlemen," said Torgesson, "gentlemen. You'll disturb little Rollo."

They turned to the typewriter, which was still tapping

steadily: ''—the stars whelled in ther mightie orb its as stalnees earthbound senses insis ted the rotating ship sto od still.''

The typewriter carriage whipped back to begin a new line. Marmie held his breath. Here, if anywhere, would come—

And the little finger moved out and made: *

Hoskins yelled, ''Asterisk!''

Marmie muttered, ''Asterisk.''

Torgesson said, ''Asterisk?''

A line of nine more asterisks followed.

''That's all, brother,'' said Hoskins. He explained quickly to the staring Torgesson, ''With Marmie, it's a habit to use a line of asterisks when he wants to indicate a radical shift of scene. And a radical shift of scene is exactly what I wanted.''

The typewriter started a new paragraph: ''within the ship—''

''Turn it off, Professor,'' said Marmie.

Hoskins rubbed his hands. ''When do I get the revision, Marmie?''

Marmie said coolly, ''What revision?''

''You said the monk's version.''

''I sure did. It's what I brought you here to see. That little Rollo is a machine; a cold, brutal, logical machine.''

''Well?''

''And the point is that a good writer is not a machine. He doesn't write with his mind, but with his heart. His heart.'' Marmie pounded his chest.

Hoskins groaned. ''What are you doing to me, Marmie? If you give me that heart-and-soul-of-a-writer routine, I'll just be forced to turn sick right here and right now. Let's keep all this on the usual I'll-write-anything-for-money basis.''

Marmie said, ''Just listen to me for a minute. Little Rollo corrected Shakespeare. You pointed that out yourself. Little Rollo wanted Shakespeare to say, 'host of troubles,' and he was right from his machine standpoint. A 'sea of troubles' under the circumstances is a mixed metaphor. But don't you suppose Shakespeare knew that, too? Shakespeare just happened to know when to *break* the rules, that's all. Little Rollo is a machine that can't break the rules, but a good writer can, and *must*. 'Sea of troubles' is more impressive; it has roll and power. The hell with the mixed metaphor.

"Now, when you tell me to shift the scene, you're following mechanical rules on maintaining suspense, so of course little Rollo agrees with you. But I know that I must break the rules to maintain the profound emotional impact of the ending as I see it. Otherwise I have a mechanical product that a computer can turn out."

Hoskins said, "But—"

"Go on," said Marmie, "vote for the mechanical. Say that little Rollo is all the editor you'll ever be."

Hoskins said, with a quiver in his throat, "All right, Marmie, I'll take the story as is. No, don't give it to me; mail it. I've got to find a bar, if you don't mind."

He forced his hat down on his head and turned to leave. Torgesson called after him, "Don't tell anyone about little Rollo, please."

The parting answer floated back over a slamming door, "Do you think I'm crazy . . . ?"

Marmie rubbed his hands ecstatically when he was sure Hoskins was gone.

"Brains, that's what it was," he said, and probed one finger as deeply into his temple as it would go. "This sale I enjoyed. This sale, Professor, is worth all the rest I've ever made. All the rest of them together." He collapsed joyfully on the nearest chair.

Torgesson lifted little Rollo to his shoulder. He said mildly, "But, Marmaduke, what would you have done if little Rollo had typed your version instead?"

A look of grievance passed momentarily over Marmie's face. "Well, damn it," he said, "that's what I *thought* it was going to do."

HAPGOOD'S HOAX

Allen Steele

Allen Steele, who entered the science fiction field with all the subtlety of a supernova, took time off from his string of brilliant novels long enough to produce this idiosyncratic look at a gentleman who is not L. Ron Hubbard, but whose career shows certain remarkable parallels.

HAPGOOD, H.L. (Harold LaPierre),—1911-1966; *American pulp SF writer of the 1930s and 1940s. Although most of his short fiction is obscure today, Hapgood is best known (as Dr. H. LaPierre Hapgood) as the author of several allegedly non-fictional works on UFO contact, including* Abducted to Space *(1950) and* UFO! *(1952). These works were based on Hapgood's claim that he was seized by aliens from space in 1948, which is widely regarded as a hoax.*

> —*The Encyclopedia of Science Fiction and Fantasy*
> URSULA MAY, editor (1981)

Lawrence R. Bolger; Professor of English, Minnesota State University, and science fiction historian.

Harry Hapgood. *(Sighs.)* It would figure that someone would want to interview me about Harry Hapgood, especially since the new collection of his work just came out. The field may not be able to get rid of him until someone digs up his coffin and hammers a stake in his heart. . . .

Okay, since you've come all this way, I'll tell you about

H.L. Hapgood, Jr. But, to tell the truth, I'd just as soon leave the bastard in his literary grave.

There were pulp writers from the '30s who managed to survive the times and outlast the pulps, to make the transition from pulp fiction to whatever passes as literature in this genre. Jack Williamson, Clifford Simak, Ray Bradbury . . . those are some of the ones whose work eventually broke out of the pulp mold. They're regarded as the great writers of the field and we still read their stories. They still find their audience. Their publishers keep their classics, like *City* and *The Humanoids* and *The Martian Chronicles,* in print.

Those are the success stories. Yet for every Bradbury or Williamson, there's a hundred other writers—some of them big names back then, you need to remember—who didn't make it out of the pulp era. For one reason or another, their careers faded when the pulps died at the end of the '40s. H. Bedford-Jones, Arthur K. Barnes, S.P. Meek . . . all obscure authors now. Just like H.L. Hapgood, Jr.

Not that they were necessarily bad writers, either. I mean, some of their stories are no more crap than a lot of the stuff that gets into print today. But when the field started to grow up, when John Campbell began to demand that his *Astounding* contributors deliver realistic SF or else . . . well, Harry was one of those writers who fell into the ''or else'' category.

But before that, he had been extraordinarily successful, especially when you consider the times. The Depression nearly killed a lot of writers, but those years were kind to him. He had a nonstop imagination and fast fingers, and, for a penny a word, Harry Hapgood cranked out stories by the bushel. I was reading all the SF pulps at the time—I was in high school in Ohio then—so I can tell you with personal authority that there was rarely a month that went by without H.L. Hapgood's byline appearing somewhere. If not in *Amazing* or *Thrilling Wonder,* then in the pre-Campbell era *Astounding* or *Captain Future* or someplace else. ''The Sky Pirates of Centaurus,'' ''Attack of the Giant Robots,'' ''Mars or Bust!''—those were some of his more memorable stories. Rock-jawed space captains fighting Venusian tiger-men while mad scientists with Z-ray machines menaced ladies in bondage. Greasy kid stuff, sure, but a hell of a lot of fun when

you were fourteen years old. Harry was the master of the
space opera. Not even Ed Hamilton or Doc Smith could tell
'em like he could.

You can still find some of his older work in huckster rooms
at SF conventions, if you look through the raggy old pulps
some people have on the tables. That's about the only place
you can find Harry Hapgood's pulp stories anymore. I think
his last published story, at least in his lifetime, was in *Amazing* in '45 or '46. The last time any of his early work was
reprinted was when somebody put together a pulp anthology
about ten years ago. When he died in '66, his career in science fiction had been long since over.

That's the main reason why he's been obscure all these
years. But there was also the New Hampshire hoax. He died
a rich man because of that stunt, but he also blackened his
name in the field. I don't think anyone wanted to remember
Hapgood because of that. At least, not until recently . . .

*Startled and dazzled by the sudden burst of light, I looked
up and saw a monstrous disk-shaped vehicle descending toward me. Rocket-fighters raced from the sky to combat the
weird machine, but as they got close, scarlet rays flashed
from portals along the side of the spaceship. The rockets
exploded!*

*"Dirk, oh Dirk!" Catherine screamed from the bunker next
to me, fearful of the apparition. "What can it be?"*

*Before I could answer, Captain Black of the United Earth
Space Force spoke up. "The Quongg death machine, Miss
Jones," he said, his chin thrust out belligerently.*

*I reached for my blaster. "Oh, yeah?" I snarled. "Well,
they'll never take us alive!"*

*Captain Black stared at me. "They'll take us alive, all
right!" he snarled. "They want us as specimens!"*

—"Kidnappers From The Stars",

by H.L. HAPGOOD JR.
Space Tales; December, 1938

Joe Mackey; retired electrical engineer.
If I remember correctly, I first met Harry Hapgood back

in 1934 or 1935, when we both lived in the same three-decker in Somerville, Massachusetts, just outside of Boston. I was about nineteen at the time and was working a day-job in a deli on Newbury Street to put myself through M.I.T. night school. So, y'know, when I wasn't making grinders or riding the trolley over to classes in Cambridge, I was at home hitting the books. I got maybe four hours of sleep in those days. The Depression was a bitch like that.

I met Harry because he lived right upstairs. His apartment was directly above mine and he used to bang on his typewriter late at night, usually when I was studying or trying to sleep. Every time he hit the carriage return, it sounded like something was being dropped on the floor. I had no idea what he was doing up there . . . practicing somersaults or something.

Anyway, one night I finally got fed up with the racket, so I marched upstairs and hammered on his door, planning on telling him to cut it out 'cause I was trying to catch a few winks. Well, he opened his door—very timidly—and I started to chew him out. Then I looked past him and saw all these science fiction magazines scattered all over the place. Piled on the coffee table, the couch, the kitchen table, the bed . . . *Amazing, Astonishing, Thrilling Wonder, Planet Stories, Startling Stories.* Heaps of them. My jaw just dropped open because, though I read all those magazines when I could afford to buy 'em, I thought I was the only person in Boston who read science fiction.

So I said something like, "Holy smoke! You've got the new issue of *Astounding!*" I remember that it was lying open on the coffee table. Brand new issue. I was too broke to pick it up myself.

Harry just smiled, then he walked over and picked it up and brought it to me. "Here, you can borrow it if you want," he said. Then he added, very slyly, "Read the story by H.L. Hapgood. You might like it."

I nodded and said, "Yeah, I really like his stories." He just blushed and coughed into his fist and shuffled his feet and then he told me who he was.

Well, I didn't say anything about his typing after that, but once he found out I was taking night classes at M.I.T., he stopped typing late at night so I could get some sleep. He figured it out for himself. Harry was a good guy like that.

Margo Croft; literary agent; former assistant editor, *Rocket Adventures*.

I was the first-reader at *Rocket* back then, so I read Harry's stories when they came in through the mail, which was once every week or two. Seriously. In his prime, he was more prolific than Bob Silverberg or Isaac Asimov ever were. But the difference was, Silverberg and Asimov were good writers, even in their pulp days.

No, no, scratch that. At a certain level, Harry *was* good. He knew how to keep a story going. He was a master of pacing, for one thing. But it was all formula fiction, even if he didn't recognize the formula himself. Anyone who compares him to E.E. Smith or Edmond Hamilton is fooling you. His characters were one-dimensional, his dialogue was vintage movie serial. "Ah-ha, Dr. Zoko, I've got you now!"—that sort of thing. His understanding of real science was nonexistent. In fact, he usually ignored science. When it was convenient, say, for a pocket of air to exist in a crater on the Moon, there it was.

But his stories were no worse than the other stuff we published, and he got his share of fan mail, so we sent him lots of checks. For a long time, he was in our stable of regular writers. Whenever we needed a six thousand-word story to fill a gap in the next issue, there was always an H.L. Hapgood yarn in the inventory. He was a fiction factory.

I finally met him at the first World Science Fiction Convention, in New York back in '39. I think it was Donald Wollheim who introduced us. I was twenty years old then, flat-chested and single, ready to throw myself at the first writer who came along, so I developed a crush on Harry at once. He might have been a hack, but he was a good-looking hack *(Laughs)*.

He had fans all around him, though, because he was such a well-known writer. I spent the better part of Saturday following him around Caravan Hall, trying to get his attention. It was hard. Harry was shy when it came to one-on-one conversation, but he soaked up the glory when a mob was around.

Anyway, I finally managed to get him into a group that was going out to dinner that night. We found an Italian restaurant a few blocks away and took over a long table in the back room. There were a whole bunch of us—I think Ray Bradbury was in the group, though nobody knew who he was then—and I managed to get myself positioned across the table from Harry. Like I said, he was very shy when it came to one-on-one conversation, so I gave up on talking to him like a pretty girl and tried speaking to him like an editor. He began to notice me then.

His lack of—well, for lack of better term, literary sophistication—was mind-boggling. He had barely heard of Ernest Hemingway, and he only recognized Steinbeck as the name of his neighborhood grocer. The only classics he had read were by H.G. Wells and Jules Verne. In fact, the only thing Harry seemed to have ever read was science fiction or *Popular Mechanics,* and that was all he wanted to talk about. I mean, there I was trying to show off my legs—maybe I had no chest back then, but my legs were Marlene Dietrich's—and Harry only wanted to discuss the collected work of Neil R. Jones.

So I lost a little interest in him during that talk, and after a while I started paying attention to other people at the table. I *do* distinctly remember two things Harry said that night. One was that his ambition was to get rich and famous. He was convinced that he would write for the pulps forever. "Science fiction will never change," he proclaimed.

The other was a comment which sounds routine today. Every other SF writer has said it at least once, but I recall Harry saying it first, at least as far as I can remember. It probably sticks in my mind because of what happened years later.

"If aliens ever came to Earth to capture people," he said offhandedly at one point, "they wouldn't have to hunt for me. I'd volunteer for the trip."

Joe Mackey:

Harry Hapgood was a hell of a good person back then. You can quote me on that. He put me up to a lot of meals when I was starving, and he always had a buck to spare even

when his own rent was due. But the day I saw him begin to
hurt was the day John Campbell rejected one of his stories.

I had dropped by his place after work. It was in the middle
of winter . . . 1940, I think . . . and the M.I.T. semester
hadn't yet started, so I had some time to kill. The mail had
just come, and when I came into Harry's apartment he was
sitting at his kitchen table, bent over a manuscript which had
just come back in the mail. It was a rejection from *Astounding*.

This almost never happened to him. Harry thought he was
rejection-proof. After all, his stories usually sold on the first
shot. That, and the fact that *Astounding* had always been one
of his most reliable markets. But Harry's old editor, F. Orlin
Tremaine, had left a couple of years earlier, and the new guy,
John W. Campbell, was reshaping the magazine . . . and that
meant getting rid of the zap-gun school of science fiction.

So here was Harry, looking at this story which had been
bounced back, "Enslaved On Venus." Just staring at it, that's
all. "What's going on?" I asked, and he told me that Campbell had just rejected this story. "Did he tell you why?" I
said. Harry told me he had received a letter, but he wouldn't
show it to me. I think it was in the trash. "Well, just send it
out again to some other magazine," I said, because this is
what he had always told me should be done when a story gets
rejected.

But he just shook his head. "No," he said. "I don't think
so."

Something John Campbell had written in that letter had
really gotten to Harry. Whatever Campbell had written in that
letter, it had cut right to the bone. I don't think Campbell
ever consciously tried to hurt writers whose work he rejected,
but he was known to be tough . . . and now he had gotten
tough on Harry.

Anyway, Harry told me that he wanted to be alone for a
while, so I left his place. I wasn't really worried. I had confidence that "Enslaved On Venus" would be published
somewhere else. But I never saw that story make it into print,
and Harry never mentioned it to me again. I think he trashed
it along with Campbell's letter. It wasn't even found in his
files.

Lawrence Bolger:

Harry Hapgood became a dinosaur. His literary career died because he couldn't adapt. The World War II paper shortage killed the pulps, so there went most of his regular markets, and the changes in the genre swept in by John Campbell, H.L. Gold, Frederik Pohl, and other editors made his kind of SF writing unpopular. Raymond Palmer continued to buy his stories for *Amazing* until Palmer, too, left the field in the late '40s. By then, science fiction had grown up.

But Hapgood didn't grow with the genre. His stories were pure romanticism. He paid no attention to scientific accuracy or character development. He persisted in trying to write Buck Rogers stuff. Other writers learned the new rules, changed their styles to fit the times, but Harry Hapgood wouldn't—probably couldn't—change chords. So while Robert Heinlein was creating his "Future History" series and Ted Sturgeon was writing classics like "Baby Is Three," Harry was still trying to get away with space heroes and bug-eyed monsters. The more sophisticated SF mags wouldn't touch that stuff.

It was sad. He still went to science fiction conventions on the East Coast, but he was no longer surrounded by fans. They just didn't want to talk to him anymore.

The magazine editors tried to tell him where he was going wrong, why they weren't buying his stories any more. I remember, at one science fiction convention in Philadelphia, overhearing John Campbell patiently trying to explain to Harry that, as long as he persisted in writing stories which claimed that rockets could travel to another solar system in two days or that Jupiter had a surface, he simply could not accept any of Harry's work.

Harry never listened. He stubbornly wanted to play by his own rules. Gregory Benford once criticized science fiction that "plays with the net down," SF stories which ignore basic scientific principles like the theory of relativity. In Harry Hapgood's case, he was playing on a different court altogether. All he could write were stories in which lizard-men kidnapped beautiful women and the Space Navy always saved the day. But he was playing ping-pong among Wimbledon champs, and he wouldn't realize that he was in a new game.

Margo Croft:

After *Rocket Adventures* folded, I went down the street to work as an associate editor at Doubleday, helping to edit their mystery line. That was in '48. I had all but completely withdrawn from the science fiction scene by then, but I still had a few contacts in the field, people with whom I'd touch bases now and then.

Anyway . . . one of Doubleday's whodunnit writers lived in Boston and I occasionally took the train up there to meet with her. On one of those trips I had some time to kill before catching the train back to New York. I had my address book in my purse and Harry's number was written in it, so I called him up and told him I'd buy him lunch downtown. It was mainly for old time's sake, but also I wondered if he had recovered from the collapse of the pulp market. By then, I hadn't seen him in a few years.

Harry wasn't looking good. He had lost weight and he had started chain-smoking. He wore a suit which looked as if it had been new in 1939, and I knew it had to be his best suit. The last time he had made an SF magazine sale had been the year before. He wouldn't admit it, but I knew that he had been trying to pay the bills by writing articles for some furniture trade magazine. It was ironic. Harry, who had practically thrived during the Depression, was on the skids during the postwar boom. Ironic, but not funny.

It was a painful lunch. He didn't want to talk much. He knew I was paying, so he ordered the biggest item on the menu. It was probably the best meal he had eaten in months. I told him that I had married—my first husband, Phillip—and though he tried to take it well, I could see that he was disappointed. I suppose he had noticed that girlish crush I'd had on him ten years before, and was sorry now that he hadn't done anything about it then. *(Shakes her head.)* Poor man.

His personal life was a wreck, so I tried to talk to him about his writing. I told him that Doubleday was starting to publish science fiction and that they were looking for established authors; he should take a crack at it. He didn't say much, and I got the impression that he had lost interest in SF. Somehow that didn't make sense. Harry was a science fiction writer top to bottom. He should have jumped at the chance.

He had stopped at a newsstand before meeting me at the restaurant, and he had picked up a handful of magazines. It was his usual reading matter—all the SF magazines—but in the stack was also the first issue of a new magazine which I had heard about through the grapevine. That was *Fate*, the UFO digest that Ray Palmer started publishing after he left *Amazing* to take advantage of the flying saucer craze.

Sure, it was the type of thing which Harry Hapgood would read. Nothing sinister about that. But I remember, over dessert, watching him absently pick it up and thumb through the pages. Then he casually asked me what it would take for him to write a bestseller.

"I'm talking about a science fiction novel," he said. "I mean, something that would sell like crazy."

Coming from Harry Hapgood, that would have been hysterical if it hadn't been so sad. I didn't really think he was capable of writing an SF novel that was even publishable— and it would be years before science fiction scratched the bestseller lists. But I told him that he had answered his own question.

"Write something that a lot of people will want to read," I said. The obvious answer, of course. Harry just nodded his head and kept flipping through *Fate*.

Joe Mackey:

I remember Harry's disappearance very well.

By then I was working as a draftsman for a refrigerator company in Boston, but I still lived downstairs from Harry, in that three-decker in Somerville. I had gotten home from work and was settling down on the couch to read. Harry knocked on my door, stuck his head in, and said that he was going out for ice cream. Did I want to come along? I told him, no, thanks anyway, and so he left. I heard the front door downstairs open and close . . . and that was it. That was the last time I heard from him for five days.

Next morning I went up to his place for coffee before going to work—something I did every morning—and found his door unlocked. His lights were still on, but he was missing. I was a little worried, but I figured, what the hell. I turned off the lights and went to my job. But when I got home that evening and found that he still hadn't returned, I called the police.

Nothing was missing. His suitcase was still in the closet, his toothbrush was still next to the sink in the bathroom, there was even a half-finished furniture article in his typewriter. He had just walked out to get ice cream and . . . *phhtt!* Vanished. The cops searched the neighborhood, thinking he had been mugged, maybe killed and left in an alley somewhere, but there was no trace of him. He hadn't checked into any hospitals and the cab drivers didn't report picking him up anywhere. The newspapers reported his disappearance the next day, as a minor item buried in the back pages. Nobody seemed to be really concerned, though. Except me. I was worried sick about the whole thing. Y'know, maybe Harry was going to be found floating in the Charles River or something.

Then . . . well, you know what happened next. He turned up in the boonies of New Hampshire, saying that he had been kidnapped by a flying saucer.

A lone pedestrian, found on Route 202 in Hillsboro, was brought to Hillsboro Police station Tuesday night, after he wandered out of the woods and flagged down a driver. The man, identified as a Somerville, Massachusetts, writer, has been sought by Massachusetts police as a missing person since last week.

Harold LaPierre Hapgood, Jr., 38, of 19 Waterhouse St., Somerville, was found on the roadside near the Antrim town line by the Rev. Lucius Colby, minister of the First Episcopal Church in Henniker. According to Hillsboro Police Chief Cyril G. Slater, Mr. Hapgood stumbled out into the highway in front of the Rev. Colby's automobile, waving his arms and forcing the driver to halt. The Rev. Colby then drove Mr. Hapgood to the Hillsboro police station.

Chief Slater says that Mr. Hapgood, a magazine writer, has been sought by the Somerville, Boston, and Massachusetts state police departments since Friday, May 7, when he apparently vanished after leaving his residence in Somerville. Chief Slater says that although Mr. Hapgood appears to be in good health, he was delirious when brought to his office.

Mr. Hapgood claims that he was kidnapped by a space-ship piloted by creatures from another planet . . .
> —*Hillsboro News-Register*,
> Hillsboro, N.H.
> Thursday, May 13, 1948

Lawrence Bolger:

Did Harry Hapgood really get kidnapped by a UFO? Not a chance. If he got kidnapped by anything, it was the Trailways bus he caught at the station in Boston.

When a reporter from one of the Boston papers retraced Hapgood's trail, he found that the driver remembered someone who looked like Harry getting on in Boston and getting off in Keene, New Hampshire. He used false names when he bought the ticket and when he checked into a hotel in Keene for four days, but his description was matched by the bus driver, the hotel clerk and chambermaids, even the waitress at the diner where he ate breakfast and dinner. The only thing which wasn't established was how he got from Keene to Hillsboro, so one can only assume that he hitched a ride . . . and it sure as hell wasn't in a flying saucer.

It wasn't an iron-clad story at all. Hell, it was a blatant fraud. He didn't have a shred of evidence to support his claim that he had been teleported off the street in Somerville, taken into space in a UFO, and examined by strange little men for four days.

On the other hand, he didn't need any proof. The country was in the midst of its first big flying-saucer flap, started by Kenneth Arnold's sighting of UFOs over Mt. Rainier the year before. There were a lot of true believers like the Fortean Society, and whenever newspapers or the Air Force debunked a sighting or a kidnap story, these people would claim that it was part of a government conspiracy to cover up the UFO "invasion" or whatever.

Harry Hapgood knew what he was doing. First, he sold a first-hand account of his experience to Ray Palmer at *Fate*. After that story was printed and enough newspapers had written about his "ordeal," he wrote his book and sold it to a minor hardback publisher, changing his byline to H. LaPierre

Hapgood so that he wouldn't get confused with H.L. Hapgood, Jr., the pulp writer.

(Laughs). No one noticed the name change, because no one paid any attention to science fiction in those days. The only people who really knew that H. LaPierre Hapgood had started his career as a science fiction hack were SF fans. Since they were considered to be even further out on the fringe than the UFO cultists, no one paid any attention to them.

And what do you know? It became a runaway bestseller . . .

Margo Croft:
The odd thing about Harry's first book is, if you take it as science fiction, it's a pretty good yarn. His narrative skills, developed from all those years of grinding out stories for the pulps, really lent themselves to this sort of thing. It has an almost-convincing sense of realism. I mean, if you checked your skepticism at the door, you could have ended up believing him. And a lot of people did.

If Harry had applied himself to writing science fiction, he could have re-emerged in the field as one of the major writers of the '50s. *(Shrugs.)* But maybe he was fed up with science fiction. I dunno. I guess he was more interested in making money, at that point.

One of the funnier stories about the hoax was that, after *Abducted to Space* was published and made it to the bestseller lists, he got invited to be the commencement speaker at graduation ceremonies at some small liberal-arts college in Illinois. As academic tradition sometimes has it, for his services he was presented an honorary doctorate in astronomy from the school. It didn't mean a damn thing, but Harry and his publisher milked it for all it was worth. So Harry overnight became Dr. H. LaPierre Hapgood, the professional astronomer. *(Laughs.)* He didn't even graduate from high school!

When I awoke, I found myself lying in a circular chamber. The walls rose around me as a hemispherical dome, white and featureless except for a pulsing red orb suspended from the apex of the ceiling.

The room seemed to hum, just above the range of audibil-

*ity. I was lying on a raised platform which seemed to be made
out of metal, except that it was soft where I lay. I attempted
to move my arms, then my legs, but discovered to my alarm
that I was completely paralyzed. Yet there were no visible
restraints on my arms or legs.*

*Then, directly in front of me, a section of the wall faded
and became a screen. I saw the black expanse of outer space.
In the center of the screen hung Earth, and I realized that I
was thousands of miles out in space. I was terrified. How did
I get here? What would be done to me? Most importantly,
would I ever be released?*

*A few moments later, a low section of the wall to my right
slid upward, and the first of the Aliens slowly walked into the
chamber . . .*

—H. LaPierre Hapgood;
Abducted to Space

Joe Mackey:

Harry moved out of the place in Somerville as soon as he
got the advance money for *Abducted to Space*, but by then
he and I weren't on speaking terms. I was pretty upset with
him by that time. I thought we were friends, but he had used
me to establish credibility for that cock-and-bull story of his.
Hell, when the reporters starting showing up to interview him
about his experience, he would send them downstairs to interview me as a "reliable source." Of course, they never
printed my opinion that he was making the whole thing up.
Just the part about how I found his place empty one morning.

So I didn't really mind when he moved out to one of the
ritzier parts of Chestnut Hill, but I did keep up with him,
from a distance. I'm sure you know a lot of this already,
right? After he and his publisher made a mint from *Abducted
to Space*, he did *UFO!*, which was just a rehash of the first
book, except that he embellished the story a little. Seems he
"remembered" a lot of details in his dreams, which he
claimed were buried in his subconscious by the aliens. That's
a lot of horseshit—excuse my French—because I could see
he was just recycling stuff from his old pulp stories. Probably

had his copies of *Thrilling Wonder* and *Amazing* right there
on his desk when he was writing the thing.

It was after he put out *Odd Visitors,* the third book, that
he really went for the nugget. He started that UFO cult of
his—whachacallit, the International Center For Extraterres-
trial Studies—and soon had every dingbat in the country sending him donations. Ten dollars got you a mimeographed
newsletter every couple of months, and a hundred bucks put
you on a list of "honorary contactees."

The money was supposedly going for the construction of
a "UFO spaceport" on some land he had purchased out in
the western part of the state. The line was that, when the
spacearks arrived, they would land at the spaceport and take
aboard human passengers for a voyage to another planet,
which Harry called Nirvanos. Complete crap—but, y'know,
there's a lot of mixed-up people out there who'll buy into
just that sort of thing.

My wife and I drove out there one Sunday to check it out.
Found a three-acre plot in Leicester, off a dirt road in the
middle of nowhere. Just a big cleared cow pasture, surrounded by a barb-wire fence with an empty shack in the
middle and a big billboard at the end. It had some weird
symbols painted on it and was strung with Christmas lights.
Some local kid was hired to switch them on each night. And
that was his spaceport.

I bet Harry spent no more than five hundred dollars on the
thing . . . and he probably took a million to the bank, in
donations from a lot of sick, gullible folks.

I can't tell you how much I despised the son of a bitch.

Margo Croft:
Harry dropped out of sight for about a dozen years, and while
he did the UFO craze of the '50s ran its course. By the time Alan
Shephard went up in space, flying saucers were a joke. The company which put out Harry's three UFO books went under—I think
the publisher went to jail for tax fraud—and no respectable house
would touch the ravings of Dr. H. LaPierre Hapgood. He kept
his UFO cult going for a little while longer, after he moved it to
Mexico to escape the IRS, but eventually it ran out of steam. On
occasion I heard scuttlebutt about some millionaire American ex-

patriate who had made his money writing UFO books, now living in a mansion-compound just outside of Mexico City, and never seen by outsiders. I knew who he was, and I didn't give a damn.

Then it was 1965, and I had left Doubleday and was starting my own literary agency. I wanted to take on some science fiction writers as clients, so I started hitting the major SF conventions, trying to find the next Robert Heinlein or Isaac Asimov. I found myself at an SF convention in the Chicago area, in a private party filled with the hot young writers of the day—Roger Zelazny, Harlan Ellison, Larry Niven, some others I can't recall. The hotel room was crowded and smoke-filled, so I went in search of a quiet corner of the room. And when I got there, I found Harry Hapgood.

He was old, old before his time. I was only a few years younger than him, but he seemed *(long pause)* so wasted. Used up, like something had been sucking blood out of him for fifteen years. If he was a millionaire, it didn't show. His clothes looked like they had been bought off the rack at Woolworth's, and he was so thin, so pale . . . I might not have recognized him if it hadn't been for his nametag.

"H.L. Hapgood, Jr." it read. He had gone back to his old byline, but if anyone had recognized his name, they didn't want to meet him. "Hapgood" was a foul name to conjure in SF circles. Science fiction writers and fans had long been misassociated by the general public with the UFO crazies, just as they're now lumped in with the New Age crystal-freaks. H.L. Hapgood was the name of one of their own, a writer who had turned Quisling and sold out to the lunatic fringe. In a crowded party, he was all alone. I couldn't believe that he had dared to show his face at an SF convention.

He recognized me at once. He might have even been waiting for me. I wanted to turn and walk away. But then he said my name, and I stayed. I sat down on the windowsill next to his chair, and listened to a dying old man.

He said . . .

(Sighs). I'm sorry. I can't go on. Will you turn off the recorder now, please?

"I've been asked, 'Why did you try, when you knew 99 percent of the people wouldn't believe you?' My reply, when

it wasn't self-incriminating to answer the question, was simple. 'You're missing the point,' I said. "It doesn't matter if 99 percent of the people won't believe you. It only takes the remaining 1 percent to make you a rich man."

"I have done many terrible things to become rich, and I won't apologize for all of them. The New Hampshire hoax was only the first of many. I have deceived and manipulated countless people. I have no regrets about bilking total strangers for their money. If they were silly enough to send me money for the privilege of hearing more of my lies, then they deserved what they received. You get what you pay for.

"Yet, for those whose friendship I betrayed, I feel a vast, unspeakable shame. The wealth I reaped is a poor substitute for the friends I have lost. The debt I owe them can never be repaid, even by the division of my estate.

"The greater part of my estate, though, I bequeath to Minnesota State University, for the continuance of its English department's science fiction research program. My actions have tarnished the genre. Perhaps this will help to make amends. However, there is no reason why the program should be blackened by the name of a liar, which is why this donation will be made anonymously.

"As for my three UFO books, I commend them to death. I have appointed Margo Croft to be my literary executor, and she had been instructed to make sure that they are never again reprinted. They will follow me into the grave, never again to rot anyone's mind.

"As for my remaining works . . . Margo, you may do with them as you please."

—HAROLD L. HAPGOOD, JR.
Last will and testament
(Recorded July 28, 1966)

Lawrence Bolger:

Shortly after Harry Hapgood's funeral, the University sent a couple of graduate researchers from the SF program down to Mexico, to visit Hapgood's mansion. They went along with Margo Croft, who had yet to set foot in Harry's house, even though the two of them had reached sort of a reconciliation just before he died. Both our students and Margo were interested in the same thing, the vague reference to "remaining work" Hapgood had alluded to in his will.

Outside the high walls of the compound, a few of Harry's remaining followers were still holding vigil—wild-haired old ladies clutching frayed copies of *Abducted to Space,* intense young men with madness lurking behind their eyes, a smiling married couple wearing aluminum-foil spacesuits, waiting for Harry's spaceark to arrive and carry them to the promised land in the sky. Within the mansion, men were packing in crates his furniture and belongings—jade and porcelain vases, Spanish iron sculptures, Elizabethan tapestries—in preparation for Sotheby's auction of the estate. As Hapgood had directed, the house itself and its grounds would be donated to Mexico for a mental institute. Perhaps this was a final, wry joke on his part.

Margo and the researchers found Harry's office virtually untouched. Only the lawyers had been in there, to retrieve the file cabinets containing Harry's financial records. There was another file cabinet in the office, though, and a desk; in the drawers, they found the last literary work of H.L. Hapgood, Jr.

They counted sixty-four short stories and three novels: meticulously typed, almost all completed, and none previously published. All had been written since the early 1950s, most in the last few years of his life when Harry had been fighting his cancer. All science fiction . . . not a UFO book in the whole bunch. Enough writing to fill a career.

Yet there were no rejection slips in the files, nor were there copies of cover letters. No indication that Harry had ever submitted any of these stories to magazine or book publishers. It was as if he would write a story, then simply stash it away and start another one. Hapgood had lived alone; there had been no one to read his work.

Why? *(Shrugs.)* Who knows? Maybe he couldn't face rejection . . . he didn't want to see any of those stories come back in the mail. But they were good stories, nonetheless. Hapgood had obviously learned something about writing in the intervening years.

You know the rest, of course. Margo brought the manuscripts back to New York, and one of her clients culled the best short stories from the stack, edited them into a posthumous collection, and managed to get it published. The damn thing's been selling like crazy ever since. *(Laughs.)* Perhaps Harry's legion of UFO cultists is still out there, loyally buying multiple copies from the bookstores. That's the only explanation I have for the new book getting on the New York *Times* bestseller list last week. And now the same publisher is going to issue his novels in a uniform edition. They'll probably become bestsellers, too. So go figure . . .

So who got the last laugh? Maybe this is Harry's final revenge. His place in the genre's history has been revised, and hardly anyone out there remembers the New Hampshire hoax. That's the conventional wisdom. But, y'know, he didn't survive to see his new acceptance in the field. Literary success doesn't do you much good if you're dead, right?

Look at it this way. Harry always said that the UFOs were coming back to get him. And he was right. The flying saucers got him in the end.

WATERSPIDER

Philip K. Dick

Philip K. Dick was one of our most respected authors during his lifetime, and one of our most revered since his tragic death. In addition to such off-the-wall novels as Ubik *and* Do Androids Dream of Electric Sheep?, *he also wrote more than his share of disconcerting short stories. Like the one in which his fellow science fiction writer Poul Anderson, who has solved scientific problems galore in his own fiction, is called upon to do so in Dick's universe . . .*

I

THAT MORNING, AS he carefully shaved his head until it glistened, Aaron Tozzo pondered a vision too unfortunate to be endured. He saw in his mind fifteen convicts from Nachbaren Slager, each man only one inch high, in a ship the size of a child's balloon. The ship, traveling at almost the speed of light, continued on forever, with the men aboard neither knowing nor caring what became of them.

The worst part of the vision was just that in all probability it was true.

He dried his head, rubbed oil into his skin, then touched the button within his throat. When contact with the Bureau switchboard had been established, Tozzo said, "I admit we can do nothing to get those fifteen men back, but at least we can refuse to send any more."

His comment, recorded by the switchboard, was passed on to his co-workers. They all agreed; he listened to their voices chiming in as he put on his smock, slippers and overcoat. Obviously, the flight had been an error; even the public knew that now. But—

"But we're going on," Edwin Fermeti, Tozzo's superior, said above the clamor. "We've already got the volunteers."

"Also from Nachbaren Slager?" Tozzo asked. Naturally the prisoners there would volunteer; their lifespan at the camp was no more than five or six years. And if this flight to Proxima were successful, the men aboard would obtain their freedom. They would not have to return to any of the five inhabited planets within the Sol System.

"Where does it matter where they originate?" Fermeti said smoothly.

Tozzo said, "Our effort should be directed toward improving the U.S. Department of Penology, instead of trying to reach other stars." He had a sudden urge to resign his position with the Emigration Bureau and go into politics as a reform candidate.

Later, as he sat at the breakfast table, his wife patted him sympathetically on the arm. "Aaron, you haven't been able to solve it yet, have you?"

"No," he admitted shortly. "And now I don't even care." He did not tell her about the other ship loads of convicts which had fruitlessly been expended; it was forbidden to discuss that with anyone not employed by a department of the government.

"Could they be re-entering on their own?"

"No. Because mass was lost here, in the Sol System. To re-enter they have to obtain equal mass back, to replace it. That's the whole point." Exasperated, he sipped his tea and ignored her. Women, he thought. Attractive but not bright. "They need mass back," he repeated. "Which would be fine if they were making a round trip, I suppose. But this is an attempt to colonize, it's not a guided tour that returns to its point of origin."

"How long does it take them to reach Proxima?" Leonore asked. "All reduced like that, to an inch high."

"About four years."

Her eyes grew large. "That's marvelous."

Grumbling at her, Tozzo pushed his chair back from the

table and rose. I wish they'd take her, he said to himself, since she imagines it's so marvelous. But Leonore would be too smart to volunteer.

Leonore said softly, "Then I was right. The Bureau *has* sent people. You as much as admitted it just now."

Flushing, Tozzo said, "Don't tell anybody; none of your female friends especially. Or it's my job." He glared at her.

On that hostile note, he set off for the Bureau.

As Tozzo unlocked his office door, Edwin Fermeti hailed him. "You think Donald Nils is somewhere on a planet circling Proxima at this very moment?" Nils was a notorious murderer who had volunteered for one of the Bureau's flights. "I wonder—maybe he's carrying around a lump of sugar five times his size."

"Not really very funny," Tozzo said.

Fermeti shrugged. "Just hoping to relieve the pessimism. I think we're all getting discouraged." He followed Tozzo into his office. "Maybe we should volunteer ourselves for the next flight." It sounded almost as if he meant it, and Tozzo glanced quickly at him. "Joke," Fermeti said.

"One more flight," Tozzo said, "and if it fails, I resign."

"I'll tell you something," Fermeti said. "We have a new tack." Now Tozzo's co-worker Craig Gilly had come sauntering up. To the two men, Fermeti said, "We're going to try using pre-cogs in obtaining our formula for re-entry." His eyes flickered as he saw their reaction.

Astonished, Gilly said, "But all the pre-cogs are dead. Destroyed by Presidential order twenty years ago."

Tozzo, impressed, said, "He's going to dip back into the past to obtain a pre-cog. Isn't that right, Fermeti?"

"We will, yes," his superior said, nodding. "Back to the golden age of pre-cognition. The twentieth century."

For a moment Tozzo was puzzled. And then he remembered.

During the first half of the twentieth century so many precogs—people with the ability to read the future—had come into existence that an organized guild had been formed with branches in Los Angeles, New York, San Francisco and Pennsylvania. This group of pre-cogs, all knowing one an-

other, had put out a number of periodicals which had flourished for several decades. Boldly and openly, the members
of the pre-cog guild had proclaimed in their writings their
knowledge of the future. And yet—as a whole, their society
had paid little attention to them.

Tozzo said slowly, "Let me get this straight. You mean
you're going to make use of the Department of Archaeology's time-dredges to scoop up a famous pre-cog of the past?"

Nodding, Fermeti said, "And bring him here to help us,
yes."

"But now can he help us? He would have no knowledge
of our future, only of his own."

Fermeti said, "The Library of Congress has already given
us access to its virtually complete collection of pre-cog journals of the twentieth century." He smiled crookedly at Tozzo
and Gilly, obviously enjoying the situation. "It's my hope—
and my expectation—that among this great body of writings
we will find an article *specifically dealing with our re-entry
problem*. The chances, statistically speaking, are quite good
. . . they wrote about innumerable topics of future civiliza-
tion, as you know."

After a pause, Gilly said, "Very clever. I think your idea
may solve our problem. Speed-of-light travel to other star
systems may yet become a possibility."

Sourly, Tozzo said, "Hopefully, before we run out of convicts." But he, too, liked his superior's idea. And, in addition, he looked forward to seeing face to face one of the
famous twentieth century pre-cogs. Theirs had been one brief,
glorious period—sadly, long since ended.

Or not so brief, if one dated it as starting with Jonathan
Swift, rather than with H.G. Wells. Swift had written of the
two moons of Mars and their unusual orbital characteristics
years before telescopes had proved their existence. And so
today there was a tendency in the textbooks to include him.

II

It took the computers at the Library of Congress only a
short while to scan the brittle, yellowed volumes, article by
article, and to select the sole contribution dealing with dep-

rivation of mass and restoration as the modus operandi of interstellar space travel. Einstein's formula that as an object increased its velocity its mass increased proportionally had been so fully accepted, so completely unquestioned, that no one in the twentieth century had paid any attention to the particular article, which had been put in print in August of 1955 in a pre-cog journal called *If.*

In Fermeti's office, Tozzo sat beside his superior as the two of them pored over the photographic reproduction of the journal. The article was titled *Night Flight,* and it ran only a few thousand words. Both men read it avidly, neither speaking until they had finished.

"Well?" Fermeti said, when they had come to the end.

Tozzo said, "No doubt of it. That's our Project, all right. A lot is garbled; for instance he calls the Emigration Bureau 'Outward, Incorporated,' and believes it to be a private commercial firm." He referred to the text. "It's really uncanny, though. You're obviously this character, Edmond Fletcher; the names are similar but still a little off, as is everything else. And I'm Alison Torelli." He shook his head admiringly. "Those pre-cogs . . . having a mental image of the future that was always askew and yet in the main—"

"In the main correct," Fermeti finished. "Yes, I agree. This *Night Flight* article definitely deals with us and the Bureau's Project . . . herein called *Waterspider,* because it has to be done in one great leap. Good lord, that would have been a perfect name, had we thought of it. Maybe we can still call it that."

Tozzo said slowly, "But the pre-cog who wrote *Night Flight* . . . in no place does he actually give the formula for mass-restoration or even for mass-deprivation. He just simply says that 'we have it.' " Taking the reproduction of the journal, he read aloud from the article:

Difficulty in restoring mass to the ship and its passengers at the termination of the flight had proved a stumbling block for Torelli and his team of researchers and yet they had at last proved successful. After the fateful implosion of the *Sea Scout,* the initial ship to—

"And that's all," Tozzo said. "So what good does it do us? Yes, this pre-cog experienced our present situation a hundred years ago—*but he left out the technical details."*

There was silence.

At last Fermeti said thoughtfully, "That doesn't mean he didn't *know* the technical data. We know today that the others in his guild were very often trained scientists." He examined the biographical report. "Yes, while not actually using his pre-cog ability he worked as a chicken-fat analyst for the University of California."

"Do you still intend to use the time-dredge to bring him up to the present?"

Fermeti nodded. "I only wish the dredge worked both ways. If it could be used with the future, not the past, we could avoid having to jeopardize the safety of this pre-cog—" He glanced down at the article. "This Poul Anderson."

Chilled, Tozzo said, "What hazard is there?"

"We may not be able to return him to his own time. Or—" Fermeti paused. "We might lose part of him along the way, wind up with only half of him. The dredge has bisected many objects before."

"And this man isn't a convict at Nachbaren Slager," Tozzo said. "So you don't have that rationale to fall back on."

Fermeti said suddenly, "We'll do it properly. We'll reduce the jeopardy by sending a team of men back to that time, back to 1954. They can apprehend this Poul Anderson and see that *all of him* gets into the time-dredge, not merely the top half or the left side."

So it had been decided. The Department of Archaeology's time-dredge would go back to the world of 1954 and pick up the pre-cog Poul Anderson; there was nothing further to discuss.

Research conducted by the U.S. Department of Archaeology showed that in September of 1954 Poul Anderson had been living in Berkeley, California, on Grove Street. In that month he had attended a top-level meeting of pre-cogs from all over the United States at the Sir Francis Drake Hotel in San Francisco. It was probable that there, in that meeting, basic policy for the next year had been worked out, with Anderson, and other experts, participating.

"It's really very simple," Fermeti explained to Tozzo and Gilly. "A pair of men will go back. They will be provided with forged identification, showing them to be part of the nation-wide pre-cog organization . . . squares of cellophane-enclosed paper which are pinned to the coat lapel. Naturally, they will be wearing twentieth-century garments. They will locate Poul Anderson, single him out and draw him off to one side."

"And tell him what?" Tozzo said skeptically.

"That they represent an unlicensed amateur pre-cog organization in Battlecreek, Michigan, and that they have constructed an amusing vehicle built to resemble a time-travel dredge of the future. They will ask Mr. Anderson, who was actually quite famous in his time, to pose by their humbug dredge, and then they will ask for a shot of him within. Our research shows that according to his contemporaries, Anderson was mild and easy-going and also that at these yearly top-strategy assemblies he often became convivial enough to enter into the mood of optimism generated by his fellow pre-cogs."

Tozzo said, "You mean he sniffed what they called 'airplane dope?' He was a 'glue-sniffer?' "

With a faint smile, Fermeti said, "Hardly. That was a mania among adolescents and did not become widespread in fact until a decade later. No, I am speaking about imbibing alcohol."

"I see," Tozzo said, nodding.

Fermeti continued, "In the area of difficulties, we must cope with the fact that at this top-secret session, Anderson brought along his wife Karen, dressed as a Maid of Venus in gleaming breast-cups, short skirt and helmet, and that he also brought their new-born daughter Astrid. Anderson himself did not wear any disguise for purposes of concealing his identity. He had no anxieties, being a quite stable person, as were most twentieth century pre-cogs.

"However, during the discussion periods between formal sessions, the pre-cogs, minus their wives, circulated about, playing poker, and arguing, some of them it is said stoning one another—"

"Stoning?"

"Or, as it was put, becoming stoned. In any case, they gathered in small groups in the antechambers of the hotel, and it is at such an occasion that we expect to nab him. In the general hubbub his disappearance would not be noted. We would expect to return him to that exact time, or at least no more than a few hours later or earlier . . . preferably not earlier because *two* Poul Andersons at the meeting might prove awkward."

Tozzo, impressed, said, "Sounds foolproof."

"I'm glad you like it," Fermeti said tartly, "because you will be one of the team sent."

Pleased, Tozzo said, "Then I had better get started learning the details of life in the mid-twentieth century." He picked up another issue of *If*. This one, May of 1971, had interested him as soon as he had seen it. Of course, this issue would not be known yet to the people of 1954 . . . but eventually they would see it. And once having seen it they would never forget it . . .

Ray Bradbury's first textbook to be serialized, he realized as he examined the journal. *The Fisher of Men*, it was called, and in it the great Los Angeles pre-cog had anticipated the ghastly Gutmanist political revolution which was to sweep the inner planets. Bradbury had warned against Gutman, but the warning had gone—of course—unheeded. Now Gutman was dead and the fanatical supporters had dwindled to the status of random terrorists. But had the world listened to Bradbury—

"Why the frown?" Fermeti asked him. "Don't you want to go?"

"Yes," Tozzo said thoughtfully. "But it's a terrible responsibility. These are no ordinary men."

"That is certainly the truth," Fermeti said, nodding.

III

Twenty-four hours later, Aaron Tozzo stood surveying himself in his mid-twentieth century clothing and wondering if Anderson would be deceived, if he actually could be duped into entering the dredge.

The costume certainly was perfection itself. Tozzo had even been equipped with the customary waist-length beard and handlebar mustache so popular circa 1950 in the United States. And he wore a wig.

Wigs, as everyone knew, had at that time swept the United States as the fashion note par excellence; men and women both had worn huge powdered perukes of bright colors, reds and greens and blues and of course dignified grays. It was one of the most amusing occurrences of the twentieth century.

Tozzo's wig, a bright red, pleased him. Authentic, it had come from the Los Angeles Museum of Cultural History, and the curator had vouched for it being a man's, not a woman's. So the fewest possible chances of detection were being taken. Little risk existed that they would be detected as members of another, future culture entirely.

And yet Tozzo was still uneasy.

However, the plan had been arranged; now it was time to go. With Gilly, the other member selected, Tozzo entered the time-dredge and seated himself at the controls. The Department of Archaeology had provided a full instruction manual, which lay open before him. As soon as Gilly had locked the hatch, Tozzo took the bull by the horns (a twentieth century expression) and started up the dredge.

Dials registered. They were spinning backward into time, back to 1954 and the San Francisco Pre-cog Congress.

Beside him, Gilly practiced mid-twentieth century phrases from a reference volume. "Diz muz be da blace . . ." Gilly cleared his throat. "Kilroy was here," he murmured. "Wha' hoppen? Like man, let's cut out; this ball's a drag." He shook his head. "I can't grasp the exact sense of these phrases," he apologized to Tozzo. "Twenty-three skidoo."

Now a red light glowed; the dredge was about to conclude its journey. A moment later its turbines halted.

They had come to rest on the sidewalk outside the Sir Francis Drake Hotel in downtown San Francisco.

On all sides, people in quaint archaic costumes dragged along on foot. And, Tozzo saw, there were no monorails; all the visible traffic was surface-bound. What a congestion, he thought, as he watched the automobiles and buses moving inch by inch along the packed streets. An official in blue waved traffic ahead as best he could, but the entire enterprise, Tozzo could see, was an abysmal failure.

"Time for phase two," Gilly said. But he, too, was gaping at the stalled surface vehicles. "Good grief," he said, "look at the incredibly short skirts of the women; why, the knees are virtually exposed. Why don't the women die of whisk virus?"

"I don't know," Tozzo said, "but I do know we've got to get into the Sir Francis Drake Hotel."

Carefully, they opened the port of the time-dredge and stepped out. And then Tozzo realized something. There had been an error. Already.

The men of this decade were clean-shaven.

"Gilly," he said rapidly, "we've got to shed our beards and mustaches." In an instant he had pulled Gilly's off, leaving his bare face exposed. But the wig; that was correct. All the men visible wore headdress of some type; Tozzo saw few if any bald men. The women, too had luxurious wigs . . . or were they wigs? Could they perhaps be *natural* hair?

In any case, both he and Gilly now would pass. Into the Sir Francis Drake, he said to himself, leading Gilly along.

They darted lithely across the sidewalk—it was amazing how slowly the people of this time-period walked—and into the inexpressibly old-fashioned lobby of the hotel. Like a museum, Tozzo thought as he glanced about him. I wish we could linger . . . but they could not.

"How's our identification?" Gilly said nervously. "Is it passing inspection?" The business with the face-hair had upset him.

On each of their lapels they carried the expertly made false identification. It worked. Presently they found themselves ascending by a lift, or rather elevator, to the correct floor.

The elevator let them off in a crowded foyer. Men, all clean-shaven, with wigs or natural hair, stood in small clusters everywhere, laughing and talking. And a number of attractive women, some of them in garments called leotards, which were skin-tight, loitered about smilingly. Even though the styles of the times required their breasts to be covered, they were a sight to see.

Sotto voce, Gilly said, "I am stunned. In this room are some of the—"

"I know," Tozzo murmured. Their Project could wait, at least a little while. Here was an unbelievably golden opportunity to see these pre-cogs, actually talk to them and listen to them . . .

Here came a tall, handsome man in a dark suit that sparkled with tiny specks of some unnatural material, some variety of synthetic. The man wore glasses and his hair, everything about him, had a tanned, dark look. The name on his identification. Tozzo peered.

The tall, good-looking man was A. E. Van Vogt.

"Say," another individual, perhaps a pre-cog enthusiast, was saying to Van Vogt, stopping him. "I read both versions of your *World of Null A* and I still didn't quite get that about it being *him;* you know, at the end. Could you explain that part to me? And also when they started into the tree and then just—"

Van Vogt halted. A soft smile appeared on his face and he said, "Well, I'll tell you a secret. I start out with a plot and then the plot sort of folds up. So then I have to have another plot to finish the rest of the story."

Going over to listen, Tozzo felt something magnetic about Van Vogt. He was so tall, so spiritual. Yes, Tozzo said to himself; that was the word, a healing spirituality. There was a quality of innate goodness which emanated from him.

All at once Van Vogt said, "There goes a man with my pants." And, without a further word to the enthusiast, stalked off and disappeared into the crowd.

Tozzo's head swam. To actually have seen and heard A. E. Van Vogt—

"Look," Gilly was saying, plucking at his sleeve. "That enormous, genial-looking man seated over there; that's Howard Browne, who edited the pre-cog journal *Amazing* at this time-period."

"I have to catch a plane," Howard Browne was saying to

anyone who would listen to him. He glanced about him in
worried anxiety, despite his almost physical geniality.

"I wonder," Gilly said, "if Doctor Asimov is here?"

We can ask, Tozzo decided. He made his way over to one
of the young women wearing a blonde wig and green leotards. "Where Is Doctor Asimov?" he asked clearly in the
argot of the times.

"Who's to know?" the girl said.

"Is he here, miss?"

"Naw," the girl said.

Gilly again plucked at Tozzo's sleeve. "We must find
Poul Anderson, remember? Enjoyable as it is to talk to this
girl—"

"I'm inquiring about Asimov," Tozzo said brusquely.
"After all, Isaac Asimov had been founder of the entire
twenty-first century positronic robot industry. How could he
not be here?"

A burly outdoorish man strode by them, and Tozzo saw
that this was Jack Vance. Vance, he decided, looked more
like a big game hunter than anything else . . . we must beware of him, Tozzo decided. If we got into any altercation
Vance could take care of us easily.

He noticed now that Gilly was talking to the blonde-wigged
girl in the green leotards. "Murray Leinster?" Gilly was asking. "The man whose paper on parallel time is still at the
very forefront of theoretical studies; isn't he—"

"I dunno," the girl said, in a bored tone of voice.

A group had gathered about a figure opposite them, the
central person whom everybody was listening to was saying,
". . . all right, if like Howard Browne you prefer air travel,
fine. But I say it's risky. I don't fly. In fact even riding in a
car is dangerous. I generally lie down in the back. The man
wore a short-cropped wig and a bow tie; he had a round,
pleasant face but his eyes were intense.

It was Ray Bradbury, and Tozzo started toward him at once.

"Stop!" Gilly whispered angrily. "Remember what we
came for."

And, past Bradbury, seated at the bar, Tozzo saw an older,
care-weathered man in a brown suit wearing small glasses

and sipping a drink. He recognized the man from drawings in early Gernsback publications; it was the fabulously unique pre-cog from the New Mexico region, Jack Williamson.

"I thought *Legion of Time* was the finest novel-length science-fiction work I ever read," an individual, evidently another pre-cog enthusiast, was saying to Jack Williamson, and Williamson was nodding in pleasure.

"That was originally going to be a short story," Williamson said. "But it grew. Yes, I liked that one, too."

Meanwhile Gilly had wandered on, into an adjoining room. He found at a table, two women and a man in deep conversation. One of the women, dark-haired and handsome, with bare shoulders, was—according to her identification plate— Evelyn Paige. The taller women he discovered was the renowned Margaret St. Clair, and Gilly at once said:

"Mrs. St. Clair, your article entitled *The Scarlet Hexapod* in the September 1959 *If* was one of the finest—" And then he broke off.

Because Margaret St. Clair had not written that yet. Knew in fact nothing about it. Flushing with nervousness, Gilly backed away.

"Sorry," he murmured. "Excuse me, I became confused."

Raising an eyebrow, Margaret St. Clair said, "In the September 1959 issue, you say? What are you, a man from the future?"

"Droll," Evelyn Paige said, "but let's continue." She gave Gilly a hard stare from her black eyes. "Now Bob, as I understand what you're saying—" She addressed the man opposite her, and Gilly saw now to his delight that the dire-looking cadaverous individual was none other than Robert Bloch.

Gilly said, "Mr. Bloch, your article in *Galaxy, Sabbatical,* was—"

"You've got the wrong person, my friend," Robert Bloch said. "I never wrote any piece entitled *Sabbatical.*"

Good lord, Gilly realized. I did it again; *Sabbatical* is another work which has not been written yet. I had better get away from here.

He moved back toward Tozzo . . . and found him standing rigidly.

Tozzo said, "I've found Anderson."

At once, Gilly turned, also rigid.

Both of them had carefully studied the pictures provided by the Library of Congress. There stood the famous pre-cog, tall and slender and straight, even a trifle thin, with curly hair—or wig—and glasses, a warm glint of friendliness in his eyes. He held a whiskey glass in one hand, and he was discoursing with several other pre-cogs. Obviously he was enjoying himself.

"Um, uhh, let's see," Anderson was saying, as Tozzo and Gilly came quietly up to join the group. "Pardon?" Anderson cupped his ear to catch what one of the other pre-cogs was saying. "Oh, uh, yup, that's right." Anderson nodded. "Yup, Tony, uh, I agree with you one hundred per cent."

The other pre-cog, Tozzo realized, was the superb Tony Boucher, whose pre-cognition of the religious revival of the next century had been almost supernatural. The word-by-word description of the Miracle in the Cave involving the robot . . . Tozzo gazed at Boucher with awe, and then he turned back to Anderson.

"Poul," another pre-cog said. "I'll tell you how the Italians intended to get the British to leave if they did invade in 1943. The British would stay at hotels, the best, naturally. The Italians would overcharge them."

"Oh, yes, yes," Anderson said, nodding and smiling, his eyes twinkling. "And the British, being gentlemen, would say nothing—"

"But they'd leave the next day," the other pre-cog finished, and all in the group laughed, except for Gilly and Tozzo.

"Mr. Anderson," Tozzo said tensely, "we're from an amateur pre-cog organization at Battlecreek, Michigan and we would like to photograph you beside our model of a time-dredge."

"Pardon?" Anderson said, cupping his ear.

Tozzo repeated what he had said, trying to be audible above the background racket. At last Anderson seemed to understand.

"Oh, um, well, where is it?" Anderson asked obligingly.

"Downstairs on the sidewalk," Gilly said. "It was too heavy to bring up."

"Well, uh, if it won't take too awfully long," Anderson said, "which I doubt it will." He excused himself from the group and followed after them as they started toward the elevator.

"It's steam-engine building time," a heavy-set man called to them as they passed. "Time to build steam engines, Poul."

"We're going downstairs," Tozzo said nervously.

"Walk downstairs on your heads," the pre-cog said. He waved good-by goodnaturedly, as the elevator came and the three of them entered it.

"Kris is jolly today," Anderson said.

"And how," Gilly said, using one of his phrases.

"Is Bob Heinlein here?" Anderson asked Tozzo as they descended. "I understand he and Mildred Clingerman went off somewhere to talk about cats and nobody has seen them come back."

"That's the way the ball bounces," Gilly said, trying out another twentieth century phrase.

Anderson cupped his ear, smiled hesitantly, but said nothing.

At last, they emerged on the sidewalk. At the sight of their time-dredge, Anderson blinked in astonishment.

"I'll be gosh darned," he said, approaching it. "That's certainly imposing. Sure, I'd, uh, be happy to pose beside it." He drew his lean angular body erect, smiling that warm, almost tender smile that Tozzo had noticed before. "Uh, how's this?" Anderson inquired, a little timidly.

With an authentic twentieth century camera taken from the Smithsonian, Gilly snapped a picture. "Now inside," he requested, and glanced at Tozzo.

"Why, uh, certainly," Poul Anderson said, and stepped up the stairs and into the dredge. "Gosh, Karen would, uh, like this," he said as he disappeared inside. "I wish to heck she'd come along."

Tozzo followed swiftly. Gilly slammed the hatch shut, and, at the control board, Tozzo with the instruction manual in hand punched buttons.

The turbines hummed, but Anderson did not seem to hear them; he was engrossed in staring at the controls, his eyes wide.

"Gosh," he said.

The time-dredge passed back to the present, with Anderson still lost in his scrutiny of the controls.

IV

Fermeti met them. "Mr. Anderson," he said, "this is an incredible honor." He held out his hand, but now Anderson was peering through the open hatch past him, at the city beyond; he did not notice the offered hand.

"Say," Anderson said, his face twitching. "Um, what's, uh, this?"

He was staring at the monorail system primarily, Tozzo decided. And this was odd, because at least in Seattle there had been monorails back in Anderson's time . . . or had there been? Had that come later? In any case, Anderson now wore a massively perplexed expression.

"Individual cars," Tozzo said, standing close beside him. "Your monorails had only group cars. Later on, after your time, it was made possible for each citizen's house to have a monorail outlet; the individual brought his car out of its garage and onto the rail-terminal, from which point he joined the collective structure. Do you see?"

But Anderson remained perplexed; his expression in fact had deepened.

"Um," he said, "what do you mean 'my time'? Am I dead?" He looked morose now. "I thought it would be more along the lines of Valhalla, with Vikings and such. Not futuristic."

"You're not dead, Mr. Anderson," Fermeti said. "What you're facing is the culture-syndrome of the mid twenty-first century. I must tell you, sir, that you've been napped. But you will be returned; I give you both my personal and official word."

Anderson's jaw dropped, but he said nothing; he continued to stare.

* * *

Donald Nils, notorious murderer, sat at the single table in the reference room of the Emigration Bureau's interstellar speed-of-light ship and computed that he was, in Earth figures, an inch high. Bitterly, he cursed. "It's cruel and unusual punishment," he grated aloud. "It's against the Constitution." And then he remembered that he had volunteered, in order to get out of Nachbaren Slager. That goddamn hole, he said to himself. Anyhow, I'm out of there.

And, he said to himself, even if I'm only an inch high I've still made myself captain of this lousy ship, and if it ever gets to Proxima I'll be captain of the entire lousy Proxima System. I didn't study with Gutman himself for nothing. And if that don't beat Nachbaren Slager, I don't know what does . . .

His second-in-command, Pete Bailly, stuck his head into the reference room. "Hey, Nils, I have been looking over the micro-repro of this particular old pre-cog journal *Astounding* like you told me, this Venus Equilateral article about matter transmission, and I mean even though I was the top vid repairman in New York City that don't mean I can build one of *these* things." He glared at Nils. "That's asking a lot."

Nils said tightly, "We've got to get back to Earth."

"You're out of luck," Bailly told him. "Better settle for Prox."

Furiously, Nils swept the micro-reproductions from the table, onto the floor of the ship. "That damn Bureau of Emigration! They tricked us!"

Bailly shrugged. "Anyhow we got plenty to eat and a good reference library and 3-D movies every night."

"By the time we get to Prox," Nils snarled, "we'll have seen every movie—" He calculated. "Two thousand times."

"Well, then don't watch. Or we can run them backwards. How's your research coming?"

"I got going the micro of an article in *Space Science Fiction*," Nils said thoughtfully, "called *The Variable Man*. It tells about faster-than-light transmission. You disappear and then reappear. Some guy named Cole is going to perfect it, according to the old-time pre-cog who wrote it." He brooded about that. "If we could build a faster-than-light ship we could return to Earth. We could take over."

"That's crazy talk," Bailly said.

Nils regarded him. "I'm in command."

"Then," Bailly said, "we got a nut in command. There's no returning to Terra; we better build our lives on Proxima's planets and forget forever about our home. Thank God we got women aboard. My God, even if we did get back . . . what could one-inch high people accomplish? We'd be jeered at."

"Nobody jeers at me," Nils said quietly.

But he knew Bailly was right. They'd be lucky if they could research the micros of the old pre-cog journals in the ship's reference room and develop for themselves a way of landing safely on Proxima's planets . . . even *that* was asking a lot.

We'll succeed, Nils said to himself. As long as everyone obeys me, does exactly as I tell them, with no dumb questions.

Bending, he activated the spool of the December 1962 *If*. There was an article in it that particularly interested him . . . and he had four years ahead of him in which to read, understand, and finally apply it.

Fermeti said, "Surely your pre-cog ability helped prepare you for this, Mr. Anderson." His voice faltered with nervous strain, despite his efforts to control it.

"How about taking me back now?" Anderson said. He sounded almost calm.

Fermeti, after shooting a swift glance at Tozzo and Gilly, said to Anderson, "We have a technical problem, you see. That's why we brought here to our own time-continuum. You see—"

"I think you had better, um, take me back," Anderson broke in. "Karen'll get worried." He craned his neck, peering in all directions. "I knew it would be somewhat on this order," he murmured. His face twitched. "Not too different from what I expected . . . what's that tall thing over there? Looks like what the old blimps used to catch onto."

"That," Tozzo said, "is a prayer tower."

"Our problem," Fermeti said patiently, "is dealt with in your article *Night Flight* in the August 1955 *If*. We've been able to deprive an interstellar vehicle of its mass, but so far restoration of mass has—"

"Uh, oh, yes," Anderson said, in a preoccupied way. "I'm working on that yarn right now. Should have that off to Scott in another couple of weeks." He explained, "My agent."

Fermeti considered a moment and then said, "Can you give us the formula for mass-restoration, Mr. Anderson?"

"Um," Poul Anderson said slowly, "Yes, I guess that would be the correct term. Mass-restoration . . . I could go along with that." He nodded. "I haven't worked out any formula; I didn't want to make the yarn too technical. I guess I could make one up, if that's what they wanted." He was silent, then, apparently having withdrawn into a world of his own; the three men waited, but Anderson said nothing more.

"Your pre-cog ability," Fermeti said.

"Pardon?" Anderson said, cupping his ear. "Pre-cog?" He smiled shyly. "Oh, uh, I wouldn't go so far as to say that. I know John believes in all that, but I can't say as I consider a few experiments at Duke University as proof."

Fermeti stared at Anderson a long time. "Take the first article in the January 1953 *Galaxy*," he said quietly. *"The Defenders* . . . about the people living beneath the surface and the robots up above, pretending to fight the war but actually not, actually faking the reports so interestingly that the people—"

"I read that," Poul Anderson agreed. "Very good, I thought, except for the ending. I didn't care too much for the ending."

Fermeti said, "You understand, don't you, that those exact conditions came to pass in 1996, during World War Three? That by means of the article we were able to penetrate the deception carried on by our surface robots? That virtually every word of that article was exactly prophetic—"

"Phil Dick wrote that," Anderson said. *"The Defenders."*

"Do you know him?" Tozzo inquired.

"Met him yesterday at the Convention," Anderson said. "For the first time. Very nervous fellow, was almost afraid to come in."

Fermeti said, "Am I to understand that *none of you are aware that you are pre-cogs?"* His voice shook, completely out of control now.

* * *

"Well," Anderson said slowly, "some sf writers believe in it. I think Alf Van Vogt does." He smiled at Fermeti.

"But don't you understand?" Fermeti demanded. "You described *us* in an article—you accurately described our Bureau and its interstellar Project!"

After a pause, Anderson murmured, "Gosh, I'll be darned. No, I didn't know that. Um, thanks a lot for telling me."

Turning to Tozzo, Fermeti said, "Obviously we'll have to recast our entire concept of the mid-twentieth century." He looked weary.

Tozzo said, "For our purposes their ignorance doesn't matter. Because the pre-cognitive ability was there anyhow, whether they recognized it or not." That, to him, was perfectly clear.

Anderson, meanwhile, had wandered off a little and stood now inspecting the display window of a nearby gift store. "Interesting bric-a-brac in there. I ought to pick up something for Karen while I'm here. Would it be all right—" He turned questioningly to Fermeti. "Could I step in there for a moment and look around?"

"Yes, yes," Fermeti said irritably.

Poul Anderson disappeared inside the gift shop, leaving the three of them to argue the meaning of their discovery.

"What we've got to do," Fermeti said, "is sit him down in the situation familiar to him: *before a typewriter.* We must persuade him to compose an article on deprivation of mass and its subsequent restoration. Whether he himself takes the article to be factual or not has no bearing; it still will be. The Smithsonian must have a workable twentieth century typewriter and 8½ by 11 white sheets of paper. Do you agree?"

Tozzo, meditating, said, "I'll tell you what I think. It was a cardinal error to permit him to go into that gift shop."

"Why is that?" Fermeti inquired.

"I see his point," Gilly said excitedly. "We'll never see Anderson again; he's skipped out on us through the pretext of gift-shopping for his wife."

Ashen-faced, Fermeti turned and raced into the gift shop. Tozzo and Gilly followed.

The store was empty. Anderson had eluded them; he was gone.

As he loped silently out the back door of the gift shop, Poul Anderson thought to himself, I don't believe they'll get me. At least not right away.

I've got too much to do while I'm here, he realized. What an opportunity! When I'm an old man I can tell Astrid's children about this.

Thinking of his daughter Astrid reminded him of one very simple fact, however. Eventually he had to go back to 1954. Because of Karen and the baby. No matter what he found here—for him it was temporary.

But meanwhile . . . first I'll go to the library, *any* library, he decided. And get a good look at history books that'll tell me what took place in the intervening years between 1954 and now.

I'd like to know, he said to himself, about the Cold War, how the U.S. and Russia come out. And—space explorations. I'll bet they put a man on Luna by 1975. Certainly, they're exploring space now; heck, they even have a time-dredge so they must have *that*.

Ahead Poul Anderson saw a doorway. It was open and without hesitation he plunged into it. Another shop of some kind, but this one larger than the gift shop.

"Yes sir," a voice said, and a bald-headed man—they all seemed to be bald-headed here—approached him. The man glanced at Anderson's hair, his clothes . . . however the clerk was polite; he made no comment. "May I help you?" He asked.

"Um," Anderson said, stalling. What did this place sell, anyhow? He glanced around. Gleaming electronic objects of some sort. But what did they do?

The clerk said, "Haven't you been nuzzled lately, sir?"

"What's that?" Anderson said. *Nuzzled?*

"The new spring nuzzlers have arrived, you know," the clerk said, moving toward the gleaming spherical machine nearest him. "Yes," he said to Poul, "you do strike me as very, very faintly introve—no offense meant, sir, I mean, it's legal to be introved." The clerk chuckled. "For instance, your rather odd clothing . . . made it yourself, I take it? I must say, sir, to make your own clothing is highly introve. Did you weave it?'' The clerk grimaced as if tasting something bad.

''No,'' Poul said, ''as a matter of fact, it's my best suit.''

''Heh, heh,'' the clerk said. ''I share the joke, sir; quite witty. But what about your head? You haven't shaved your head in *weeks.*''

''Nope,'' Anderson admitted. ''Well, maybe I do need a nuzzler.'' Evidently everyone in this century had one; like a TV set in his own time, it was a necessity, in order for one to be part of the culture.

''How many in your family?'' the clerk said. Bringing out a measuring tape, he measured the length of Poul's sleeve.

''Three,'' Poul answered, baffled. ''How old is the youngest?''

''Just born,'' Poul said.

The clerk's face lost all its color. ''Get out of here,'' he said quietly. ''Before I call for the polpol.''

''Um, what's that? Pardon?'' Poul said, cupping his ear, and trying to hear, not certain he had understood.

''You're a criminal,'' the clerk mumbled. ''You ought to be in Nachbaren Slager.''

''Well, thanks anyhow,'' Poul said, and backed out of the store, onto the sidewalk; his last glimpse was of the clerk still staring at him.

''Are you a foreigner?'' a voice asked, a woman's voice. At the curb she had halted her vehicle. It looked to Poul like a bed; in fact, he realized, it was a bed. The woman regarded him with astute calm, her eyes dark and intense. Although her glistening shaved head somewhat upset him, he could see that she was attractive.

''I'm from another culture,'' Poul said, finding himself unable to keep his eyes from her figure. Did all the women dress like this here in this society? Bare shoulders, he could understand. But not—

And the bed. The combination of the two was too much for him. What kind of business was she in, anyhow? And in public. What a society this was . . . morals had changed since his own time.

"I'm looking for the library," Poul said, not coming too close to the vehicle which was a bed with motor and wheels, a tiller for steering.

The woman said, "The library is one bight from here."

"Um," Poul said, "what's a 'bight?' "

"Obviously, you're wanging me," the woman said. All visible parts of her flushed a dark red. "It's not funny. Any more than your disgustingly hairy head is. Really, both your wanging and your head are not amusing, at least not to me." And yet she did not go on; she remained where she was, regarding him somberly. "Perhaps you need help," she decided. "Perhaps I should pity you. You know of course that the polpol could pick you up any time they want."

Poul said, "Could I, um, buy you a cup of coffee somewhere and we could talk? I'm really anxious to find the library."

"I'll go with you," the woman agreed. "Although I have no idea what 'coffee' is. If you touch me I'll nilp at once."

"Don't do that," Poul said, "it's unnecessary; all I want to do is look up some historical material." And then it occurred to him that he could make good use of any technical data he could get his hands on.

What one volume might he smuggle back to 1954 which would be of great value? He racked his brains. An almanac. A dictionary . . . a school text on science which surveyed all the fields for laymen; yes, that would do it. A seventh grade text or a high school text. He could rip the covers off, throw them away, put the pages inside his coat.

Poul said, "Where's a school? The closest school." He felt the urgency of it, now. He had no doubt that they were after him, close behind.

"What is a 'school?' " the woman asked.

"Where your children go," Poul said.

The woman said quietly, "You poor sick man."

V

For a time Tozzo and Fermeti and Gilly stood in silence. And then Tozzo said in a carefully controlled voice, "You know what's going to happen to him, of course. Polpol will pick him up and mono-express him to Nachbaren Slager. Because of his appearance. He may even be there already."

Fermeti sprinted at once for the nearest vidphone. "I'm going to contact the authorities at Nachbaren Slager. I'll talk to Potter; we can trust him, I think."

Presently Major Potter's heavy, dark features formed on the vidscreen. "Oh, hello, Fermeti. You want more convicts, do you?" He chuckled. "You use them up even faster than we do."

Behind Potter, Fermeti caught a glimpse of the open recreation area of the giant internment camp. Criminals, both political and nonpol, could be seen roaming about, stretching their legs, some of them playing dull, pointless games which, he knew, went on and on, sometimes for months, each time they were out of their work-cells.

"What we want," Fermeti said, "is to prevent an individual being brought to you at all." He described Poul Anderson. "If he's monoed there, call me at once. And don't harm him. You understand? We want him back safe."

"Sure," Potter said easily. "Just a minute; I'll have a scan put on our new admissions." He touched a button to his right hand and a 315-R computer came on; Fermeti heard its low hum. Potter touched buttons and then said, "This'll pick him out if he's monoed here. Our admissions-circuit is prepared to reject him."

"No sign yet?" Fermeti asked tensely.

"Nope," Potter said, and purposely yawned.

Fermeti broke the connection.

"Now what?" Tozzo said. "We could possibly trace him by means of a Ganymedean sniffer-sponge." They were a repellent life form, though; if one managed to find its quarry it fastened at once to its blood system leech-wise. "Or do it mechanically," he added. "With a detec beam. We have a print of Anderson's EEG pattern, don't we? But that would really bring in the polpol." The detec beam by law belonged only to the polpol; after all, it was the artifact which had, at last, tracked down Gutman himself.

Fermeti said bluntly, "I'm for broadcasting a planet-wide Type II alert. That'll activate the citizenry, the average informer. They'll know there's an automatic reward for any Type II found."

"But he could be manhandled that way," Gilly pointed out. "By a mob. Let's think this through."

After a pause Tozzo said, "How about trying it from a purely cerebral standpoint? If you had been transported from the mid-twentieth century to our continuum, what would you want to do? *Where would you go?*"

Quietly, Fermeti said, "To the nearest spaceport, of course. To buy a ticket to Mars or the outplanets—routine in our age but utterly out of the question at mid-twentieth century."

They looked at one another.

"But Anderson doesn't know where the spaceport is," Gilly said. "It'll take him valuable time to orient himself. We can go there directly by express subsurface mono."

A moment later the three Bureau of Emigration men were on their way.

"A fascinating situation," Gilly said, as they rode along, jiggling up and down, facing one another in the monorail first-class compartment. "We totally misjudged the mid twentieth century mind; it should be a lesson to us. Once we've regained possession of Anderson we should make further inquiries. For instance, the Poltergeist Effect. What was their interpretation of it? And table-tapping—did they recognize it for what it was? Or did they merely consign it to the realm of so-called 'occult' and let it go at that?"

"Anderson may hold the clue to these questions and many others," Fermeti said. "But our central problem remains the same. We must induce him to complete the mass-restoration formula in precise mathematical terms, rather than vague, poetic allusions."

Thoughtfully, Tozzo said, "He's a brilliant man, that Anderson. Look at the ease by which he eluded us."

"Yes," Fermeti agreed. "We mustn't underestimate him. We did that, and it's rebounded." His face was grim.

* * *

Hurrying up the almost-deserted sidestreet, Poul Anderson wondered why the woman had regarded him as sick. And the mention of the children had set off the clerk in the store, too. Was birth illegal now? Or was it regarded as sex had been once, as something too private to speak of in public?

In any case, he realized, if I plan to stay here I've got to shave my head. And, if possible, acquire different clothing.

There must be barbershops. And, he thought, the coins in my pockets; they're probably worth a lot to collectors.

He glanced about, hopefully. But all he saw were tall, luminous plastic and metal buildings which made up the city, structures in which incomprehensible transactions took place. They were as alien to him as—

Alien, he thought, and the word lodged chokingly in his mind. Because—something had oozed from a doorway ahead of him. And now his way was blocked—deliberately, it seemed—by a slime mold, dark yellow in color, as large as a human being, palpitating visibly on the sidewalk. After a pause the slime mold undulated toward him at a regular, slow rate. A human evolutionary development? Poul Anderson wondered, recoiling from it. Good lord . . . and then he realized what he was seeing.

This era had space travel. He was seeing a creature from another planet.

"Um," Poul said, to the enormous mass of slime mold, "can I bother you a second to ask a question?"

The slime mold ceased to undulate forward. And in Poul's brain a thought formed which was not his own. "I catch your query. In answer: I arrived yesterday, from Callisto. But I also catch a number of unusual and highly interesting thoughts in addition . . . you are a time traveler from the past." The tone of the creature's emanations was one of considerate, polite amusement—and interest.

"Yes," Poul said. "From 1954."

"And you wish to find a barbershop, a library and a school. And at once, in the precious time remaining before they capture you." The slime mold seemed solicitous. "What can I do to help you? I could absorb you, but it would be a permanent symbiosis, and you would not like that. You are thinking of your wife and child. Allow me to inform you as to the problem regarding your unfortunate mention of children. Terrans of this period are experiencing a mandatory moratorium on childbirth, because of the almost infinite sporting of the previous decades. There was a war, you see. Between Gutman's fanatical followers and the more liberal legions of General McKinley. The latter won.''

Poul said, ''Where should I go? I'm confused.'' His head throbbed and he felt tired. Too much had happened. Just a short while ago he had been standing with Tony Boucher in the Sir Francis Drake Hotel, drinking and chatting . . . and now this. Facing this great slime mold from Callisto. It was difficult—to say the least—to make such an adjustment.

The slime mold was transmitting to him. ''I am accepted here while you, their ancestor, are regarded as odd. Ironic. To me, you look quite like them, except for your curly brown hair and of course your silly clothing.'' The creature from Callisto pondered. ''My friend, the polpol are the political police, and they search for deviants, followers of the defeated Gutman, who are terrorists now, and hated. Many of these followers are drawn from the potentially criminal classes. That is, the nonconformists, the so-called introves. Individuals who set their own subjective value-system up in place of the objective system in vogue. It is a matter of life and death to the Terrans, since Gutman almost won.''

''I'm going to hide,'' Poul decided.

''But where? You can't really. Not unless you wish to go underground and join the Gutmanites, the criminal class of bomb-throwers . . . and you won't want to do that. Let us stroll together, and if anyone challenges you, I will say you're my servant. You have manual extensors and I have not. And I have, by a quirk, decided to dress you oddly and to have you retain your head-hair. The responsibility then becomes mine. It is actually not unusual for higher out-world organisms to employ Terran help.''

''Thanks,'' Poul said tautly, as the slime mold resumed its slow forward motion along the sidewalk. ''But there are things I want to do—''

''I am on my way to the zoo,'' the slime mold continued.

An unkind thought came to Poul.

"Please," the slime mold said. "Your anachronistic twentieth century humor is not appreciated. I am not an inhabitant
of the zoo, it is for life forms of low mental order such as
Martian glebs and trawns. Since the initiation of interplanetary travel, zoos have become the center of—"

Poul said, "Could you lead me to the space terminal?"
He tried to make his request sound casual.

"You take a dreadful risk," the slime mold said, "in going
to any public place. The polpol watch constantly."

"I still want to go." If he could board an interplanetary
ship, if he could leave Earth, see other worlds—

But they would erase his memory; all at once he realized
that, in a rush of horror. *I've got to make notes*, he told
himself. At once!

"Do, um, you have a pencil?" he asked the slime mold.
"Oh, wait, I have one. Pardon me." Obviously the slime
mold didn't.

On a piece of paper from his coat pocket—it was convention material of some sort—he wrote hurriedly, in brief, dis-
jointed, phrases, what had happened to him, what he had
seen in the twenty-first century. Then he quickly stuck the
paper back in his pocket.

"A wise move," the slime mold said. "And now to the
spaceport, if you will accompany me at my slow pace. And,
as we go, I will give you details of Terra's history from your
period on." The slime mold moved down the sidewalk. Poul
accompanied it eagerly; after all, what choice did he have?
"The Soviet Union. That was tragic. Their war with Red
China in 1983 which finally involved Israel and France . . .
regrettable, but it did solve the problem of what to do with
France—a most difficult nation to deal with in the latter half
of the twentieth century."

On his piece of paper Poul jotted that down, too.

"After France had been defeated—" The slime mold went
on, as Poul scratched against time.

Fermeti said, "We must glin, if we're to catch Anderson
before he boards a ship." And by "glin" he did not mean
glinning a little; he meant a full search with the cooperation
of the polpol. He hated to bring them in, and yet their help

now seemed vital. Too much time had passed and Anderson had not yet been found.

The spaceport lay ahead, a great disk miles in diameter, with no vertical obstructions. In the center was the Burned Spot, seared by years of tail-exhausts from landing and departing ships. Fermeti liked the spaceport, because here the denseness of the close-packed buildings of the city abruptly ceased. Here was *openness*, such as he recalled from childhood . . . if one dared to think openly of childhood.

The terminal building was set hundreds of feet beneath the rexeroid layer built to protect the waiting people in case of an accident above. Fermeti reached the entrance of the descent ramp, then halted impatiently to wait for Tozzo and Gilly to catch up with him.

"I'll nilp," Tozzo said, but without enthusiasm. And he broke the band on his wrist with a single decisive motion.

The polpol ship hovered overhead at once.

"We're from the Emigration Bureau," Fermeti explained to the polpol lieutenant. He outlined their Project, described—reluctantly—their bringing Poul Anderson from his time-period to their own.

"Hair on head," the polpol lieutenant noted. "Quaint duds. Okay, Mr. Fermeti; we'll glin until we find him." He nodded, and his small ship shot off.

"They're efficient," Tozzo admitted.

"But not likeable," Fermeti said, finishing Tozzo's thought.

"They make me uncomfortable," Tozzo agreed. "But I guess they're supposed to."

The three of them stepped onto the descent ramp—and dropped at breathtaking speed to level one below. Fermeti shut his eyes, wincing at the loss of weight. It was almost as bad as takeoff itself. Why did everything have to be so rapid, these days? It certainly was not like the previous decade, when things had gone leisurely.

They stepped from the ramp, shook themselves, and were approached instantly by the building's polpol chief.

"We have a report on your man," the gray-uniformed officer told them.

"He hasn't taken off?" Fermeti said. "Thank God." He looked around.

"Over there," the officer said, pointing.

At a magazine rack, Poul Anderson was looking intently at the display.

It took only a moment for the three Emigration Bureau officials to surround him.

"Oh, uh, hello," Anderson said. "While I was waiting for my ship I thought I'd take a look and see what's still in print."

Fermeti said, "Anderson, we require your unique abilities. I'm sorry, but we're taking you back to the Bureau."

All at once Anderson was gone. Soundlessly, he had ducked away; they saw his tall, angular form become smaller as he raced for the gate to the field proper.

Reluctantly, Fermeti reached within his coat and brought out a sleep-gun. "There's no other choice," he murmured, and squeezed.

The racing figure tumbled, rolled. Fermeti put the sleep-gun away and in a toneless voice said, "He'll recover. A skinned knee, nothing worse." He glanced at Gilly and Tozzo. "Recover at the Bureau, I mean."

Together, the three of them advanced toward the prone figure on the floor of the spaceport waiting room.

"You may return to your own time-continuum," Fermeti said quietly, "when you've given us the mass-restoration formula." He nodded, and a Bureau workman approached, carrying the ancient Royal portable typewriter.

Seated in the chair across from Fermeti in the Bureau's inner business office, Poul Anderson said, "I don't use a portable."

"You must cooperate," Fermeti informed him. "We have the scientific know-how to restore you to Karen; remember Karen and remember your newly-born daughter at the Congress in San Francisco's Sir Francis Drake Hotel. Without full cooperation from you, Anderson, there will be no co-operation from the Bureau. Surely, with your pre-cog ability you can see that."

After a pause Anderson said, "Um, I can't work unless I

have a pot of fresh coffee brewing around me at all times, somewhere.''

Curtly, Fermeti signaled. ''We'll obtain coffee beans for you,'' he declared. ''But the brewing is up to you. We'll also supply a pot from the Smithsonian collection and there our responsibility ends.''

Taking hold of the carriage of the typewriter, Anderson began to inspect it. ''Red and back ribbon,'' he said. ''I always use black. But I guess I can make do.'' He seemed a trifle sullen. Inserting a sheet of paper, he began to type. At the top of the page appeared the words:

NIGHT FLIGHT
—Poul Anderson

''You say *If* bought it?'' he asked Fermeti.

''Yes,'' Fermeti replied tensely.

Anderson typed:

Difficulties at Outward, Incorporated had begun to nettle Edmond Fletcher. For one thing, an entire ship had disappeared, and although the individuals aboard were not personally known to him he felt a twinge of responsibility. Now, as he lathered himself with hormone-impregnated soap

''He starts at the beginning,'' Fermeti said bitingly. ''Well, if there's no alternative we'll simply have to bear with him.'' Musingly, he murmured, ''I wonder how long it takes . . . I wonder how fast he writes. As a pre-cog he can see what's coming next; it should help him to do it in a hurry.'' Or was that just wishful thinking?

''Have the coffee beans arrived yet?'' Anderson asked, glancing up.

''Any time now,'' Fermeti said.

''I hope some of the beans are Colombian,'' Anderson said.

Long before the beans arrived the article was done.

Rising stiffly, uncoiling his lengthy limbs, Poul Anderson said, ''I think you have what you want, there. The mass restoration formula is on typescript page 20.''

Eagerly, Fermeti turned the pages. Yes, there it was; peering over his shoulder, Tozzo saw the paragraph:

If the ship followed a trajectory which would carry it into the star Proxima, it would, he realized, regain its mass through a process of leeching solar energy from the great star-furnace itself. Yes, it was Proxima itself which held the key to Torelli's problem, and now, after all this time, it had been solved. The simple formula revolved in his brain.

And, Tozzo saw, there lay the formula. As the article said, the mass would be regained from solar energy converted into matter, the ultimate source of power in the universe. The answer had stared them in the face all this time.

Their long struggle was over.

"And now," Poul Anderson asked, "I'm free to go back to my own time?"

Fermeti said simply, "Yes."

"Wait," Tozzo said to his superior. "There's evidently something you don't understand." It was a section which he had read in the instruction manual attached to the time-dredge. He drew Fermeti to one side, where Anderson could not hear. "He can't be sent back to his own time with the knowledge he has now."

"What knowledge?" Fermeti inquired.

"That—well. I'm not certain. Something to do with our society, here. What I'm trying to tell you is this: the first rule of time travel, according to the manual, is don't change the past. In this situation just bringing Anderson here has changed the past merely by exposing him to our society."

Pondering, Fermeti said, "You may be correct. While he was in that gift shop he may have picked up some object which, taken back to his own time, might revolutionize their technology."

"Or at the magazine rack at the spaceport," Tozzo said. "Or on his trip between those two points. And—*even the knowledge that he and his colleagues are pre-cogs.*"

"You're right," Fermeti said. "The memory of this trip must be wiped from his brain." He turned and walked slowly

back to Poul Anderson. "Look here," he addressed him.
"I'm sorry to tell you this, but everything that's happened to
you must be wiped from your brain."

After a pause, Anderson said, "That's a shame. Sorry to
hear that." He looked downcast. "But I'm not surprised,"
he murmured. He seemed philosophical about the whole af-
fair. "It's generally handled this way."

Tozzo asked, "Where can this alteration of the memory
cells of his brain be accomplished?"

"At the Department of Penology," Fermeti said.
"Through the same channels we obtained the convicts."
Pointing his sleep-gun at Poul Anderson he said, "Come
along with us. I regret this . . . but it has to be done."

VI

At the Department of Penology, painless electroshock removed from Poul Anderson's brain the precise cells in which
his most recent memories were stored. Then, in a semicon-
scious state, he was carried back into the time-dredge. A
moment later he was on his trip back to the year 1954, to his
own society and time. To the Sir Francis Drake Hotel in
downtown San Francisco, California and his waiting wife and
child.

When the time-dredge returned empty, Tozzo, Gilly and
Fermeti breathed a sigh of relief and broke open a bottle of
hundred-year-old Scotch which Fermeti had been saving. The
mission had been successfully accomplished; now they could
turn their attention back to the Project.

"Where's the manuscript that he wrote?" Fermeti said,
putting down his glass to look all around his office.

There was no manuscript to be found. And, Tozzo noticed,
the antique Royal portable typewriter which they had brought
from the Smithsonian—it was gone, too. But why?

Suddenly chill fear traveled up him. He understood.

"Good lord," he said thickly. He put down his glass.
"Somebody get a copy of the journal with his article in it.
At once."

Fermeti said, "What is it, Aaron? Explain."

"When we removed his memory of what had happened we

made it impossible for him to write the article for the journal," Tozzo said. "He must have based *Night Flight* on his experience with us, here." Snatching up the August 1955 copy of *If* he turned to the table-of-contents page.

No article by Poul Anderson was listed. Instead, on page 78, he saw Philip K. Dick's *The Mold of Yancy* listed instead.

They had changed the past after all. And now the formula for their Project was gone—gone entirely.

"We shouldn't have tampered," Tozzo said in a hoarse voice. "We should never have brought him out of the past." He drank a little more of the century-old Scotch, his hands shaking.

"Brought who?" Gilly said, with a puzzled look.

"Don't you remember?" Tozzo stared at him, incredulous.

"What's this discussion about?" Fermeti said impatiently. "And what are you two doing in my office? You both should be busy at work." He saw the bottle of Scotch and blanched. "How'd that get open?"

His hands trembling, Tozzo turned the pages of the journal over and over again. Already, the memory was growing diffuse in his mind; he struggled in vain to hold onto it. They had brought someone from the past, a pre-cog, wasn't it? But who? A name, still in his mind but dimming with each passing moment . . . Anderson or Anderton, something like that. And in connection with the Bureau's interstellar mass-deprivation Project.

Or was it?

Puzzled, Tozzo shook his head and said in bewilderment, "I have some peculiar words in my mind. *Night Flight*. Do either of you happen to know what it refers to?"

"Night Flight," Fermeti echoed. "No, it means nothing to me. I wonder, though—it certainly would be an effective name for our Project."

"Yes," Gilly agreed. "That must be what it refers to."

"But our Project is called *Waterspider*, isn't it?" Tozzo said. At least he thought it was. He blinked, trying to focus his faculties.

"The truth of the matter," Fermeti said, "is that we've never titled it." Brusquely, he added, "But I agree with you;

that's an even better name for it. *Waterspider.* Yes, I like that.''

The door of the office opened and there stood a uniformed, bonded messenger. ''From the Smithsonian,'' he informed them. ''You requested this.'' He produced a parcel, which he laid on Fermeti's desk.

''I don't remember ordering anything from the Smithsonian,'' Fermeti said. Opening it cautiously he found a can of roasted, ground coffee beans, still vacuum packed, over a century old.

The three men looked at one another blankly.

''Strange,'' Torelli murmured. ''There must be some mistake.''

''Well,'' Fletcher said, ''in any case, back to Project *Waterspider.*''

Nodding, Torelli and Gilman turned in the direction of their own office on the first floor of Outward, Incorporated, the commercial firm at which they worked and the project on which they had labored, with so many heartaches and setbacks, for so long.

At the Science Fiction Convention at the Sir Francis Drake Hotel, Poul Anderson looked around him in bewilderment. Where had he been? Why had he gone out of the building? And it was an hour later; Tony Boucher and Jim Gunn had left for dinner by now, and he saw no sign of his wife Karen and the baby, either.

The last he remembered was two fans from Battlecreek who wanted him to look at a display outside on the sidewalk. Perhaps he had gone to see that. In any case, he had no memory of the interval.

Anderson groped about in his coat pocket for his pipe, hoping to calm his oddly jittery nerves—and found, not his pipe, but instead a folded piece of paper.

''Got anything for our auction, Poul?'' a member of the Convention committee asked, halting beside him. ''The auction is just about to start—we have to hurry.''

Still looking at the paper from his pocket, Poul murmured, ''Um, you mean something here with me?''

''Like a typescript of some published story, the original

manuscript or earlier versions or notes. You know.'' He paused, waiting.

"I seem to have some notes in my pocket,'' Poul said, still glancing over them. They were in his handwriting but he didn't remember having made them. A time-travel story, from the look of them. Must have been from those bourbons and water, he decided, and not enough to eat. "Here,'' he said uncertainly, "it isn't much but I guess you can auction these.'' He took one final glance at them. "Notes for a story about a political figure called Gutman and a kidnapping in time. Intelligent slime mold, too, I notice.'' On impulse, he handed them over.

"Thanks,'' the man said, and hurried on toward the other room, where the auction was being held.

"I bid ten dollars,'' Howard Browne called, smiling broadly. "Then I have to catch a bus to the airport.'' The door closed after him.

Karen, with Astrid, appeared beside Poul. "Want to go into the auction?'' she asked her husband. "Buy an original Finlay?''

"Um, sure,'' Poul Anderson said, and with his wife and child walked slowly after Howard Browne.

HARK! WAS THAT THE
SQUEAL OF
AN ANGRY THOAT?

Avram Davidson

*A martian thoat from Edgar Rice Burroughs's Barsoom,
striding down the streets of Greenwich Village? In a story
that also contains Calvin M. Knox, a pseudonym of the
youthful Robert Silverberg, and Wendall Garrett, who is
most certainly to be confused with Randall Garrett, Silverberg's sometime collaborator? How can this be?*

*It can be because you're about to read a story by
Avram Davidson, writer, editor, Hugo-winner, and one
of the Grand Old Wits of science fiction.*

AT A TIME subsequently I was still living back East, we were
so many of us then Living Back East, and I was still living
on the seventh floor of a seven-floor walk-up in Greenwich
Village. Edward lived down the hall: Fox-fire Edward. Fiduciary Debenture III lived downstairs. Gabriel Courland lived
around the corner in the hay-loft of the Old De Witt Clinton
Livery Stable, a location ideally suited and situate—he said—
to pour boiling oil down upon unwelcome visitors: bill collectors, indignant fathers of daughters, people with Great
Ideas For Stories ("All you got to do is write it down and
we'll split the money, I'd do it myself if I had the time."),
editors with deadlines, men come to turn off the electric-
ity.(the gas) (the water) (the whale-oil)—

"Doesn't it *smell* a little in here, Gabe?" asked Edward.

"It smells a *lot*—but look! Look!" Here he'd point to the neat trap-door through which hay had once been hauled (and maybe smuggled bombazine and who knows what, poled up Minetta Stream, midnights so long long ago). "You can pour boiling *oil* down on people!"

Edward gives me to understand that Gabe never actually *did* pour boiling oil or even *un*boiling oil, down on people; although occasionally, Edward said, G. would allow trickles of water to defoliate the importunate, as who? put it. Someone else.

Fiduciary Debenture III lived downstairs, and across the narrow street dwelt Wendell Garrett, in the parlor of a once-huge apartment deftly cut up and furnished by his Great-aunt Ella, relict of his Great-uncle Pat Garrett, yes! The very same Sheriff Pat Garrett Who; Aunt Ella was in the Canary Islands at the time, teaching (I understand) the two-step to the wives of the Spanish officials, to whom, in that not-exactly-then-in-the-beating-heart-of-things archipelago, it—the two-step—represented Modern Culture, if not Flaming Youth in Revolt, and one of the few (very few) occupations or occasions for which their husbands would let them out of the patio.

"The Moors may have been driven out of Spain," Aunt Ella had said, or, rather, written; "but they haven't been driven out of the Spaniards. For God's sake, Wendell, see to it that Mary Teresa empties the pan under the ice-box."

Mary Teresa was the, so to speak, concièrge, and refused to allow an electric, gas, or even kerosene fridge to be installed in her own kitchen: slightly larger than a commemorative stamp. This devotion to tradition was much appreciated by the sole remaining Iceman in The Village, whose clientèle by that time consisted of several fish markets and a dozen or so other ladies of the same age and model as Mary Teresa; the Iceman was related by ties of spiritual consanguinity to all the prominent mafiosi—a godfather to godfathers, so to speak—and this in turn enabled her to do as she liked and had been accustomed to do, in a manner which would be tolerated in no one else, nowhere else.

Wendell lived rent-free in the former parlor of the house in return for his acting as an Influence upon Mary Teresa and curbing in some few important particulars her turn-of-the-century vigor.

When asked where he lived, he would say, bland as butter, "In a parlor house."

Round the corner in a decayed Federalist Row located behind an equally decayed non-Federalist row (Whig, perhaps, or, as Wendell once suggested, brushing himself, Free Soil), lived the retired Australian sanitary scientist and engineer called Humpty Dumpty. He had indeed once had a lot of cards printed:

Sir Humphrey Dunston
Remittance Man
Privies Done Cheap Retail and to the Trade

But, he had observed, these last phrases had been subject to most gross interpretations by members of one of the Village's non-ethnic minorities; so the only card still in evidence was tacked to his greasy front door. Humpty patronized the Iceman, too, Sangiaccomo Bartoldi, but not for ice: Jockum retained the antique art of needling beer, an alchemy otherwise fallen into desuetude since the repeal of the 18th (or Noble Experiment) Amendment, and which—Humpty Dumpty said—alone could raise American lager to the kick of its Australian counterpart ("Bandicoot's Ballocks," or something like that).

If you stood on what had once been the Widow's Walk atop the only one of the Federalists which still had one, you could toss a rubber ball through the back window of the Death House and into the Muniments Room of Calvin M. Knox. This great granite sarcophagus of a building had once, it was said, carried across the front of it the advice that THE WAGES OF SIN IS DEATH: but only the last of those words remained. Mary Teresa, that repository of local arcane information, sometimes claimed that "The Patriot Boys" had torn off the others to hurl them at the Invalid Corps of the Union Army during what she termed "the Rebellion"—not, indeed, the entire Civil War, but that part of it fought thereabouts and called by others The Draft Riots. Not, of course, by Mary Teresa.

Nor, in fact, did she ever use the name Invalid Corps of the Union Army.

She called them "the Prodissint Bastids."

"I understand that this used to be a House for Fallen Women," Fiduciary Debenture III had once said to Calvin Knox.

"Yes," said C. Knox, gloomily, "and if you're not careful, you're going to fall through the very same place in the floor, too. It quivers when my cat walks across it." It was in consequence of this statutory infirmity of part of the front floor that the back chamber was called the Muniments Room and was heaped high with pulp magazines in neat piles, each bearing some such style and label as (it might be) *Influences of Ned Buntline on Doc Savage,* or *Foreshadowings of Doc Savage in Ned Buntline,* or *Seabury Quinn Type Stories Not Written By Seabury Quinn,* and *J. Sheridan Le Fanu Plot Structures Exemplified in Spicy Detective Stories.*

And, as Mary Teresa so often put it, ecKt, ecKt, ecKt.

"I have reduced," C. Knox said, entirely without boastfulness, "the Basic Short Story to its essential salts."

The last, the very very last of the Hokey Pokey Women practiced in the basement. Edward often patronized her.

Wendell at that time was devoting less time to writing fiction than to his great project of reconciling the Indo-European Exarchate with the Dravidian Rite of the Sanscrit Church (Lapsed Branch) in Exile. Bengali archimandrites in cruciform dhoties and deaconesses in the Proscribed Saffron Sari fluttered round about his doors like exotic butterflies—*could* chrismation be administered in ghee?—*was* the bed of nails a legitimate form of penance?—their collective presence a great perturbation to Mary Teresa, who referred to the entire *kehilla* as Them Gypsies. The only thing which indeed prevented her taking her broom to the lot of them was that a genuine Monsignor of the True Church as recognized by the Police Department had chanced by: whereat the whole ecclesia had knelt as one and collectively kissed his brogans.

"Ah well, nobody is all bad," was her philosophic comment, as she resheathed her besom and, clearing her nasal passages, skillfully swamped a fly in the gutter.

It was to this picturesque scene, as yet unstirred by Beat, Hippy, Freak, Funk, RadLib or LibRad influences (and, indeed, only still faintly tinctured by the froth of the waves which once had beaten ceaselessly upon the Seacoasts of Bohemia) that there came one day clad only in his harness and his sword that strange brave man known, very simply, as John Carter of Mars.

Some few of the readership may have figured out, all by themselves, that Fiduciary Debenture III (who lived downstairs) was not *really* named Fiduciary Debenture III. His *real* name was in fact A. Cicero Guggenhimer, Jr. He was not related to the *the* Guggenhimers. In fact I do not know, even, if there are, or were, any *the* Guggenhimers. The people who peddled lace, smolt copper, leisurely migrated between the State of Colorado, the US Senate, and the Venetian Litoral, now and then pausing to found an art museum or transport a monastary to a choicer location, are *Guggenheims*. With *ei*. Without *er*. However, A. Cicero's grandmother was the last surviving granddaughter of old John Jacob You-Know-*Who*, and she had left A.C. her half of Manhattan Island, plus the bed of the East River, which Yon Yockoob had bought cheap in between grifting furs from the Redskins and whisking from the Knickerbockers (who had guffawed in Hudson Dutch when thinking how *they* were taking *him* in) those hay meadows and swamp-lots on which now stands *the* most valuable real estatery in the world.

Bar none.

Hence the A.

As for the Cicero, he always claimed his grandmother got it out of a dream-book.

It may not be generally known that every, but I spit you not, *e*very commercial vessel which plies or "stands" up and down the East River pays through the hawse-hole for the privilege: because if not, trolls will come up and *eat* them. Naturally, when you got this kind of money, no matter how tied up in trusts and annuities and danegeld it may be, estates mean nothing, penthouses mean nothing, fancy cars and yachts mean nothing: so naturally you come to live in Greenwich Village, where everything is so, well, Interesting.

People would snort when I told them that Edward and I lived on the seventh story of a seven-story walk-up: but we did. On the ground floor was the Dante Alighieri Association, the door of which in those days opened only wide enough to

admit one small man with well-shined shoes at a time: doubtless to discuss Canto II, or whichever. As to its subsequent
career as a coffee-house, of this I know nothing, I say nothing, I've heard nothing, wild horses would drag nothing out
of me, so don't even ask.

"Seven stories and no *el*evator?" people would exclaim,
rolling eyes and clutching chests. "That's *got* to be il*leg*al!"

"It does got," I would agree. "But it didn't used to got."
Furthermore it was made of cast-iron and not wood, and was
not mouldering at all: it was indeed a tenement house, probably one of the last of the Old Law or the first of the New
Law tenements, but it was a tenement house in good condition, I should only be in half such good condition at the same
age. I was younger in them days and had more than my memories, and thought nothing of charging up or down the full
seven story mountain, heigh ho. Maurice with his Biblical
beard used to pass by with his arms full of publications from
the four or five quarters of the earth, the sales of which, such
as they were, sustained him in scraps of food and the rents
on the dozens if not scores of public coin lockers in which
he stored the paper memorabilia of decades:

Eheu, Maurice, Maurice! Where are you now?

You were ahead of your time, as well as the wrong age
and appearance, these were your only faults: had you lived
today, had you been younger, were your beard not white nor
your locks long, had you the proper academical affiliations,
an academician of the academicians (they should plotz), or a
friend or a protegé of a bevy of academicians and critticks:
see how fast the Guggenfutzes (they should plotz) would be-
stow upon you Foundlingship after Foundlingship, weevils
should only eat their navels: may you, o contrare, O Rare
Maurice, flourish in eternal life.

Amidst the Crash of Matter.

And the Wrack of Worlds.

G. (for Gabriel) Courland . . . the Moriarity Expert? That
same. Whom else? G. Courland was then much exercised (if
that is not too vigorous a word) in the matter of his trousers:
yea cuffs? nea cuffs? He wanted no cuffs, his tailors wanted
cuffs. "But they *trip* when you run fast," he would explain.

This cut neither ice nor worsted with Morris, Max, and Rocco. "So don't *run* fast," they said.

All very well for *them:* staid old cockers with their wild, wild youths behind them. Gabriel G. was at that time running (there! that *verb* again!) a sort of Consolation Service. For listless wives. And the energy displayed by (now and then, though only now and then) some of them husbands on learning All, would, if devoted on behalf of their wives, have left them (the wives) quite listful. And McCourland *ohn* a Consolation Service.

In Bleecker Street the Open Air Market how it flourished! Greens galore. Greens (as Butch Gyrene he put it) up the ass. Flowers in bloom, too. Nearbye, the old-established markets, all the names ending in vowels. Wendell Garrett, scarlet vest well-filled, cap of maintenance on his audacious head, would stroll in and out, tweaking the poultry. "Have you any," this he would ask of the Sons of Sicily and the Abruzzi, you or me they would *kill:* "Have you any *guinea* fowl?"

Dandelion greens, fresh-made latticini, lovely reeky old pastafazool, no, had some other name, *cheese,* hm, mm, ah! Provalon'! **Smekk** Mussels in icy pools with water always a drip-drip-drip-a-drip, pizza—you let the word pass you by without your lips trembling, your nostrils pirouetting and corvetting, your salivary glands drooling and your eyes rolling? You must be dead, *dead.* . . .

Or else, for your sins and your bad karma, you have known nothing but *Protestant* pizza, may God help you. *Not* baked in a stone oven according to the Rules of the Council of Trent. *Not* with the filling so firmly bonded to the crust—and the crust brown and crisp and bubbly round the rim, Marón!, that wild horses could not part filling from crust: *No!* What do you know of pizza, you with your heritage of Drive-ins, and McDonald's, and the Methodist Church, pizza, you think *that* is pizza, that franchised flop, comes frozen, is thawed, is redone in an ordinary metal quick-a-buck oven, with the cheese from Baptist cows, the tomatoes by Mary Worth, the filling rolling back from off the crust limper than a deacon's dick: *this* you call *pizza?*

Marón.

As for the fruit bread for the Feast of St. Joseph—

"Whats a matta you no shame?" screamed Philomena Rappini, of the Fresh Home-Made Sausage Today Market. "Put a some clothes on! You some kine comuniss? Marón, I no look!" But between her fingers, plump and be-ringed, ahaah, oh ho: she *did* look! And why not? So there he was, dark and well-thewed and imperially slim.

(Well-hung, too.)

"Your pardon, Matron, and a daughter to a Jeddak of Jeddaks I perceive you must be by your grace and slender high-arched feet: may I place my sword in pawn? A message to Ed Burroughs? Magnetic telegraph message to muh nevvew Ed Burroughs? Jest tell him it's Uncle John. John Cyarter.

"Of Mars."

As to how he had gotten here, *here,* I mean *there,* in The Village, across the countless leagues and aeons and ions of interstellar freezing space, who knows? Who knows, in fact, what song the sirens sang? Who gives a shit?

When one tired of the coffee-house scene in The Village, there was always The Museum. And by "The Museum" neither I nor any denizen of the Old Village Scene as it then obtained meant one of the sundry establishments displaying genuine old art or artifacts or modern exempla of the Dribble, Splotch, Drool, or Ejaculate, School(s): no. We meant *The* Museum, there on Great Jones Street, *Bar*num's Museum. A mere shadow of itself, you say? May be. May have *been.* Old William Phineas, Jr. himself was then alive, great-nephew to the Yankee Showman himself. Billy Finn. The most recently painted sign was the one reading: *Veterans of the World War, One-Half Price*—and to this had been added by pen a new *s* after *War,* plus the words, in between lines, *And of the Korean Conflict.* These letters had a pronounced wobble, so indicative of the State of the Nation as well as of old Bill Barnum's hand not being quite so firm as it once was. Inside? Jumbo's hay-rack. A corset belonging to one of the Dolly Sisters. Anna Held's bath-tub plus one of her milk bills for same. Genuine rhinestone replica of the famed Bicycle Set which Diamond Jim had given Lillian Russell. William Jennings Bryan's hat. Calvin *Cool*idge's hat. Old Cool Cal. The oldest wombat in the world, right this way, folks.

And so on.

Across the street the incredible wooden Scotchman, no mere

Indian being good enough, was the emblematic figure in front of the establishment of MENDEL MOSSMAN, SNUFF AND SEGARS, *also Plug, Cut-Plug, Apple Twist and Pigtail Twist*. Also (though not openly designated as such, of course), behind the third mahogany door with opaque crystal glass window from the left, an entrance to a station of the Secret Subway System.

Officially, no, it was not officially *called* the Secret Subway System, officially it was called Wall Street, Pine Street, Bowling Green and Boulevard Line. The Boulevard, ask any old-timer in them days, was *upper* Broadway. Ask any one or more old-timer as to at what point ''upper'' Broadway begins: watch them flail at each other with their walking-sticks and ear-trumpets.

There is a Secret Station in the State Bank Notes Registry Room of the old Counting House (Where no state bank notes have been registered since about 1883, owing to a confiscatory Federal Tax on the process).

There is a Secret Station in the marble men's room of the *original* Yale Club.

There is one beneath Trinity Church and one behind the North River Office of the State Canal Authority and one next to the Proving Room (Muskets) of the Mercantile Zouaves and Armory.

There are a few others. Find out for yourself . . . if you can.

The fare is and has been and always will be, one silver dollar each way. *Or.* For a six-day ticket good for round trips, one half-eagle (a five-dollar gold piece, to the ignorant).

The ticket agents are the color of those fungi which grow in the basements of old wood-and-stone houses on Benefit Street in Providence, Rhode Island and Providence Plantations. It is intimated that these agents once held offices of responsibility above grounds, but Blotted Their Copy Books.

One of them is named Crater.

Crater, if you just think about it a moment, is very much like Carter.

La Belle Belinda lived upstairs over Mossman's, which she insisted had the loveliest smell in the world.

And there are those who say that this distinction belonged to The Fair Belinda herself.

The Sodality of the Decent Dress (a branch of the Legion

of Utmost Purity) had just let out into the street after its monthly meeting at Our Lady of Leghorn, and was threatening to cut up rough with John Carter: just then Gabriel C., Wendell G., Edward and myself chanced by; we caught his arcane references at once—although, of course, we did not believe a word of them, still, it was a madness which we not only recognized but respected—and, under pretense of assisting the man to send his message, we spirited him away; after having first clothed his virility under Wendell's naval cloak.

We told the man that it had belonged to the Commanding Officer of the Confederate Ram *Pamunkey*. A faint mist of tears rose in his sparkling eyes, and his protests died away on his lips. His finely-chiseled lips.

"They're after me, boys, you know," he said, simply. "But they mustn't find me. Not until I've obtained a replacement for the wore-out part of the oxygen machine. All Mars depends on that, you know."

Exchanging significant glances, we assured him that we did indeed know.

We further assured him that we would with despatch arrange for sleeping silks and furs; meanwhile he consented to doss down for a much-needed nap on Gabriel's Murphy bed (for once, not occupied by a listing wife). Edward agreed to stand by. Just In Case.

There we left him, his strong chest rhythmically rising and falling, and stepped down to the courtyard, where we exchanged a few more significant glances, also shaking our lips and pursing our heads. We were thus occupied when Mary Teresa passed by, holding Kevin Mathew Aloysius, her great-grand-nephew, in a grip which would have baffled Houdini.

"Stop tellin them lies," she was adjuring him, "or yez'll burn in Hell witt the Prodissint Bastidds."

"No I won't either, because I'm still below the age of reason, nyaa, and anyway, I did *too* seen it, Aunty Mary T'resa, it was as tall as the second-floor window and it looked in at me but I made the sign of the cross, I blessed myself, so it went away," said Kevin Mathew Aloysius, rubbing some more snot on his sleeve.

Wendell, august and benevolent, asked, "What was it that you saw, my man?"

Kevin Mathew Aloysius looked at him, his eyes the same color as the stuff bubbling from his nostrils. "A mawnster," he said. "A real mawnster, cross my heart and hope to die. It was green, Mr. Garrett. And it had four arms. And tux growing out of its mouth."

Did some faint echo, some dim adumbration or vibration of this reach the sleeping man? Edward said some had. Edward said that the sleeping man stirred, half-roused himself, flung out an arm, and, before falling back into deep slumber, cried out:

"Hark! Was that the squeal of an angry thoat? Or the sound of a hunting banth in the hills? *Slave! My harness—and my sword!*"

CORRIDORS

Barry N. Malzberg

We close, as we opened, with a story by Barry Malzberg, perhaps the master of the recursive science fiction story. This one takes place, fittingly, at a Worldcon, and tries to resolve Barry's long-standing love-hate relationship with the field.

RUTHVEN USED TO have plans. Big plans: turn the category around, arrest the decline of science fiction into stereotype and cant, open up the category to new vistas and so on. So forth. Now, however, he is, at fifty-four, merely trying to hold on; he takes this retraction of ambition, understanding of his condition as the only significant change in his inner life over two decades. The rest of it—inner and outer too—has been replication, disaster, pain, recrimination, self-pity and the like: Ruthven thinks of these old partners of the law firm of his life as brothers. At least, thanks to Replication & Disaster, he has a brief for the game. He knows what he is and what has to be done, and most of the time he can sleep through the night, unlike that period during his forties when 4 A.M. more often than not would see him awake and drinking whiskey, staring at his out-of-print editions in many languages.

The series has helped. Ruthven has at last achieved a modicum of fame in science fiction and for the first time—he would not have believed this ever possible—some financial security. Based originally upon a short novel written for *Astounding* in late 1963, which he padded for quick paper-

231

back the next year, *The Sorcerer* has proven the capstone of his career. Five or six novels written subsequently at low advances for the same firm went nowhere, but: the editor was fired, the firm collapsed, releasing all rights, the editor got divorced, married a subsidiary rights director, got a consultant job with her firm, divorced her, went to a major paperback house as science fiction chief and through a continuing series of coincidences known to those who (unlike Ruthven) always seemed to come out a little ahead commissioned three new Sorcerers from Ruthven on fast deadline to build up cachet with the salesmen. They all had hung out at the Hydra Club together, anyway. Contracts were signed, the first of the three new Sorcerers (written, all of them in ten weeks) sold 150,000 copies, the second was picked up as an alternate by a demented Literary Guild and the third was leased to hardcover. Ruthven's new, high-priced agent negotiated a contract for five more Sorcerers for $100,000.

Within the recent half decade, Ruthven has at last made money from science fiction. One of the novels was a Hugo finalist, another was filmed. He has been twice final balloted for a *Gandalf.* Some of his older novels have been reprinted. Ruthven is now one of the ten most successful science fiction writers: he paid taxes on $79,000 last year. In his first two decades in this field, writing frantically and passing through a succession of dead-end jobs, Ruthven did not make $79,000.

It would be easier for him, he thinks, if he could take his success seriously or at least obtain some peace, but of this he has none. Part of it has to do with his recent insight that he is merely hanging on, that the ultimate outcome of ultimate struggle for any writer in America not hopelessly self-deluded is to hang on; another part has to do with what Ruthven likes to think of as the accumulated damages and injuries sustained by the writing of seventy-three novels. Like a fighter long gone from the ring, the forgotten left hooks taken under the lights in all of the quick-money bouts have caught up with him and stunned his brain. Ruthven hears the music of combat as he never did when it was going on. He has lost the contents of most of these books and even some of their titles but the pain lingers. This is self-dramatization, of course, and

Ruthven has enough ironic distance to know it. No writer was ever killed by a book.

Nonetheless, he hears the music, feels the dull knives in his kidneys and occipital regions at night; Ruthven also knows that he has done nothing of worth in a long time. The Sorcerer is a fraud; he is far below the aspirations and intent of his earlier work, no matter how flawed that was. Most of these new books have been written reflexively under the purposeful influence of Scotch and none of them possesses real quality. Even literacy. He has never been interested in these books. Ruthven is too far beyond self-delusion to think that the decline of his artistic gifts, the collapse of his promise, means anything *either*. Nothing means anything except holding on as he now knows. Nonetheless, he *used* to feel that the quality of work made some difference. Didn't he? Like the old damages of the forgotten books he feels the pain at odd hours.

He is not disgraced, of this he is fairly sure, but he is disappointed. If he had known that it would end this way, perhaps he would not have expended quite so much on those earlier books. *The Sorcerer* might have had a little more energy; at least he could have put some color in the backgrounds.

Ruthven is married to Sandra, his first and only wife. The marriage has lasted through thirty-one years and two daughters, one divorced, one divorced and remarried, both far from his home in the Southeast. At times Ruthven considers his marriage with astonishment: he does not quite know how he has been able to stay married so long granted the damages of his career, the distractions, the deadening, the slow and terrible resentment which has built within him over almost three decades of commercial writing. At other times, however, he feels that his marriage is the only aspect of his life (aside from science fiction itself) which has a unifying consistency. And only death will end it.

He accepts that now. Ruthven is aware of the lives of all his colleagues: the divorces, multiple marriages, disastrous affairs, two- and three-timing, bed-hopping at conventions; the few continuing marriages seem to be cover or mausoleum . . . but after considering his few alternatives Ruthven has

nonetheless stayed married and the more active outrage of the
earlier decades has receded. It all comes back to his insight:
nothing matters. Hang on. If nothing makes any difference
then it is easier to stay with Sandra by far. Also, she has a
position of her own; it cannot have been marriage to a science
fiction writer which enticed her when they met so long ago.
She has taken that and its outcome with moderate good cheer
and has given him less trouble, he supposes, than she might.
He has not shoved the adulteries and recrimination in her face
but surely she knows of them; she is not stupid. And she is
now married to $79,000 a year, which is not inconsiderable.
At least this is all Ruthven's way of rationalizing the fact that
he has had (he knows now) so much less from this marriage
than he might have, the fact that being a writer has done
irreparable damage to both of them. And the children. He
dwells on this less than previously. His marriage, Ruthven
thinks, is like science fiction writing itself: if there was a
time to get out that time is past and now he would be worse
off anywhere else. Who would read him? Where would he
sell? What else could he do?

Unlike many of his colleagues, Ruthven had never had
ambitions outside the field. Most of them had had literary
pretensions, at least had wanted to reach wider audiences,
but Ruthven had never wanted anything else. To reproduce,
first for his own pleasure and then for money, the stories of
the forties *Astounding* which moved him seemed to be a sen-
sible ambition. Later of course he did get serious about the
category, wanting to make it anew and etc. . . . but that was
later. Much later. It seemed a noble thing in the fifties to
want to be a science fiction writer and his career has given
him all that he could have hoped for at fourteen. Or twenty-
four.

He has seen what their larger hopes have done to so many
of his peers who started out with him in the fifties, men of
large gifts who in many cases had been blocked in every way
in their attempts to leave science fiction, some becoming quite
embittered, even dying for grief or spite, others accepting
their condition at last only at the cost of self-hatred. Ruthven
knows their despair, their self-loathing. The effects of his
own seventy-three novels have set in, and of course there was

a time when he took science fiction almost as seriously as the most serious . . . but that was *later,* he keeps on reminding himself, *after* breaking in, after publication in the better magazines, after dealing with the audience directly and learning (as he should have always known) that they were mostly a bunch of kids. His problems had come later but his colleagues, so many of them, had been ambitious from the start, which made matters more difficult for them.

But then, of course, others had come in without any designs at all and had stayed that way. And they too—those who were still checking into *Analog* or the Westercon—were just as miserable and filled with self-hatred as the ambitious, or as Ruthven himself had been a few years back. So perhaps it was the medium of science fiction itself that did this to you. He is not sure.

He thinks about things like this still . . . the manner in which the field seems to break down almost all of its writers. At one time he had started a book about this, called it *The Lies of Science Fiction,* and in that bad period around his fiftieth birthday had done three or four chapters, but he was more than enough of a professional to know that he could not sell it, was more than ready to put it away when *The Sorcerer* was revived. That had been a bad time to be sure; ten thousand words on *The Lies of Science Fiction* had been his output for almost two full years. If it had not been for a little residual income on his novels, a few anthology sales, the free-lance work he had picked up at the correspondence school and Sandra's occasional substitute teaching, things might have bottomed. At that it was a near thing, and his daughters' lives, although they were already out of the house, gave Sandra anguish.

Ruthven still shudders, thinking of the images of flight which overcame him, images so palpable that often they would put him in his old Ford Galaxie, which he would drive sometimes almost a hundred miles to the state border before taking the U-turn and heading back. He had, after all, absolutely nowhere to go. He did not think that anyone who had ever known him except Sandra would put him up for more than two nights (Felicia and Carole lived with men in odd arrangements), and he had never lived alone in his life. His parents were dead.

Now, however, things are better. He is able to produce a steady two thousand words a day almost without alcohol, his drinking is now a ritualized half a pint of scotch before dinner and there are rumors of a larger movie deal pending if the purchaser of the first movie can be bought off a clause stupidly left in his contract giving him series rights. Ruthven will be guest of honor at the Cincinnati convention three years hence if the committee putting together the bid is successful. That would be a nice crown to his career at fifty-seven, he thinks, and if there is some bitterness in this—Ruthven is hardly self-deluded—there is satisfaction as well. He has survived three decades as a writer in this country, and a science fiction writer at that, and when he thinks of his colleagues and the condition of so many with whom he started he can find at least a little self-respect. He is writing badly, *The Sorcerer* is hackwork, but he *is* still producing and making pretty big money and (the litany with which he gets up in the morning and goes to bed at night) nothing matters. Nothing matters at all. Survival is the coin of the realm. Time is a river with banks.

Now and then, usually during the late afternoon naps which are his custom (to pass the time quicker before the drinking, which is the center of his day), Ruthven is assaulted by old possibilities, old ambitions, old dread, visions of what he wanted to be and what science fiction did to him, but these are, as he reminds himself when he takes his first heavy one at five, only characteristic of middle age. Everyone feels this way. Architects shake with regret, doctors flee the reservation, men's hearts could break with desire and the mockery of circumstance. What has happened is not symptomatic of science fiction but of his age, his country. His condition. Ruthven tells that to himself, and on six ounces of scotch he is convinced, *convinced* that it is so, but as Sandra comes into the room to tell him that dinner is seven minutes away he thinks that someday he will have to get *The Lies of Science Fiction* out of his desk and look at it again. Maybe there was something in these pages beyond climacteric. Maybe he had better reconsider.

But for now the smells of roast fill the house, he must drink quickly to get down the half-pint in seven minutes, the fumes of scotch fill his breath, the scents and sounds of home fill all of the corridors and no introspection is worth it. None of it is worth the trouble. Because, Ruthven tells himself for the thirty-second time that day (although it is not he who is doing the counting) that nothing nothing nothing nothing nothing matters.

Back in the period of his depression when he was attempting to write *The Lies of Science Fiction* but mostly trying to space out his days around alcohol, enraged (and unanswerable) letters to his publishers about his out-of-print books and drives in his bald-tired Galaxie . . . back in that gray period as he drove furiously from supermarket to the state border to the liquor store, Ruthven surmised that he had hit upon some of the central deceptions which had wrecked him and reduced him and so many of his colleagues to this condition. To surmise was not to conquer, of course; he was as helpless as ever but there was a dim liberation in seeing how he had been lied to, and he felt that at least he could take one thing from the terrible years through which he had come: he was free of self-delusion.

Ruthven thought often of the decay of his colleagues, of the psychic and emotional fraying which seemed to set in between their fifth and fifteenth years of professional writing and reduced their personal lives and minds to rubble. Most were drunks, many lived in chaos, all of them in their work and persona seemed to show distress close to panic. One did not have to meet them at the conventions or hang out with them at the SFWA parties in New York to see that these were people whose lives were askew; the work showed it. Those who were not simply reconstructing or revising their old stories were working in new areas in which the old control had gone, the characters were merely filters for events or possessed of a central obsession, the plots lacked motivation or causality and seemed to deal with an ever more elaborate and less comprehended technology. Whether the ideas were old or new, they were half-baked, the novels were padded with irrelevant events and syntax, characters internalized purposelessly, false leads were pursued for thousands of words. The decay seemed to cut across all of the writers and their work; those that had been good seemed to suffer no less than the mediocre or worse, and there was hardly a science fiction writer of experience who was not—at least to Ruthven's antennae—displaying signs of mental illness.

That decay, Ruthven came to think, had to do with the very nature of the genre: the megalomaniacal, expansive visions being generated by writers who increasingly saw the disparity between Spaceways and their own hopeless condition. While the characters flourished and the science gleamed, the writers themselves were exposed to all of the abuses known to the litterateurs in America and—intelligent, even the dumbest of them, to a fault—they were no longer able to reconcile their personal lives with their vision: the vision became pale or demented. At a particularly bleak time, Ruthven even came to speculate that science fiction writing was a form of illness which, like syphilis, might swim undetected in the blood for years but would eventually, untreated, strike to kill. The only treatment would be retirement, but most science fiction writers were incapable of writing anything else after a while and the form itself was addictive: it was as if every potential sexual partner carried venereal disease. You could stop fucking but only at enormous psychic or emotional course, and *then* what? Regardless, that virus killed.

Later, as he began to emerge from this, Ruthven felt a little more sanguine about the genre. It might not *necessarily* destroy you to write it if you could find a little personal dignity and, more importantly, satisfactions outside of the field. But the counsel of depression seemed to be the real truth: science fiction was aberrant and dangerous, seductive but particularly ill-suited to the maladjusted who were drawn to it, and if you stayed with it long enough, the warpage was permanent.

After all, wasn't science fiction for most of its audience an aspect of childhood they would outgrow?

This disparity between megalomania and anonymity had been one of the causes of the decay in his colleagues, he decided. Another was the factor of truncation. Science fiction dealt with the sweep of time and space, the enormity of technological consequence in all eras, but as a practical necessity and for the sake of their editors all science fiction writers had to limit the genre and themselves as they wrote it. *True* science fiction as the intelligent editors knew (and the rest followed the smart ones) would not only be dangerous and threatening, it would be incomprehensible. How could twenty-fourth century life in the Antares system be depicted? How could the readership for an escape genre be led to understand what a black hole would be?

The *writers* could not understand any of this, let alone a young and gullible readership interested in marvels that were to be made accessible. (Malzberg had been into aspects of this in his work but Ruthven felt that the man had missed the point: lurking behind Malzberg's schematics was the conviction that science fiction *should* be able to find a language for its design, but any penny-a-word stable hack for *Amazing* in the fifties knew better and Malzberg would have known better too if he had written science fiction before he went out to smash it.) So twenty-fourth century aliens in the Antares system would speak a colloquial Brooklynese, commanders of the Black Hole Explorer would long for their Ganymede Lady. The terrific would be made manageable, the awesome shaped by the exigencies of pulp fiction into the nearby. The universe would become Brooklyn with remote dangerous sections out in Bushwick or Greenpoint but plenty of familiar stops and safer neighborhoods.

The writers, awash in the market and struggling to live by their skills, would follow the editors and map out a universe to scale . . . but Ruthven speculated that the knowledge that they had drained their vision, grayed it for the sake of publication, had filled them first with disappointment and finally self-hatred: like Ruthven they had been caught early by the *idea* of science fiction—transcendence and complexity—and however far they had gone from there, they still felt at the base that this was a wondrous and expensive genre. Deliberately setting themselves against all for which the field had once stood could not have been easy for them. Rationalization would take the form of self-abuse: drink, divorce, obesity, sadism, in extreme cases penury, drugs or the outright cultivation of death. (Only H. Beam Piper had actually pulled the trigger on himself but that made him an honest man and a gun collector.) That was your science fiction writer, then, an ecclesiastic who had been first summoned from the high places and then dumped in the mud of Calvary to cast lots with the soldiers. All for a small advance.

That had been some of Ruthven's thinking, but then he had been very depressed. He had done a lot of reading and thinking about the male mid-life crisis. Sandra and he were barely dealing with one another; they lived within the form of marriage but not its substance (didn't everyone long married end that way?). His sexual panic, drinking, terror of death and sense of futility were more characteristic, perhaps, of the climacteric than of science fiction. The poor old field had taken a lot of blame over its lifetime (a lifetime, incidentally, exactly as long as Ruthven's: he had been born on April 12, 1926) for matters not of its own making, and once again was being blamed for pain it had not created. Maybe.

It wasn't science fiction alone which had put him in the ditch at late mid-life, Ruthven thought, any more than science fiction had been responsible for Hiroshima, Sputnik, the collapse of Apollo or the rotten movies of the nineteen-fifties which had first enticed and then driven the public away. The field had been innocent witness to much of these and the target of some but it was unfair to blame the genre for what seemed (at least according to the books he read) an inevitability in middle class, middle aged, male America.

It was this ambivalence—the inability to fuse his more recondite perspective with the visceral, hateful feeling that science fiction had destroyed all of their lives—which stopped *The Lies of Science Fiction*. Ruthven does not kid himself: even if the contracts for *The Sorcerer* had not come in and his career turned around, he probably would have walked away from the book. Its unsaleability was a problem, but he knew that he might have sold it *somewhere*, an amateur press, and he had enough cachet in the field to place sections here and there in the fan magazines. It wouldn't have been much but it would have been more per diem than what Sandra was making or he from the correspondence school.

But he had not wanted to go on. His commitment, if anything, had been to stop. Ruthven, from the modest perspective of almost four years, can now admit that he was afraid to continue. He could not bear to follow it through to the places it might have taken him. At the worst, it might have demonstrated that his life, that all of their lives in science fiction, had been as the title said: a lie . . . a lie which would lead to nothing but its replications by younger writers, who in turn would learn the truth. The book might have done more than that: it could have made his personal life impossible. Under no circumstance would he have been able to write that book and live with Sandra . . . but the drives on the Interstate had made it coldly evident that he had nowhere else to go. If he were not a middle-aged, married science fiction writer, then what was he?

Oh, it was a good thing that *The Sorcerer* had come through and that he had gotten back to fiction. The novels were rotten but that was no problem: he didn't *want* to be good anymore, he just wanted to survive. Now and then Ruthven still drives the Interstate in his new Impala; now and then he is still driven from sleep to stare at the foreign editions . . . but he no longer stares in anguish or drives in fury; everything seems to have bottomed out. Science fiction can still do many things to him but it no longer has the capacity to deliver exquisite pain, and for this he is grateful.

Eventually someone else, perhaps one of the younger writers, *will* do *The Lies of Science Fiction* or something similar, but of this in his heart is Henry Martin Ruthven convinced: he will never read it. He may be dead. If not he will stay clear. Science fiction now is only that means by which he is trying to hang on in the pointless universe and that which asks that he make anything more of it (what is there to make of it?) will have to check the next bar because Henry Martin Ruthven is finished. He knows the lies of science fiction, all right. But above all and just in time, he knows the truths of it too.

Ruthven attends the Cincinnati World Convention as guest of honor. At a party the first night in the aseptic and terrifying hotel he is surrounded by fans and committee, editors and colleagues, and it occurs to him that most of the people in these crowded rooms were not born when he sold his first story, "The Hawker," to *Worlds of If* on August 18, 1952.

This realization fills him with terror: it is one thing to apprehend in isolation how long he has been around in this field and how far the field in its mad branching and expansion has gone from all of them who started in the fifties, but it is quite another to be confronted in terms that he cannot evade. Because his career has turned around in the decade, most of these people have a good knowledge of his work, he is guest of honor, he is hardly ignored, but still—

Here and there in the packed three-room suite he sees people he knows, editors and writers and fans with whom he has been at conventions for years, but he cannot break out of his curious sense of isolation, and his conversations are distracted. Gossip about the business, congratulations on having survived to be a guest of honor, that sort of thing. Ruthven would almost prefer to be alone in his room or drinking quietly at the bar but that is obviously impossible. How can a guest of honor be alone on the first night of his convention? It would be, among others things, a commentary on science fiction itself and no one, least of all he, wants to face it.

None of his family are here. Felicia is no surprise: she is starting her second year of law school in Virginia and could not possibly miss the important early classes; besides, they have had no relationship for years. Maybe never. Carole had said that she might be in from Oakland, would do what she could, but he has heard that kind of thing from Carole before and does not expect her. The second marriage is falling apart, he knows, Sandra will tell him that much, and Carole is hanging on desperately (he surmises) much as Ruthven himself hung on years ago when, however bad it might be, there was nothing else. He wishes that he could share this with Carole but of course it would be the finish of him. There are hundreds of sentences which said to the wrong people would end his marriage on the spot and that is another of them.

Sandra did want to be here but she is not. She has been feeling weak all year and now at last they have a diagnosis: she will have a hysterectomy soon. Knowing what being guest of honor meant to him Sandra had offered to go regardless, stay in the room if she could not socialize, but Ruthven had told her not to. He knew that she did not want to come, was afraid of the crowds and the hysteric pulse and was for the first time in her life truly afraid of dying. She is an innocent. She considers her own death only when she feels very ill.

Not so many years ago, being alone at a large convention, let alone as guest of honor, would have inflamed Ruthven. He would have manipulated his life desperately to get even a night away alone, a Labor Day weekend would have been redemption . . . but now he feels depressed. He can take no pleasure from the situation and how it occurred. He is afraid for Sandra and misses her a little too, wishes that his daughters, who have never understood him or his work, could have seen him just this once celebrated. But he is alone and he is beginning to feel that it is simply too late for adultery. He has had his opportunities now and then, made his luck, but well past fifty and into what he thinks of as leveling out, Ruthven has become resigned to feeling that what he should have done can be done no more—take the losses, the time is gone. There are women of all ages, appearance and potential here, many are alone, others in casual attachments, many— even more than he might imagine, he suspects—available. But he will probably sleep alone all the nights of this convention, either sleep alone or end up standing in the hotel bar past four with old friends drinking and remembering the fifties. The desperation and necessity are gone: Sandra is not much, he accepts this, but she has given him all of which she is capable, which makes her flaws in this marriage less serious than Ruthven's because he could have given more. His failure comes from the decision, consciously, to deny. Perhaps it was the science fiction that shut him down. He just does not know.

Ruthven stands in the center of the large welcoming party, sipping scotch and conversing. He feels detached from the situation and from his own condition; he feels that if he were to close his eyes other voices would overwhelm him . . . the voices of all the other conventions. Increasingly he finds that he has more to hear from—and more to say to—the dead than to the living. Now with his eyes closed, rocking, it is as if Mark Clifton, Edmond Hamilton, Kuttner and Kornbluth are standing by him glasses in hand, looking at one another in commiseration and silence. There is really no need for any of them to speak. For a while none of them do.

Finally, Ruthven says as he has before, "It hurts, doesn't it? It hurts." Kuttner nods, Kornbluth raises a sardonic eyebrow. Mark Clifton shrugs. "It hurts," Clifton says, "oh it hurts all right, Henry. Look at the record." There seems nothing more to say. A woman in red who looks vaguely like Felicia touches his arm. Her eyes are solemn and intense. She has always wanted to meet him, she says; she loves his work. She tells Ruthven her name and that she is a high school English teacher in Boston.

"Thank you," he says, "I'm glad you like the books." Everybody nods. Hamilton smiles. "You might as well," Kornbluth says with a shrug, I can't anymore and there's really nothing else." Ruthven shrugs. He tells the woman that the next scotch is on him or more properly the committee. He walks her over to the bar. Her hand is in his. Quickly, oh so quickly, her hand is in his.

At eight-fifteen the next evening Ruthven delivers his guest-of-honor speech. There are about three thousand in the large auditorium; convention attendance is just over ten thousand but 30 percent is not bad. Most attendees of modern world conventions are not serious readers now; they are movie fans or television fans or looking for a good time. Ruthven has thought for months about this speech and has worked on it painfully.

Once he thought—this was, of course, years ago—that if he were ever guest of honor at a major convention he would deliver a speech denunciatory of science fiction and what it did to its writers. Later, when he began to feel as implicated as anyone, the speech became less an attack than an elegy for the power and mystery that had been drained by bad writing and editing, debased by a juvenile audience. But after *The Lies of Science Fiction* had been put away and the edge of terror blunted, the very idea of the speech seemed childish. He was never going to be guest of honor and if he were, what right did he have to tell anyone anything? Science fiction was a private circumstance, individually perceived.

Nonetheless he had, when the time came to plan, considered the speech at length. What he decided to do, finally, was review his career in nostalgic terms, dropping in just enough humor to distract the audience from the thrust of his intention because after bringing his career up to date he wanted to share with them his conviction that it did not matter. Nothing mattered except that it had kept him around until the coincidence of *The Sorcerer,* and *The Sorcerer* meant nothing except that Ruthven would not worry about money until he was dead. "Can't you see the overwhelming futility of it?" he would ask. "The Lies of Science Fiction" seemed a good title except that it would be printed in the convention book and be taken as a slap at the committee and indeed the very field which was doing him honor. Better to memorialize his book through the speech itself. Anyway, the title would have alerted the audience to the bitterness of his conclusion. He wanted to spring it on them.

So he had called it "Me and the Cosmos and Science Fiction," harmless enough, and Ruthven delivers the first thirty-two minutes of his thirty-five minute address from the text and pretty much as he had imagined. Laughter is frequent; his anecdotes of Campbell, Gold and Roger Elwood are much appreciated. There is applause when he speaks of the small triumph of the science fiction writer the day Apollo landed. *"We* did that" he remembers telling a friend, "at three cents a word." The audience applauds. They probably understand. This much, anyway.

Then, to his astonishment and disgust, Ruthven comes off the text and loses control. He has never hated himself so. Just as he is about to lift his head and explain coldly that none of it matters his voice falters and breaks. It has happened in the terrible arguments with Sandra in the old days and in the dreams with Kornbluth, Hamilton, Kuttner and Clifton, but never before in public, and Ruthven delivers the last paragraphs of his speech in a voice and from a mood he has never before known:

"We tried," he says. "I want you to know that, that even the worst of us, the most debased hack, the one-shot writer, the fifty-book series, all the hundreds and thousands of us who ever wrote a line of this stuff for publication: we tried. We tried desperately to say something because we were the only ones who could, and however halting our language, tuneless the song, it was ours.

"We wanted to celebrate, don't you see? We wanted to celebrate the insistent, circumstantial fact of the spirit itself, that wherever and in whatever form the spirit could yet sing amidst the engines of the night, that the engines could extinguish our lives but never our light, and that in the spaces between we could still thread our colors of substantiation. In childhood nights we felt it, later we lost it, but retrieval was always the goal, to get back there, to make it work, to justify ourselves to ourselves, to give the light against the light. We tried and failed; in a billion words we failed and failed again, but throughout was our prayer and somewhere in its center lived something else, the mystery and power of what might have been flickering.

"In these spaces, in all the partitions, hear out song. Let it be known that while given breath we sang until it drew the very breath from us and extinguished our light forever."

And then, in hopeless and helpless fury, Ruthven pushes aside the microphone and cries.